Tender to the Touch

8/2013

DU

Tender to the Touch

Nicole S. Rouse

www.urbanchristianonline.com

Urban Books, LLC
97 N18th Street
Wyandanch, NY 11798

ISBN 13: 978-1-60162-765-0
ISBN 10: 1-60162-765-3

First Printing August 2013
Printed in the United States of America

10 9 8 7 6 5 4 3 2 1

This is a work of fiction. Any references or similarities to actual events, real people, living or dead, or to real locales are intended to give the novel a sense of reality. Any similarity in other names, characters, places, and incidents is entirely coincidental.

Distributed by Kensington Corp.
Submit Wholesale Orders to:
Kensington Publishing Corp.
C/O Penguin Group (USA) Inc.
Attention: Order Processing
405 Murray Hill Parkway
East Rutherford, NJ 07073-2316
Phone: 1-800-526-0275
Fax: 1-800-227-9604

As iron sharpens iron, so one man sharpens another.

~Proverbs 27:17

A good friend is not someone who has to agree with everything you say and do.

A good friend is someone who challenges you to be a better person.

This book is dedicated to all my good sister friends. . . .

Acknowledgments

My relationship with God has been the greatest blessing in my life! As I enter a new season, I have learned to trust Him a little more and complain a whole lot less.

There are so many people that have touched my life during this literary journey. I'd like to thank:

My exceptional mother and wonderful family. I am blessed to have you all in my life.

Dannette Hargraves and Jenlene Arrington for listening to my ideas at all hours of the day and keeping me motivated.

My agent, Sha-Shana Crichton, and my editor, Joylynn Jossel-Ross, for their encouragement and inspiration. I appreciate your wisdom and guidance.

My sorors and friends. Life just wouldn't be the same without your presence.

My pastor, Bishop Millicent Hunter, and The Baptist Worship Center family. What an awesome place to learn and grow stronger in Christ.

Church ministries (especially First Baptist in Jeffersontown, Kentucky), book clubs (especially Valencia Samuel's book club in Illinois. I miss you ladies!), bookstores, libraries, sororities (especially Zeta Phi Beta Sorority, Inc.), and my faithful readers and supporters.

I pray that you'll enjoy *Tender to the Touch*. . . .

Prologue

The blood covering J. Amanda's hands did not belong to her. Neither did the blotches of blood on her casual brown khakis. In total shock, she dragged her body across the recently remodeled kitchen floor, and as she leaned against the refrigerator, she stared at the faint smears of blood that had trailed her. Numb to her surroundings, J. Amanda wiped her trembling hands on her pants, then subconsciously reached for the gold cross hanging from her neck. Oh my God! What just happened? she asked herself.

As she looked around the kitchen, she covered her mouth with her red-stained hands. The smell of death surrounded her. How could she be so foolish? In her quest to find happiness, she had damaged the lives of her loved ones and close friends. What had happened in the kitchen was all her fault, and no one could convince her otherwise. "This can't be real," she mumbled in disbelief. "God wouldn't do this to me. I'm only thirty-nine years old."

Feeling like a failure, J. Amanda crawled back to the center of the room in tears and stopped by the gun that had fired the fatal shot. It was only a matter of time before the police arrived, and she knew that once they assessed the scene of the crime, she would be headed to jail.

J. Amanda had disappointed everyone—her family, her friends, her ministry, and, most of all, God.

Reaching for the gun lying by her leg, she wiped the tears from her cheeks with each arm. *This is the price I have to pay for taking my eyes off of you,* she sobbed. Then, slowly, J. Amanda closed her eyes as she lifted the gun to her temple, and in a childlike voice she moaned, "I'm so sorry, God."

~ Chapter 1 ~

J. Amanda

Instead of getting ready for bed at 11:15 on a Tuesday night, Jennifer Amanda King sat in a parked car, dressed in black sweats and combat boots, on a tiny street in West Philadelphia. With eyes glued to the clock on the dashboard, Jennifer anxiously tapped the steering wheel with her left hand. If her instincts were correct, tonight would be the beginning of her initiation into Eta Omicron Pi Sorority, Inc.

Jennifer couldn't believe the moment had finally arrived. Since she was five years old, her paternal grandmother had groomed her to be a part of the family legacy, and she couldn't wait to become a member. The sisters of Eta Omicron Pi were intelligent, driven, and creative women who had a passion for uplifting and serving the community. They were also fun-loving and the best female steppers on campus.

At 11:18, someone dressed in similar clothing rushed past Jennifer's Ford Mustang. Jennifer's eyes followed the young woman as she hurried down the street and into the house that she would soon enter as well. It was dark outside, but she recognized Kenya Harris's short auburn Afro. It was no surprise that Kenya would also be one of the interested women invited tonight. Jennifer had seen her at several of the sorority's events. Though she hadn't developed a friendship with

Kenya, they acknowledged one another in passing on campus.

When Kenya entered the house, Jennifer glanced at the clock again. Eleven twenty-three. She still had seven minutes. Jennifer played with the keys dangling from the ignition. Patience was not an inherent trait. She wanted to get out of the car and walk up and down the block to waste time, but it was late and she didn't want to risk being seen. She also didn't know much about West Philadelphia neighborhoods. Though she grew up in Camden, New Jersey, and was familiar with inner-city living, Jennifer often said, "I'm only comfortable in my hood."

Besides the fact that she was in a strange place and was wary about her surroundings, Yolanda, the current president of the sorority, had given Jennifer strict instructions. "Come to my house dressed in black sweats, black army boots, and white undergarments at eleven thirty. Not one minute earlier or later."

Before Jennifer could ask questions, Yolanda had hung up the phone. Such impolite behavior would've rubbed some people the wrong way, but Jennifer knew better. Her aunts, who pledged at different schools, had informed her that this would happen. It was also a clear indication that the pledge process was about to begin.

Jennifer turned off the car and wondered who else would be inside the house. Aside from the eight members in the chapter, the young women with whom she'd share this experience would also be in attendance. Kenya would be one of them, and so would Tionna Jenkins.

Discretion was key, and all the interested women were told not to share the details of their conversations with anyone, but Jennifer and Tionna had bonded as friends their freshmen year at Temple and made a pact to keep one another informed no matter what. Jennifer was glad Tionna was also given instructions to be at the house tonight. She couldn't think of a better person to go through the process with.

The time on the clock changed to 11:27, and Jennifer thought it was now safe to get out of her car. She'd just have to pace her walk to the house. Though nervous, she was ready. Her grandmother, aunts, and cousins all shared several pledge stories in hopes that Jennifer would be prepared for whatever happened. However, fear of the unknown still loomed over her.

With each step toward her destination, Jennifer recited the first scripture that came to mind to help ease the uneasiness in her stomach.

"Yea, though I walk through the valley of the shadow of death, I will fear no evil. . . ."

When Jennifer reached the front steps, she checked the watch on her arm. Eleven twenty-nine. "Perfect!" she mouthed as she climbed the steps and walked to the front door.

Jennifer stared at the watch until the numbers got blurry. She knew she had to follow Yolanda's instructions, and as she waited for the time to change, Jennifer could hear bouts of laughter inside. Maybe tonight wouldn't be as bad as she had imagined, after all.

A minute passed, and Jennifer didn't hesitate to ring the bell. Quickly, she took the watch off her arm and stuffed it into her left pocket. Another minute passed, and she was still waiting outside on the porch. "Can't they hear the bell?" she mumbled.

Leaning slightly to her left, Jennifer glanced through the front window. There was one light on in the living room, and she could see the shadows of several people standing around. Jennifer twisted her lips and took a deep breath. Should she ring the bell again? Jennifer stood up tall, and as she lifted her hand to ring the bell a second time, the door opened.

The jovial face that once belonged to Yolanda Miller had disappeared.

Unsure of what to say or do, Jennifer smiled and softly said, "Hello."

"Hey," Yolanda replied with a slight smirk as she slowly pushed the screen door open. Yolanda looked Jennifer up and down and then motioned for her to come inside.

Carefully, Jennifer walked past Yolanda and stopped in the center of the living room. All the darkened figures that she'd seen through the window a few seconds ago were gone. She heard murmurs coming from the kitchen, but Jennifer didn't want to walk in there ahead of Yolanda. Unsure of what to do, she faced the sorority president. "Should I—"

"Did you bring the notepad?" Yolanda interrupted as she checked Jennifer's attire more closely.

With shaking hands, Jennifer reached inside of her bra and pulled out a small notebook.

"Good," Yolanda said. "Now, follow me."

Walking a few paces behind Yolanda, Jennifer immediately noticed five women dressed in the exact same attire standing against the wall when they entered the kitchen. All but one of the women she knew.

"Okay, ladies," Yolanda said to get their attention. "Line up in size order and face your big sisters."

In less than a minute, the interested women formed a line as they were told. Jennifer stood at the front of the line, followed by the one woman she hadn't seen before. The woman was trembling, and Jennifer grabbed her hand in hopes that it would put her at ease.

With at least a dozen members surrounding her, Yolanda walked up and down the line, carefully eyeing each potential member as she spoke. "Welcome, ladies. Should you make it through this process, you will be the nineteen eighty-nine fall neophytes of Eta Omicron Pi. The women behind me are now your big sisters, and from this point forward, I am the dean of pledges," she said proudly. "You will refer to me as Dean Cyclone."

One of the big sisters handed Yolanda a dark bag. "Face the basement door," she continued as she took a bunch of blindfolds from the bag. The girls turned to their left, still in a straight line, and one by one, Yolanda blindfolded them all. When she was done, Jennifer could feel Dean Cyclone standing in front of her. "Jennifer, Cynthia, Zora, Kenya, Tionna, and Jasmine, tonight you will . . ." Yolanda stopped mid-sentence. "Wait a minute. I think we have too many Jennifers in this chapter." Yolanda tapped Jennifer's shoulder. "What's your middle name?"

"Amanda," Jennifer blurted. Anxiety caused her to speak too loudly at times.

There was a brief moment of silence, and then Yolanda spoke again. "From now on, you'll be called J. Amanda. I think I like the ring of that." Several big sisters agreed, and Yolanda continued her speech. "Like I was saying, tonight you will begin a process designed for strong and intelligent women. Once you walk down the stairs, you will enter into a new world, one of sisterhood and strength. Should you all finish this pledge process, you will be an official member of the greatest sorority in the world. You will also be a part of a sisterhood that will love you, support you, and stand by you until the end of time. Now, ladies, it's time for your journey as an Eta woman to begin."

About eleven years later . . .

J. Amanda rose from her seat on the pulpit and
strolled to the podium as Faith Tabernacle's choir
concluded a musical selection. She surveyed the two-
thousand-seat sanctuary filled with women and rested
her eyes on two special ladies seated on the front row.
Though Tionna and Kenya were members of the church
and often sat near the front every Sunday, tonight's
women's fellowship was extra special. The word God
had implanted in her spirit was inspired by their friendship. The sermon was also special, because in less than
twenty-four hours, she would be heading to Temple
University to participate in alumni weekend and reunite
with the five women with whom she had pledged Eta
Omicron Pi Sorority, Inc. Though she'd been in touch
with all of her line sisters through the years, the last time
they were all together was close to eleven years ago.

As the choir sang the last note, J. Amanda pulled
the microphone close to her mouth. "Hallelujah!" she
repeated three times. "Give the Lord a hand clap of
praise, for He has been good to all of us. If it had not
been for the Lord who was on my side, oh where would
I be? If that's your story tonight, throw your head back
and shout, 'Thank you, Lord.' For the Lord is great and
greatly to be praised."

Sounds of praise filled the sanctuary, and J. Amanda
was overwhelmed with emotion. With little warning,
she broke into a dance of praise. Every time she stood
before the women of God, she had to thank Him. Going
into the ministry was not the plan she had designed for
herself.

Growing up in a single-parent home in Camden,
New Jersey, as the youngest of five children, she took
full advantage of being the "baby" of the family. Before

meeting J. Amanda's father, her mother had been a widow for almost three years. As the story had been told, J. Amanda's mother wasn't interested in finding love again. She was focused on raising her four children: Rose, age eleven; Kyle, age ten; and twins Tanya and Tamika; age seven. Eventually, her father's charm and persistence changed her mother's mind, and the two began to date. The romance escalated, and in less than a year, J. Amanda was conceived.

This did not go over well with J. Amanda's paternal family. They didn't approve of having children out of wedlock. It didn't take long before the tension between the two families tore her parents apart. Although they never married, both parents played a crucial role in raising her.

By the time J. Amanda was a teenager, her oldest sister, Rose, was living in her own apartment. They wore the same size clothes, so she had access to all her sister's latest fashions and frequently entertained friends at her sister's apartment on the weekends. In fact, it was at Rose's apartment that J. Amanda lost her virginity at the age of fifteen.

Kyle, her older brother, didn't go out much during the week, because someone had to watch J. Amanda while their mother was working a second job at night. This didn't keep him from inviting friends over to their home. While Kyle socialized with his friends, J. Amanda would often sneak a beer or a cigarette into her room just for kicks.

J. Amanda's twin sisters enjoyed entertaining as well. Though they were the first to attend college in their family, they partied on campus just as much as they studied. On the weekends that J. Amanda wasn't at Rose's apartment, she was in New Brunswick partying with the twins.

Looking back over her life, she realized there was never a dull moment. Her past was colorful and exhilarating, to say the least, but her father's family had kept her balanced. While her mother's family was loud, bold, and social, the other side of her family was conservative and well educated. In fact, J. Amanda's paternal grandmother took an interest in her after her parents parted ways. She was determined to see that her granddaughter excelled in life. And J. Amanda was grateful. If it hadn't been for her grandmother, she wouldn't have gone to college, she wouldn't have joined a sorority, and she wouldn't have known about God's love and power.

Despite attending church most Sundays with her grandmother, J. Amanda limited her relationship with God. God was someone she talked to briefly every morning, as her grandmother had taught her to do. He was also someone she called on in the heat of trouble. She memorized key scriptures but rarely recited or applied them on a daily basis. But something happened one Sunday while she was singing in the young adult choir. As she belted out the lyrics to "I Won't Complain," J. Amanda thought about all the times God protected her during the rough seasons in her life, and began to cry. That day, God opened her eyes, and the words to the song became real.

From that day forward, she changed her lifestyle and joined several ministries in the church to keep busy. It didn't take long for her to stand out as a leader. J. Amanda became a minister at the age of twenty-eight, and God used her experiences, personality, and vigor to encourage and bless others. Ten years later she was a dynamic preacher known throughout Philadelphia and in many parts of New Jersey and Delaware. Women traveled to Faith Tabernacle Church to hear her speak at every third Sunday service and at the women's fellowship once a month.

J. Amanda stopped dancing around the pulpit and grabbed the microphone from its base. Facing Pastor Olivia T. Bowman, she willed her tears not to fall as she thanked Pastor Olivia for giving her the freedom to spread her wings. Pastor Olivia blew kisses to her protégé, and then J. Amanda turned back to the congregation.

Excited about the word in her heart, she began the sermon with fire and zeal, quickly elevating the emotions of the women. Preaching from the book of First Samuel, she focused on Jonathan, the son of Saul. When she reached the fourteenth chapter, J. Amanda couldn't keep still. She closed her Bible and then walked to the front of the podium. "The Bible tells us that there was a war going on against the Philistines, and Jonathan felt moved to go to battle without telling his father. But he doesn't go alone. His armor bearer is with him. Now, this is the part that I like," she said, dancing from side to side as the organist played a mild beat in between her phrases.

"Jonathan turns to the armor bearer, who is standing right by his side, and says, 'Let's go to the outposts. Perhaps the Lord will help us, for nothing can hinder the Lord.' Now, the armor bearer could've told Jonathan that he was crazy or that he'd have to go into battle alone, but get this. . . . The armor bearer replies, 'Do what you think is best. I am with you *completely,* whatever you decide.' I don't know about you, but that's the kind of friend I want by my side. In times of trouble, I don't want someone who'll just throw in the towel. I want someone who will cover me, *whatever* I decide."

J. Amanda shared a few quick stories about her pledge process to demonstrate how she needed her line sisters. They were forced into situations where they had to trust each other and have each other's backs, no matter how challenging things became. "Those women have been a great support system for me because they knew me when I was out all night dancing at a party and they know me now as God's servant. They don't judge me or purposefully hurt me. They keep me covered." J. Amanda was preaching so hard, she started to sweat. "They check me when I'm wrong, and they respect me when I'm right. They love me, flaws and all."

Wiping sweat from her brow, J. Amanda sauntered behind the podium to wrap up her sermon. "While we shouldn't put our friends before God, we do want to thank Him for friends that sincerely have our backs in great times and in times of struggle. When you're going through something, and you can't pray for yourself, you ought to have people you can call and just say, 'Cover me,' and they immediately go to God on your behalf. Women of God, it's important to have strong, positive friendships in your life. Friends who will keep you covered."

J. Amanda dropped the microphone on the podium and threw her head back. "Lord, I thank you," she moaned as tears fell from her eyes. As the women in the sanctuary praised God in their own way, she faced the ministers behind her. "Thank you for covering me," she cried. With tears still in her eyes, she turned back around and looked at Tionna and Kenya, who were also crying. "I got you," J. Amanda mouthed as she pointed to her friends. "I got you covered," she repeated, and from their eyes, she could tell they had her covered too.

After the service, J. Amanda waited for Tionna and Kenya in her office. As she sat alone in the room, she felt empty inside. She'd just preached a message that blessed a great number of women, yet there was still something missing in her own spirit. "God, you continue to amaze me," she whispered. Despite being in a barren place spiritually, God was still able to use her for His glory. She had challenged the women to build and maintain positive friendships, yet she was holding on to a secret. *How can my friends cover me if I don't tell them the truth?* she asked herself.

The truth was that she was growing weary but doing a good job at hiding it. For the last year, she had followed a strict schedule as her ministry flourished. She'd been preaching at different churches a few times each month, teaching leadership classes at church three times a week, and overseeing the women's ministry. Life at home was just as structured. On the evenings that she was not preaching, she cooked dinner and checked homework. In between her daily duties, she washed a load of clothes, vacuumed, or cleaned the bathroom and kitchen. And on cue, every Sunday and Thursday night, around 4:00 A.M., she made love to her husband.

J. Amanda tried not to complain, but her spirit was longing for a change. But what kind of change?

There was a knock on the door, and J. Amanda told her friends to come inside. Tionna entered the room first in her signature four-inch heels. At five foot eight, Tionna was the only woman she knew who could wear skinny heels every day, all day long. Tionna had the body of a twenty-five-year-old woman, and if her hair wasn't completely gray, she could've passed for one.

"You were on fire today," Tionna said as she placed her handbag on an empty chair.

"I was about to call the firehouse," Kenya joked as she pulled her thin, long auburn locks into a ponytail.

J. Amanda perked up in their presence. She wasn't sure when or how she wanted to share what was going through her mind. "I felt on fire," she replied in jest. "For a second, I thought I was going into early menopause."

Kenya walked to the coat closet and opened the door. She studied her curvy figure in the full-length mirror posted behind the door and laughed. "And what was up with that dance? I told Tionna I needed you to lay hands on me so I could get my dance on. I wanna feel the Holy Ghost too," she said, shaking her hands rapidly, as if they were tambourines.

"We need to cover that crazy child in prayer," Tionna teased.

"Don't play with the Holy Spirit, Kenya. Cynthia would give you a swift kick for that remark," added J. Amanda. Saying Cynthia's name reminded her of the weekend ahead. "I can't wait to see all my girls."

Kenya closed the door and stood next to J. Amanda's desk. "We're going to have so much fun," she said and loosened the first two buttons on her snug shirt. "Is Jazz coming?"

"I spoke to her last night. She's excited about seeing *everyone*," J. Amanda confirmed and then stared at Tionna. Kenya stared at her too.

"Oh, please," Tionna snarled. "That's what she told you."

Tionna and Jasmine were the only two line sisters who didn't get along, but J. Amanda prayed that would change this year. Jasmine mentioned that she was willing to work things out if a moderator controlled the conversation, and as always, J. Amanda had volunteered.

"Don't you think it's time to heal old wounds?" she asked.

"Ha!" Kenya laughed aloud and walked back to the closet to freshen up her makeup. "God's gonna have to perform a miracle."

"I'm not going to make any promises," Tionna replied. "The two of you should just be happy I even agreed to be in the suite with her."

"We should all be one big happy family," J. Amanda asserted.

"Listen, we'll always be connected, but there's no rule that says we have to be close," Tionna replied. "I have five other line sisters to keep up with. That's quite enough for me."

"I heard that," Kenya said and put on an extra coat of mascara. She loved the thick eyelash look. "But enough about you and Jasmine. I need to get out of here."

"Where are you running off to?" J. Amanda questioned.

Kenya put her makeup case back in her knockoff Gucci bag and then sashayed her full-figured body to the door. "I'm going to dinner with Alphonse."

"Alphonse?" Tionna and J. Amanda said in unison.

"You heard me right, ladies," Kenya confirmed. "We're going downtown to Del Frisco's."

"Does Mack know you're going on an expensive date?" Tionna asked.

"I don't answer to him, thank you very much. We're not together," Kenya replied, correcting her. "Besides, his old behind is probably sitting on the couch, with our son sound asleep, like he always is."

"No one told your fast tail to date a man almost fifteen years older than you," J. Amanda said and laughed. "It was cute to you when you were twenty, but now that you're thirty-four, it's a problem and you're bored."

"Y'all should go ahead and get married," added Tionna. "He's a good guy."

"Officer Wet Behind the Ears is a good guy too, but I don't see you running down the aisle," Kenya retorted. "You need to give him a *real* chance."

Tionna shook her head, and J. Amanda cracked up. Kenya should've been a comedian rather than a social worker.

"You don't have anything to say now, do ya?" Kenya said and waved good-bye as she headed out the door.

"She's right, you know," J. Amanda stated. "Casey is a *very* mature thirty-year-old man . . . *and* . . . you deserve to *really* be happy."

Tionna picked up her handbag and walked to the door. "That's my cue to leave. I don't want you to break into another sweat, trying to preach to me again."

"I thought we were going to dinner," J. Amanda said. She wasn't ready to go home.

"Not tonight. I need to pack, and Casey's bringing my favorite Thai food to the," Tionna responded with a smile. "Go home and enjoy dinner with your husband."

"I will," J. Amanda answered, and when Tionna left her office, she mumbled, "I guess I have no choice."

J. Amanda unzipped her skirt as she tiptoed into her eight-year-old daughter, Tiffany's, bedroom. Tiffany tried to wait up for her mother without success. J. Amanda covered her with a bright pink Disney comforter and then kissed her cheek.

"Night, Mommy," Tiffany said in a muffled voice. "I saved you a burger."

"Thank you," she replied and then turned off the lamp on the nightstand.

J. Amanda walked next door to her bedroom and slid off her skirt. As always, her son was sleeping soundly in the middle of her bed. David Jr. turned five last month, and he was still afraid to sleep in his own room alone.

"Hey, baby," said David, J. Amanda's husband, when he walked out of their bathroom. "How was the service?" David placed his arm around her waist and then kissed her on the lips.

"I think I did well," she replied and tossed her skirt in a pile ready to go to the cleaners.

"You're being modest. I'm sure every woman in the building would say you were great."

David always knew the right things to say. He was J. Amanda's greatest supporter. Unlike some husbands, he shared household responsibilities with little complaint. He cooked most of the meals and watched their children every time she had to preach. David was a good man with a good heart. That was why she felt guilty about her feelings. Many women would give their right arm to have a husband who paid the bills on time and supported his wife's career without question.

"I'll take him to his room in a minute, babe," David said as he changed into his nightclothes.

J. Amanda sat on the side of the bed and rubbed her son's plump cheek. He didn't move an inch when she touched him. He never did. When he was tired, David Jr. could sleep in the middle of a hurricane and not wake up. "You have to work tonight?" she asked her husband.

"Yeah, but not too long. I just have one more test to grade."

J. Amanda watched her husband get dressed for bed and sighed. David was a math education instructor at the Community College of Philadelphia. The only time he had to grade papers was late at night. J. Amanda understood his reasons for working so late, but sometimes she needed him to lie with her in bed until she fell asleep. She wanted to cuddle with him the way they did when they were newlyweds.

Once David was dressed, he walked over to the bed, standing close enough for J. Amanda to reach out and gently rub his thigh as he lifted their son. Despite the lack of attention he gave her, she was still very much attracted to him. "Don't stay downstairs too long," she said as her hand slowly left his thigh. "I'll be in the tub when you come up."

David didn't sense her need to be with him tonight. If he did, he didn't let on. Maybe she should've been more direct and just told him what she was feeling, but she didn't want to ask to make love and have him reject her. That would crush her more than his inattentiveness. Rather than get upset, J. Amanda undressed and ran her bathwater. This was her way to relax after a long day. Tomorrow she didn't have to be at the church until noon, so she could sleep in a little later than usual.

Water slowly filled the bathtub, and J. Amanda turned on the radio, then lit the vanilla-scented candle on the window ledge. As she slid into the bathtub, she hummed along as Anita Baker sang "Sweet Love." *Maybe David will change his mind and join me,* she thought as she lowered herself into the warm water and leaned back.

Jolted awake by a kiss on her forehead, J. Amanda couldn't believe that she had fallen asleep in the bathtub. She wondered how long she'd been there. "You getting in?" she asked groggily. "I'll run some hot water to warm it up a bit."

David blew out the candle. "I took a shower before you got home," he said, "and I'm just as tired as you are. I think we need to call it a night."

J. Amanda was tired, but she would've found some energy to enjoy her husband, even if it was only for ten minutes. "All right," she responded with disappointment and finished taking her bath . . . alone.

Frustrated, J. Amanda threw on her robe and walked past her king-size bed. "I'll be back," she told her husband. "I'm going to make a cup of tea."

David nodded from under the covers, and J. Amanda quietly walked downstairs to the kitchen. In the dark, she grabbed her cell phone from her purse on the table and sat down. It was almost one in the morning, but she made sure the phone was on silent and then sent her friend a text message.

Seconds later, her cell phone lit up and displayed the message: I'm up.

Can u talk? she texted back.

Her cell phone lit up again, but this time it was an incoming call. "Hello," she said softly.

"What's up, love?" a gentleman's raspy voice replied.

J. Amanda never thought she'd look forward to saying good night to a man who wasn't her husband, but when she heard the voice of an old friend she'd nicknamed Hunky, subtle chills rushed through her body.

~ Chapter 2 ~

Tionna

Dr. Tionna Jenkins pulled a suitcase from her closet and rolled it to the side of her bed. She had planned to pack the night before but had to work longer hours at the clinic all week. By the time she made it home and prepared dinner, all she wanted to do was get in bed and watch her favorite television shows until she fell asleep.

"Grandmom wants me to perm her hair tomorrow," said Brianna, her seventeen-year-old daughter, as she folded her mother's clean clothes.

Tionna opened her suitcase and put five sets of matching underwear inside. "She must trust you." She laughed. "Make sure you don't turn her hair blue."

"Don't sleep on my skills, Mom. Just because you don't trust me to perm or color your gray hair doesn't mean I don't know how. If Aunt Kenya trusts me to take care of her locks, then you know I'm legit," Brianna replied.

"Well, if you're that good, doing hair needs to be your side hustle in college." Tionna tucked a plastic bag of toiletries in the side pouch of her suitcase. "Did you get any new letters today?"

Brianna was a senior at Germantown Friends School, a private institution in the Germantown section of Philadelphia. She'd been a student there since the fifth grade. Brianna was Tionna's only child, and she had made many sacrifices to ensure her daughter received the best education possible. There were times when she felt a bit overprotective. Several public schools and charter schools in Philadelphia were known for their academic excellence, but Tionna knew several teachers in the city. They were overworked, underpaid, stressed, and responsible for more students than any one teacher should handle. There was also a higher risk of preteen jealousy, peer pressure, and silly arguments in the public and charter schools. Tionna knew these issues also surfaced in private schools, but they were few in number, giving Brianna more time to focus on getting good grades. And Brianna had exceeded Tionna's expectations. She had been an honor student since the seventh grade.

Brianna already received college acceptance letters from Penn, Princeton, Syracuse, and Temple. So keeping her daughter "sheltered," as she was often told, was well worth it.

"We didn't get any mail today, but it doesn't matter, anyway," Brianna said. "I'm going to Temple, like you."

Tionna beamed with pride. "You don't have to follow in my footsteps, you know. Wherever you decide to go will be fine with me. I trust your decisions."

Brianna put the clothes she'd folded into her mother's dresser drawers. "I know. How cool would it be if I graduated from the same medical school *and* pledged at the same school as you?"

The smile on Tionna's face slowly disappeared. Her last years of college were filled with heartache, disappointment, and struggle. Those weren't the footsteps she wanted Brianna to follow.

"Aunt Kenya said Jasmine's hanging out with all of you this weekend," Brianna continued. "You okay with that?"

"Your aunt Kenya talks too much," Tionna answered as she headed to her walk-in closet. Brianna followed behind her. "I'm fine," she lied as she recalled the promise she made to J. Amanda. *I'll go only if Jazz sleeps in a different room.*

Tionna browsed the section of her closet designated for dresses. She pulled out a strapless black dress with the price tag still attached and held it close to her body. "What do you think?"

Brianna ran her hand across the sheer sleeves of Tionna's black evening dress. "I love it!" Brianna exclaimed.

God had gifted Tionna with great metabolism, which kept her weight below 150 pounds. For a woman nearly six feet tall in heels, that was great. Sometimes she wondered if God wanted to make up for the head full of gray hairs that had grown in by her early thirties.

Brianna had inherited many of her genes as well. Though she had a hefty appetite, her weight rarely wavered. She'd been a proportional size ten since the ninth grade. Brianna was like her mother in many other ways too. She had a guarded personality and coarse hair, which relied on a good perm to make it lie straight. Strands of early gray had also appeared in the past year, and Tionna prayed her daughter wouldn't go completely gray before she reached her midtwenties.

Much like her mother, Brianna was an overachiever. Since she was ten years old, she wanted to be an ob-gyn doctor, like her mother. But as she grew older and had the opportunity to research different specialties, Brianna realized that she wanted to focus on internal medicine.

"What about these shoes?" Brianna asked, holding up a pair of sparkling silver stilettos. "These would be perfect."

Tionna agreed and handed Brianna the dress. "Put this dress and the heels in the suitcase for me," she ordered.

When Brianna walked away, Tionna walked to the back of her closet and got down on her knees. She crawled under the suits that were hanging and pulled out a box stored behind a bag of clothes she needed to give to Goodwill. The box hadn't been opened in ten years.

Slowly, Tionna lifted the lid, and immediately memories of her sorority life surfaced. The box was filled with pictures, pins, notebooks, and other paraphernalia. J. Amanda wanted everyone to bring the pins they'd received the night they crossed the "burning sands" and became official members of the sorority. Tionna prayed she hadn't thrown hers away.

Hidden underneath a frilly pillow was the sorority handbook and the notepad she had kept on her at all times when she was pledging. Though it was worn and had several ripped pages, she was the only one of her line sisters who managed to keep her notepad intact. When they crossed, half of Zora's notepad had been stripped of its pages. Tionna laughed at the thought of the days when all six women lived in her tiny campus apartment. Having grown up an only child, Tionna thought living with her sisters would be lots of fun. It was quite the opposite. Although she loved them, she had their bags packed and at the front door the day after they crossed.

Brianna walked into the closet and sat down next to her mother. She reached inside the box and pulled out a twenty-four-inch paddle. The wood had been stained black, and down its center were three raised white Greek letters, along with Tionna's line name: Changing Faces. The big sisters had given her that name because she could twist and rearrange her facial expressions in ways that could keep them entertained for hours.

Tionna traced the number five that was positioned beneath her line name, and sighed. She regretted that she let one person distance her from all the advantages the sorority had to offer. The happy times she shared with her sisters far outweighed the bad. If only she had been mature enough back then to realize that, she wouldn't have disassociated herself completely.

Tionna put the paddle back inside the box and took out a plastic jewelry box. When she opened it, the sorority pin she was looking for was inside.

"Aunt Kenya said that you would pin me when I cross," Brianna said.

Tionna smiled. Pledging was no longer what it used to be, and she was glad. The process she endured brought her closer to her line sisters, but parts of the process were, in her opinion, unnecessary and too physical. "Kenya tells you too much," Tionna noted. She was careful not to share pledge stories with her daughter. There were some things she just shouldn't know. Brianna wasn't a naive child, but she didn't think her daughter would be able to handle pledging old-school style, the way she had. "But of course, I'll be at your ceremony."

"Will my big sisters be extra mean to me when I pledge, because I'm a legacy?"

Tionna put the jewelry box back and then closed the box of memories. "You're not going to pledge, Brianna. People don't do that anymore."

"That's not what Aunt Kenya said," Brianna replied as she stood up.

"I'm gonna have to have a word with your aunt," Tionna said. "All I want is for you to graduate cum laude. Joining a sorority is not that important to me."

"Are you saying that because of Jasmine?"

Tionna walked out of the closet, and Brianna followed. "No," she answered blandly.

Brianna's cell phone rang, and she told the person she'd call them back in a few minutes. "You really need to move on. What happened between you and Jasmine is in the past," she said and walked to the door. "I mean, I understand why you're upset with her, but you shouldn't give her the satisfaction of knowing you're still holding a grudge."

Tionna twisted her lips and then stuck out her tongue, imitating an immature child. Until Brianna said those words, making amends with Jasmine hadn't been a serious consideration. "When did you become such a mature grown-up?" she asked. "Is that what they teach you in school?"

"I'm serious, Mom. I don't like what Jasmine did, either, but—"

"Let me stop you there," Tionna said. "Just because your stepmother and I aren't friends doesn't mean you can't like her."

"Mom . . . you taught me to be cordial, so I am, but I can't forget that she's the reason you and Daddy aren't together."

There was no debating that fact. Tionna and Brian had been the darling couple on campus for two years straight. "Jasmine was young. . . . We all were, so we all made some bad decisions."

"I'm young, Mom," Brianna replied. "There are just some things you don't do to friends."

Tionna checked her suitcase and made a note of the items she was missing. Brianna was causing her to think about a painful time in her life. "Go call your friend back," she said. "I can't take all this grown-up talk."

Brianna reminded her mother that she would be eighteen in a couple of months, and then walked out of the bedroom. Tionna shook her head. Where did all the years go? It seemed like yesterday when she held Brianna in her arms for the first time.

Thinking about the day she and Jasmine severed their friendship, Tionna couldn't help but wonder if she and Brian would still be together if Jasmine hadn't interfered. Even after Tionna learned about the affair, she and Brian tried to make their relationship work. They were about to be parents, so Tionna figured it was worth a try. Besides, she still loved him.

Tionna heard a dog barking outside, and she walked to the window to see what was going on. The neighbor's dog often found his way into her backyard and made himself at home in her rose garden. As she suspected, the overgrown Lhasa-poo was in her yard chasing after squirrels. As she watched the fluffy black dog run back and forth, she felt a sense of sadness. The last time she talked to Jasmine, they were at Brianna's first birthday party.

While everyone enjoyed the Winnie-the-Pooh cake Brian's mother spent hours decorating, Tionna overheard Jasmine ask Brian about a letter. Without knowing all the details, Tionna stormed across the room, to where Brian and Jasmine were standing, and screamed harsh words at the top of her lungs. She was so irate that everyone quickly cleared the apartment. As she watched her family and friends leave, Tionna realized that she hadn't forgiven Brian, and that whoever left the letter under her door the day she caught him cheating had caused more turmoil than relief.

I wonder who sent that letter, Tionna thought as she replayed that night in her head.

***

Tionna woke up in the middle of the night and wad-dled out of her bedroom and into the bathroom right outside her door. One of the joys of being five months pregnant was waking up from a deep sleep several times during the night because of an urge to pee.

On the way back to her bedroom, she noticed that someone had slid an envelope under the front door. She walked to the door and squatted low enough to pick up the envelope, which had her name on it. She didn't recognize the handwriting and could tell that someone had rushed to scribble her name. Tionna opened the envelope as she stood to her feet, and then turned on the hall light to read the letter. Whoever had written it knew her well, and they knew a lot about Brian. As she continued to read, her eyes stopped at one sentence.

"Brian has been sleeping with Jasmine."

As she read those words, Tionna fell back into the wall. She didn't believe it at first, but the information was something that her pregnant hormones couldn't let go of without investigation

"This can't be true. They wouldn't do this to me," she said aloud as she rubbed her swollen belly.

Tionna and Brian hadn't been sleeping in the same bed for several weeks. This was at Tionna's request. She'd gained so much weight in her second semester that she enjoyed having the bed to herself. It was just temporary, and she never considered that Brian would find someone else to sleep with every night in her place. Especially not one of her line sisters.

With tears in her eyes, Tionna called Kenya and read the letter to her.

"Meet me outside in two minutes," Kenya said, full of anger. "I can't let you drive over to Nineteenth and Diamond alone at four in the morning."

As Tionna drove her used Chevette three blocks to Brian's house, she wished she'd made herself a key. She wanted to walk in unannounced and catch him in the act. That way he couldn't lie about what he'd done to the mother of his unborn child.

There was no place to park at that hour, so Tionna double-parked in front of his brownstone apartment. It was a good thing Brian lived on the first floor. In case she needed to leave in a hurry, she wouldn't be slowed down by stairs.

"Let me do the talking," Kenya said as she jumped out of the car. "I don't need you going into labor."

Tionna was about to the ring the bell when Kenya moved in front of her and banged on the door. Impatient, Kenya banged on the door harder and with both fists.

"He's supposed to be home," Tionna said. "He called me at one to say he was in for the night."

"Yeah, I bet he is in for the night," Kenya asserted and banged on the door a third time. As she prepared to knock again, the window facing the street opened and Brian's roommate poked out his head.

"Where is he, Frank?" Kenya demanded.

From the look of the dried drool coming from his mouth, they had interrupted his sleep, but neither of the women really cared. Tionna needed answers, and she needed them tonight.

"You can't be serious. He's not here," Frank replied with an attitude.

"I can wait for him to come home. Just let me in," Tionna said as nicely as she could, but Frank wasn't buying her kindness. He could tell the women were there to start trouble. After all, it was four in the morning.

"He's not here. I'm going back to bed, and so should you," Frank snapped and closed the window.

"Oh, I can stand here all night," Kenya remarked and resumed banging on the door. This time she didn't pause to give anyone time to answer the door. "I'll wake up everyone in the building if Brian doesn't let us in."

Tionna was nervous but glad that Kenya was with her. Her hormones were so unpredictable that she would have either sat on Brian's step and cried until he showed up or busted down the door to let herself inside.

Frank opened the window again and threatened to call the police if they didn't leave, but Kenya wasn't scared. "If Brian is in there with someone, you're gonna need the police," she fired back.

A tenant from the second floor opened her window and pleaded with Frank too. "Just let them in so we can all get some sleep!"

Frank huffed and slammed his window shut. When they heard footsteps, Kenya stopped banging on the door. Expecting to see Frank, Tionna couldn't believe her eyes when the door opened. But there Brian stood, barefoot and wearing nothing but a shabby cotton robe. How could he let her stand outside at such an early hour making a fool of herself? And why wasn't he wearing boxers and a T-shirt? Brian didn't like to sleep in the nude. Seeing him angered Tionna, and she pushed him aside with all her might as she marched into the apartment.

"Why didn't you answer the door the first time?" Tionna questioned.

Brian played it cool as he fiddled with the belt holding the robe closed. "You know my room is in the back. I thought I was dreaming when I heard all that banging."

Kenya twisted her lips. "That's bull, and you know it. Frank said you weren't here."

"He thought I was still out. My room is in the back of the apartment. How would he know for sure? We don't check on each other every night," he explained.

"Where is she, Brian?" Tionna said coolly, although her blood was boiling.

"Who is she?" he asked, looking confused.

Kenya walked around Brian and headed to his bedroom. Tionna silently followed. "We don't have time for your mess," Kenya growled. "For your sake, you better hope I don't find anyone back here."

"What is she doing?" Brian questioned and followed them down the hall.

On the way to his room, Kenya stopped at the bathroom and pulled back the shower curtain. Tionna stayed out of her way. If anyone could solve a mystery, it was Kenya. She was inquisitive by nature and had been named Sherlock Holmes by their big sisters.

Deciding that the bathroom was clear, Kenya continued down the hall and walked into Brian's room. There was nothing he could do to stop her, so he lingered nervously behind them. Still keeping his composure, Brian leaned on the door while Kenya searched beneath his bed and in his closets.

"Are you satisfied now?" he remarked when Kenya ran out of places to look.

Ignoring him, Kenya walked to the window and tried to lift it, but it was locked. Since Brian lived on the first floor, it was possible that someone could've jumped out the window and run away. That would've been her final verdict, but as she scanned the room, she noticed a black and white T-shirt on the back of a chair by Brian's desk.

Kenya charged to the chair and snatched up the shirt. "Want to explain this?"

Brian's facial expression didn't change. "Isn't that Tionna's?"

Tionna grabbed the shirt and held it up so Brian could see the name on the back. "Do you think I'm stupid? Fame is Jazz's line name. Now, where is she?"

"She may have jumped out the window, Tee. But that's okay. Let's head to her house," Kenya replied.

Brian tried to explain how the shirt had ended up in his bedroom, but Tionna didn't want to hear it. She pulled the letter from her pocket and shoved it in his face. "You're such a liar. I thought you were different."

"Just stay calm," Brian said.

"Save it!" Tionna shouted. "I'm not stupid. You're standing here practically naked, with Jazz's shirt on your chair. I know what's going on!"

Kenya tugged at Tionna's arm, and the two women left the bedroom. As they approached the living room, they saw Jasmine creeping down the hall toward Frank's room, dressed in nothing but Brian's fraternity sweatshirt. She must've been hiding in one of the hall closets.

When Kenya screamed her name, Jasmine had no choice but to deal with her line sisters face-to-face.

Tionna couldn't speak for fear that she would get too riled up and would try to break every bone in Jasmine's body. Kenya lunged forward, eager to give Jasmine the beating Tionna couldn't because she was pregnant, but her path down the hall was blocked by Brian. Kenya tried to wiggle around him, but Brian used all his strength to hold her back.

"You're a disgrace to our sisterhood," Kenya shouted, still tangled in Brian's grip. "A real woman would never stab her pregnant sister in the back."

"Mom," Brianna called, snapping Tionna out of her trance. "Casey's here. Are you okay?"

"Yes," Tionna responded. "The neighbor's dog got into our yard again. Why don't you go and take him back home."

"Sure thing," Brianna said as she skipped back downstairs.

Tionna walked to the vanity and combed her hair. She prayed that she could get through the weekend without snapping at Jasmine. As far as Tionna was concerned, she still owed Jasmine a beat down or, at the very least, a hard smack.

Tionna wished she could resolve her issues with her line sister, but the pain was too deep. After she and Brian broke up for good, Jasmine had claimed him as her man in less than a year. As crazy as it sounded, Tionna really believed that Jasmine would come to her and apologize for what she'd done, not pick up where she and Brian had left off.

To this day, Tionna had been unable to maintain a serious relationship. She just couldn't pour so much of herself into another person and risk being betrayed. The breakup with Brian was a heartache she never wanted to visit again.

This was unfortunate for Casey, a detective she'd been seeing for the past six months. He was doing all the things a man should do in a relationship, but Tionna remained guarded. She expected him to disappear slowly, like all the suitors did, but Casey was different. He seemed to know how to handle her trust issues. Though he was only thirty years old, Casey had proven that he could be the man that she needed. Only, Tionna was too blind to see that. She couldn't believe that a young, handsome churchgoing man would want to be faithful to a woman with a head full of gray hairs.

As Tionna walked down the stairs, she had a clear view of the kitchen. Casey had already fixed her plate and was pouring them each a glass of Perrier sparkling water. Thinking of the damage Jasmine and Brian had caused, she prayed that God would help her finally forgive them before her hard exterior pushed Casey away for good.

~ Chapter 3 ~

Zora

"Will you hurry up!" Cynthia shouted from the living room of her best friend's swanky bi-level Manhattan condo.

Dr. Zora Thomas sat in the home office she shared with her husband and shook her head. "Cynthia Clark," Zora sang with slight laughter as she read through her e-mails. "I'll be down in five minutes."

Zora should've known better. Waiting was something her line sister had little patience for, especially when there was a place she had to be at a specific time. No sooner had Zora made her comment, Cynthia started walking up the stairs. Typing at a faster speed, Zora didn't look up from the laptop keyboard when Cynthia entered the room.

"My students have an assignment due on Monday, so I want to make sure I answer all their questions before we head out, just in case I don't have time to check e-mail at the hotel."

"Just hurry," Cynthia replied and walked to the large oval mirror on the wall. She fingered through her tapered bob cut, lifting a few of the newly highlighted strands. This was the first time she'd dyed her hair to cover up the grays, so it took some time to get used to. "We told J. Amanda that we'd be there by seven. If we don't leave in the next fifteen minutes, we'll hit that awful weekend traffic."

Zora looked up from her laptop. Cynthia hadn't been in the house a good ten minutes and already her anal tendencies were getting on Zora's nerves. "I don't think she's going to be upset if we're a little late," she replied. "And relax. This is supposed to be a fun weekend. Everything doesn't have to follow a rigid plan."

"*You* remember that, Professor Thomas," Cynthia retorted as she faced her friend. "You need to leave that laptop here. I bet not one of your Columbia University students is thinking about writing a paper over the weekend."

"We'll get there on time," Zora softly huffed, trying to concentrate. "Cute hair, by the way."

"You think so?" Cynthia asked and headed back to the mirror. "My stylist wanted to go a lighter brown, but I told her that would be too bold for me."

"I think that color's perfect," Zora added.

"Yeah, I kinda like it. I wish I was bold enough to wear natural locks like you and Kenya," Cynthia replied, still admiring her new hairdo. "I get tired of going to the salon every week."

Zora chuckled to herself. Just as much as Cynthia enjoyed serving others, she enjoyed being pampered even more. Every Tuesday, without fail, Cynthia went to the same salon for a fresh manicure, pedicure, and wash and curl. Though they were best friends, Zora and Cynthia were complete opposites. Zora learned how to maintain her curly locks and visited a salon only for special occasions.

Cynthia walked over to Zora's desk and stood behind her chair. "You should've taken the day off."

"Okay, Cyn. You win," Zora coolly replied, then closed all the open programs on her laptop. As she waited for her computer to shut down, Zora eased the printed essays she hadn't graded into the briefcase beside her left foot. She didn't have any intention to work while she was in Philadelphia, but she took work with her everywhere she went. Every down moment was a chance for her to catch up on one of the four freshmen courses she was teaching this semester.

Cynthia repositioned a picture and the sorority centerpiece on Zora's desk.

"All right, Perfect Patty," Zora said, using the name her big sisters had given Cynthia during their pledge process. "Let's go before you start finding things to straighten up."

"You know how I am," Cynthia responded and moved to the other desk in the room. Staring at the papers that were seemingly out of place, Cynthia shook her head. "Your husband can definitely use my help. It's a wonder Reggie knows where anything is."

"His desk always looks that way before he leaves for a road trip with the team. He'll organize things when he gets back on Sunday," Zora replied in his defense.

Cynthia pointed to a bright orange envelope from the City of New York. "I see Reggie got a ticket. I got one last week for not coming to a complete stop. Those darn cameras are getting everyone."

"That could be mine," said Zora. "I've been driving to work for the past month. I got tired of carrying so many bags on the train every day."

In her wedge sandals Cynthia walked steadily across the room and toward the door. "Lawrence has been driving too. His office parking lot is being renovated. . . ."

Zora placed her laptop in its protective case and then straightened her desk. Once Cynthia got started talking about her husband, there was no way to interrupt her flow. All the line sisters were used to this and had learned how to tune her out.

Cynthia was the only line sister who didn't graduate from college, and yet she seemed to be in a better position financially than everyone else. Not long after they pledged, Cynthia met a law student from NYU. One year later, and to everyone's surprise, Cynthia decided to postpone her education and become Mrs. Lawrence T. Clark, Esq.

Zora bet the others that Cynthia wouldn't last more than two years as a housewife, but something happened after she gave birth to her only child. The woman everyone knew as Perfect Patty gave up her pursuit of a career in industrial engineering in order to raise her son. By the time Lawrence Jr., or LJ, was two years old, Cynthia had become the poster mom for stay-at-home mothers. She was a member of Jack and Jill, the Links, and Drifters, and volunteered as the Northeast director for Mocha Moms.

"I don't want to work for anyone but my husband and little LJ," she'd say whenever she was questioned about joining the workforce. And as a senior partner at one of the top law firms in New York, Lawrence made sure his wife was well taken care of and happy.

Looking at Cynthia's life, Zora sometimes wondered if she had made some mistakes in her own marriage. She married the man she'd loved since junior high school, and for her, marriage wasn't a smooth stroll in the park. Much like Cynthia, Zora left Temple before graduating and followed Reggie to Chicago. Only, she didn't give up on pursuing her education. While in Chicago, she earned a doctorate in creative writing from the University of Illinois, and when Reggie accepted a physical therapist position with the New York Knicks, she didn't put up a fuss about moving again. New York was closer to her family and her line sisters.

To an outsider, Zora and Reggie were the model couple. No one knew the challenges they faced behind closed doors, and this year had been especially troubling. The pressure to start a family had become a constant battle. Every time the subject came up, the conversation ended in a heated argument. Reggie wanted kids now, but Zora didn't. Having children would require a commitment that neither of them was ready for. Reggie traveled frequently for work, and Zora was writing her first novel. Neither had time to dedicate fully to raising a child, and Zora refused to push back her dream of becoming a published author. Especially when she had direct contact with an editor at one of the largest publishing companies in New York. If she didn't jump on the opportunity now, another chance might not come around again. As far as Zora was concerned, she had already made enough sacrifices for her husband. It was time for him to compromise and let her shine, just as he'd promised to do when they got married.

It didn't help matters that Reggie's mother questioned her at least once a week. Although she had three grandchildren already, she couldn't wait for her oldest son to be a father. Yes, the pressure was great, but Zora held her ground. Still, whenever she was around Cynthia and Lawrence, she questioned whether or not she'd made the right decision. She was almost forty years old. How much longer could she realistically put off having children?

Zora prayed every day for answers. She didn't want the issue of starting a family to cause a permanent rift in her marriage, but she also had to be true to herself. At times she felt guilty for her feelings, but she believed that God wouldn't have given her such strong opinions about having a child for no reason. In her heart, she trusted that God would soften her heart when the time was right. But the tension between Zora and Reggie had become overwhelming lately, and she prayed that she hadn't allowed her pride to close her ear and prevent her from hearing what God had to say.

"I hate to leave LJ, but I convinced Lawrence's mother to spend the weekend at our house while I'm gone," Zora heard Cynthia say.

Pretending that she had been present during the entire conversation, Zora grabbed her briefcase and stood up. "It's only two days, Cyn. LJ is in very capable hands," she assured her friend as she walked toward Reggie's desk. "You have nothing to worry about."

"When you have children, you'll understand what I'm going through right now," Cynthia said.

Zora ignored Cynthia's comment and picked up the traffic ticket. More than any of her line sisters, Cynthia understood Zora's position about children, and although they didn't agree, Cynthia respected her opinions. "I hope this isn't mine," Zora said as she removed the ticket from the envelope. She unfolded the letter and was relieved to see a picture of Reggie's Lincoln Navigator. *Whew!* she said to herself. Before returning the letter to the envelope, she caught a glimpse of the location where Reggie had been ticketed. The car was parked in a neighborhood at the opposite end of Manhattan. She was really familiar with the area. Valencia Lambert, one of the players on New York's female basketball team, lived there. At least once a month she and Reggie would attend a social gathering hosted by the basketball star.

Zora started to put the ticket away without giving it a second thought, but then something made her look at the time and the date it was issued. Three twenty-eight in the morning on March 16th.

"You all right?" asked Cynthia.

Zora hadn't realized the expression on her face had changed. March 15th was a Tuesday. She knew that because that was her mother's birthday, and she had gone to Philly to spend the day with her. It was also the day she and Reggie had an argument and he decided to stay in New York. "I'm fine," Zora lied. "You ready?"

"I've been ready!" exclaimed Cynthia.

Zora forced herself to smile as she stuffed the ticket into her briefcase. "Go ahead downstairs. I just need to get my luggage from the bedroom."

"Good," Cynthia replied. "And make it quick. It's two forty-seven. If we don't get out of here by three, we can count on sitting in traffic."

"I'm driving," Zora reminded her. "You can just sit back and relax. Traffic will be my problem."

"I'm still riding with you. That's just as painful, if not more," Cynthia said as she walked out of the room.

Zora walked next door to her bedroom and stared at the luggage by the door. What was Reggie doing in Valencia Lambert's neighborhood at three in the morning? And why hadn't he mentioned that he was there? Had she not remembered the argument they had that day, she wouldn't have suspected that anything out of the ordinary had happened. But now she wondered if Reggie was having an affair.

Zora wasn't an insecure woman, and during the ten years that she'd been married, she never felt threatened by another woman. But with all the tension between them lately, she had to be honest with herself. The possibility that Reggie was seeking the attention of another woman was there. Zora couldn't remember the last time that she'd had sex with her husband. Maybe four months ago?

Zora prayed that she wasn't overreacting. There were no overt signs that Reggie and Valencia were having an affair, yet Zora began to replay all the times Valencia had been in her presence. Did she hug Reggie a little tighter than she did the other men? Did she kiss his cheek a little longer? Laugh harder at his jokes? Nothing jumped out at her as strange, yet there was something in her spirit that didn't feel right.

Many women would've broken down in tears at the thought of their husband having an affair. Not Zora. When she pledged, her big sisters had given her the name "Nonchalant," because she rarely showed emotion. One night the big sisters tried everything in their power to make Zora cry, but she never crumbled. She always kept a straight face, until Cynthia whispered in her ear one night, "Just fake cry, and they'll leave you alone." And so Zora shed a few tears. It wasn't that Zora didn't feel things or connect to someone else's pain. She did, and she possibly had deeper feelings than the others. But she expressed her emotions more in terms of physical actions than words or tears.

"Lord, if there is any truth to what I'm thinking, please open my eyes," Zora prayed and took a deep breath. "Now, please help me to put this behind me until I get back on Sunday."

The three-hour ride to Philadelphia temporarily helped Zora relieve her mind, of thoughts that Reggie was cheating. Cynthia told stories about her husband and son the entire trip, and this time Zora didn't mind listening. But as much as she wanted to bury thoughts of Reggie and Valencia, they instantly returned the moment she parked the car and Cynthia stopped talking.

Unloading her car, Zora realized that she had to speak to Reggie. There was no way she was going to enjoy the weekend unless she cleared the air. "Go upstairs without me," Zora said. Cynthia looked confused.

"What's going on?" Cynthia asked. She could tell something had been on Zora's mind since they left New York, but she knew better than to pressure her to divulge any part of her life. Zora didn't share information until she was good and ready, so there was no point in trying to force her to.

"Nothing. I just forgot to call Reggie."

"You sure you don't want me to wait for you? I can sit in the lobby until you're done."

"You've been sitting for three hours. . . ."

"And another ten minutes won't kill me. Besides, I want us to walk in together."

Realizing that this was a battle she wasn't going to win, Zora agreed and got back in her car. She waited for Cynthia to leave the garage and then called her husband.

When Reggie answered his phone, Zora immediately prayed he had a reasonable and innocent explanation for being at Valencia's at 3:00 A.M. "Hey," she said loudly in order to compete with the background noise on Reggie's end. She hated to call him before a game, but she needed answers.

"Hey, babe," Reggie replied. "You make it to Philly yet?"

"I did."

"Okay. Tell the girls I said what's up," Reggie said. He was used to his wife's even temper, so her blandness didn't strike him as odd.

Knowing that Cynthia was waiting for her in the hotel lobby, Zora decided to get to the point of the call. "Are you having an affair?"

The silence on the line caused a surge of waves to roll through Zora's stomach. His unresponsiveness had to mean that he was guilty, she thought.

"What's going on, Zora?" Reggie questioned. But it was too late. The damage had already been done.

"Don't try to play me like I'm someone you just met. I saw your car parked in front of Valencia's house at three in the morning," she snapped, without revealing the true source of her knowledge. "Why else would you be there?"

"This isn't something we should talk about now."

"If you're cheating, there's nothing to talk about. I'll make arrangements to stay with Cynthia for a while," Zora responded with a slight attitude. "Now, let me go so I can try to enjoy the weekend."

"Nothing happened between Valencia and me," Reggie mumbled so that the people around him couldn't hear his words.

Adamantly, Zora answered, "I don't believe you."

"I know what this looks like, but honestly . . . I didn't sleep with her. We just had dinner a couple times. You've got to believe me," pleaded Reggie.

Zora felt her chest tighten. Even if Reggie were telling the truth, who was to say that he wouldn't have gone on more dinners if he hadn't gotten caught? "That doesn't explain why you were at her house that early in the morning, Reggie. And you haven't slept with her *yet*. Going to dinner is just preparation for the inevitable."

The argument they had that morning came to mind, and Zora couldn't help but wonder if that was the reason why he sought the company of another woman.

"Will you at least stop taking those birth control pills?" Reggie had begged hours before he left for the airport that morning. "You've been taking them for so long, it's gonna take at least a year for your body to get ready to hold a baby. With your age and—"

Zora had quickly cut him off. She knew where he was heading next, and she wasn't in the mood to argue about the risks of having a child after thirty-five. "Don't go there, Reggie," she'd urged. "You sound like one of your medical journals. We'll be fine. Can't you wait until my book is done before we have this conversation again?"

"I'm tired of having the conversation at all. Are you waiting for me to retire?"

The veins in Reggie's neck stood at alert as he talked, and that put Zora on the defensive. "Why can't I do something I want to do, for a change? I moved to Chicago because of you. I moved to New York because of you. All of our decisions have been to further *your* career. What about what *I* want? I want to do more than teach at Columbia. I have passions too, and I want to explore them before I bring a child into our lives."

Reggie never replied to her outburst. He just snatched his suitcase off the bed and stormed out of the house, leaving Zora alone to get herself together before Cynthia showed up.

"I need to go," Zora said into the phone. "I'll try to have some kind of fun with my sorors."

"I'm coming out there," he replied.

"Please don't bother," insisted Zora. "You've ruined my weekend enough. We'll just talk on Sunday."

Without saying good-bye, Zora disconnected the call and turned off her phone. She didn't want to hear him say another word. As best she could, Zora checked her sour mood and pulled herself together. She had planned a wonderful weekend with a group of women she loved with all her heart, and she was going to do her best to enjoy her time with them.

~ Chapter 4 ~

Jasmine

Jasmine Monroe had her back turned to her three daughters as she listened to Brian yell through the phone. She didn't want her children to see the disgusted look on her face. The last time Jasmine rolled her eyes while her husband scolded her for something, Amber, her middle child, imitated her expression during a huge family dinner. That was the first night Brian had busted Jasmine's lip with his fist.

Jasmine rested her hand on the countertop and waited for Brian to stop talking. When he was done complaining about his "busy" workday, she calmly asked, "What time do you think you'll be able to leave?"

"Did you hear *anything* I told you?" Brian barked. "I'm short on workers today, and a manager needs to close out the place. I'm the only manager on duty, so I have to stay until we close."

Jasmine took a deep breath. She knew her husband was lying. This was his way of ruining her plans. Since he had chosen not to go to the college reunion, he wanted to make it so that she couldn't go, either. But Jasmine wasn't going to let anything stop her from participating in the weekend events. She hadn't seen or spoken to most of her line sisters in years, and she was eager to see them.

Brian continued to rant about his long day, and as he talked, Jasmine rolled her eyes for the fifth time in the past five minutes. If this was something that he really wanted to do, he would've clocked out on time or just taken the day off, but because Jasmine had asked him to watch their children so she could be with her friends, he pretended to be overwhelmingly busy. Just last night, after a few rounds of intense lovemaking, Jasmine made him confirm that it was all right for her to spend the weekend with her sorority sisters. Without hesitation, Brian had pleasantly given her permission to go. He had even given her one hundred dollars to buy a new outfit for the occasion.

"I heard you, Brian," Jasmine replied. "I just need to know what time so that I can—"

"Why are you in such a rush?" he snapped.

Jasmine sighed silently. How could Brian have forgotten that quickly? "You know I've been planning to go to the reunion for almost a month. We just talked about this last night."

Disregarding her comment, Brian came up with a different excuse. "You don't need to be with those women all weekend, anyway. You need to be with your kids. You're too old for that college stuff. You see I'm not pressed about going."

Biting her bottom lip, Jasmine struggled not to respond negatively. The truth was that he wasn't going because he was embarrassed. He had an accounting degree, and yet he had been one of three managers at a local Home Depot for the past eight years. His fraternity brothers, on the other hand, had all excelled in white-collar careers. Working at a home improvement company was not the plan Brian and Jasmine had agreed upon. He was supposed to finish the MBA program he'd started several years ago. Those plans were shattered when Jasmine unexpectantly became pregnant with Amber. Brian tried again when Amber turned five, but then Jasmine got pregnant with Gabrielle. With four girls and a wife to take care of, Brian couldn't afford to go back to school. The cost of day care alone ate up the money he planned to use for school.

Jasmine was growing tired of Brian's random volatile acts. He was no longer the man she had fallen in love with. Trying to "save" him from himself was pointless. Whatever advice she offered was shot down and regarded as foolish or as an attempt to control him. Living with Brian proved to be more work than raising her children. He'd single-handedly drained Jasmine of her once exuberant spirit. Now *she* was the one who desperately needed saving. That was why it was so important for her to spend time with her line sisters. Jasmine needed them more than they would ever know.

"Brian," she said, careful not to let him sense her frustration, "I just need to know what time you'll be home."

"I'll be home when I get there," he blurted and then hung up.

Jasmine stood still, with the phone attached to her ear. Sensing that Sasha, her oldest daughter, was staring at her, Jasmine pretended that Brian was still on the phone. "Okay, sweetie. I'll see you soon," she said, then placed the cordless on the counter. When Jasmine turned around, Sasha was staring directly at her, just as she'd suspected.

"Daddy on his way?" Sasha asked, although she already knew the answer.

"Yes," Jasmine mumbled and picked up the damp rag hanging across the faucet. From the corner of her eye, Jasmine saw Sasha twist her lips, but she didn't reprimand her for this behavior in front of her siblings. She didn't have the energy or the time to address the situation. The only thing on her mind at the moment was getting to Temple for the weekend.

"Hurry, girls," Jasmine said as she cleaned up the loose peas Amber had tossed across the kitchen table. "Mommy needs to get dressed."

"Where you going?" Amber whined, still playing with the vegetables on her plate.

"She's going out with her friends," Sasha answered for her mother.

Jasmine cut her eyes in Sasha's direction. As soon as she returned from her mini vacation, she'd have to talk to her twelve-year-old daughter about her grown-up attitude.

"Mommy's going to a college reunion," Jasmine said, correcting Sasha, as she lifted Gabrielle from her high chair. "I'm going to see friends I haven't seen in a very long time."

"Can I go?" Amber asked with excitement.

Jasmine positioned Gabrielle on her left hip as she wiped down the high chair. "Not this time, sweetie."

"Six-year-olds can't go where Mommy's going tonight," Sasha remarked.

Jasmine threw the rag in her hand on the table and stared at her oldest child. "That's enough, Sasha. Now, quit worrying about where I'm going and clean up this kitchen for me."

Jasmine could hear Sasha's groans as she walked upstairs. If she believed in spankings, Sasha would've received one tonight.

Once inside her bedroom, Jasmine placed Gabrielle in her playpen and turned the television on so Amber could watch the Cartoon Network. The meet and greet

at Temple started in four hours, and she was supposed to meet her line sisters in less than two hours.
If Jasmine didn't hurry, she'd have to meet her line
sisters at Mitten Hall on campus instead of at the hotel, as planned. Luckily, Jasmine anticipated Brian's
response and had taken a shower before cooking the
girls' dinner. All she needed to do now was finish packing and get dressed.

Jasmine pulled out an old suitcase from the back of
her closest and wiped off the dust with her hands. She
rolled the suitcase to the center of the room and then
loaded the clothes she had already folded the night
before. She hoped the outfits she chose weren't too out-
dated. She hadn't bought anything trendy for herself
since Amber was born. And although Brian had given
her money to buy something new, Jasmine had no idea
what was in style. So, instead of dragging the girls to
the mall, she decided to wait and go shopping with her
sorority sisters.

"What should I do about makeup?" Jasmine asked
herself aloud as she walked to the vanity. She rummaged through a wooden basket full of miscellaneous
items and pulled out a tube of neutral-colored foundation. Sadly, that was the only kind of makeup she
owned. Jasmine remembered a time when friends
would borrow her products. She threw the tube back in
the basket and made a mental note to use some of the
money Brian gave her to buy eye shadow and lipstick.

"It's after five, Mom," Sasha announced as she entered the room. "Where's Daddy?"

"He's coming," Jasmine replied, annoyed. "That
kitchen better be spotless."

Sasha plopped on her parents' queen-size bed and
lay next to Amber. "I bet he won't show up," she said.
"You should go anyway, and let us stay with Kierra. I'm
sure her mom won't mind."

"Watch that mouth," Jasmine told her daughter. Sasha didn't know that her mother had already come up with a plan B. Before going to bed last night, Jasmine had packed the girls' clothes and put them in the trunk of her car. She had thought of everything. Nothing was going to keep her from getting to the reunion.

Jasmine hoped her line sisters were just as excited about seeing her. Over the years they had had their share of problems, but the love between them never faded. Even Tionna still had love for Jasmine, though she'd never admit it.

Of all the line sisters, Jasmine most regretted losing Tionna's friendship. Sure, because of the sorority, they would always be bonded, but Jasmine feared they would never have again the genuine sister connection they once shared. Why Jasmine had betrayed her, she still couldn't explain. Back then, Jasmine and Brian partied a lot, often leaving Tionna behind while they hopped from one party scene to the next.

The night Jasmine and Brian were intimate, they had both consumed one too many cups of "Beta juice," a special alcoholic mixture that Brian's fraternity had made up. Blaming what happened on the alcohol, they had promised one another never to repeat the act again. But that one time turned into two, and before long they became a secret item.

Life takes some surprising turns, Jasmine thought as she closed her suitcase. In college Brian was considered a great catch and was supposed to be her knight in shining armor. He was supposed to have a six-figure job, and their family was supposed to enjoy the pleasures of living in a gated suburban community. Instead, Brian had turned out to be extremely temperamental. Jasmine's teacher salary carried the family, and they lived in a small townhouse development ten minutes outside of Philadelphia.

Jasmine often wondered how her life would be different if she'd never deceived Tionna. Maybe Tionna and Brian belonged together, just as everyone had said. Maybe Tionna was the better woman for him, because she knew how to encourage and motivate him in ways Jasmine wasn't equipped to.

Truth be told, Jasmine should've divorced Brian after Amber was born. It was around that time that living with him became unbearable. He was drinking more, staying out late, and abusing her emotionally. It was only a matter of time after those habits were formed that he began with the physical abuse. Jasmine came close to leaving him many times, even had a suitcase packed in the trunk of her car, but when she looked at her daughters, she changed her mind. There was no point in turning their world upside down because she was unhappy. Besides, Jasmine blamed herself for the unfortunate situation she found herself in, and accepted her troubled marriage as punishment for the pain she had caused a once trusted and dear friend.

Jasmine rolled her suitcase into the hallway and then walked to the girls' bathroom at the end of the hall. That was where she had hidden the outfit she was wearing to the party tonight. Quickly, she changed into a black cocktail dress she hadn't worn since her twenty-fifth birthday. It was a little snug, but in all the right places. For shoes, Jasmine had to dig out an old pair of black pumps from a storage bin in the attic. The only accessories she had found were a pair of faux diamond earrings and a bracelet set that Brian had given Sasha for her birthday. Jasmine prayed no one would notice they weren't real.

Jasmine stared in the bathroom mirror and wondered when she had changed. In her prime, she was often compared to the lovely actress Pam Grier. At some point, she lost herself and any hope that life would get better.

After twisting her hair into a neat French roll, Jasmine curled a few strands of hair and let them spiral on each side of her head. She unplugged the curling iron and then turned to her side. A girdle would've held the baby bulge together, but overall, she was pleased. She felt like a beautiful woman again. All that was missing was makeup, and she could borrow some from Kenya when she got to the hotel.

Jasmine winked at herself in the mirror and then headed back to her bedroom. It was clear Brian wasn't coming home anytime soon, so it was time to execute plan B.

"Okay, girls," she said as she entered the bedroom. "Put on your shoes and meet me at the front door."

"Oooh, Mommy, you look pretty," Amber cooed as she sat up on the bed.

"Thanks, baby," she answered.

"So we're leaving him?" Sasha asked.

Jasmine lifted Gabrielle from the playpen, careful not to wake her. "That *him* is your father, Sasha. What have I told you about your mouth? Now, stop with all the questions and get your sister ready to leave."

Doing as she was told, Sasha rolled off the bed and headed to her room.

Carrying her suitcase in one hand and a sleeping child in the other, Jasmine tiptoed downstairs. "Make sure your sister has on matching shoes," she ordered when she reached the front door.

An hour later Jasmine parked in front of her mother-in-law's house. Brianna, her stepdaughter, was sitting on the porch, talking on her cell phone. It was no surprise that she was there. Still, there was a slight feeling of jealousy that surfaced within her spirit. Jasmine often felt that her mother-in-law favored Brianna over her other grandchildren.

Before Jasmine could get out of the car, Sasha had opened the door and run up to the porch. With the car still running, Jasmine got out and yelled for Sasha to give her a hand with the girls. It was 7:40 P.M., so she had to hurry. She was supposed to meet the girls at seven.

"Hey," Brianna greeted with a warm smile intended more for Amber and Gabrielle than Jasmine.

Jasmine replied with a friendly hello. "I don't have time to go in the house," she said as she unloaded the trunk. Jasmine quickly kissed her daughters and then waved to her mother-in-law, who was standing on the porch.

"We'll be fine, Mom," Sasha told her mother as she walked away. "Go have fun with your friends."

As soon as the girls were inside the house, Jasmine put on a pair of shades and sped off.

Full of nervous energy, Jasmine strolled through the Marriott lobby. While standing at the elevator, she recognized Anthony Jacobs, one of Brian's fraternity brothers, and lowered her head. Avoiding Brian's fraternity brothers was going to be impossible, but she would still try.

"Hey, Jazzy!" Anthony called as he walked toward her. "Is my man here?"

Jasmine mustered up some enthusiasm and gave Anthony a hug. "Hey! Good to see you," she said, because it was the right thing to do. "Brian decided to stay home with our daughters," she lied, guessing that

Brian was more than likely at the bar with some new neighborhood friends.

Anthony gazed at her dress, and she willed the elevator to reach the lobby level soon, before she was forced to tell another lie. "And he let you out in that dress?"

Jasmine blushed. It had been years since she had received a compliment from a man. "He trusts me," she answered, telling another lie.

The elevator doors opened, and Jasmine was relieved that she could escape the conversation.

"Well, I'll have to keep an eye on you in his absence," Anthony said as he watched Jasmine enter the elevator. "Make sure you tell frat I said hello."

Jasmine promised that she would as the doors closed, and prayed that would be the last lie she'd have to tell one of Brian's brothers this weekend. Though she hadn't wanted to speak to Anthony, one thing was certain. He had boosted her ego a few notches.

As she stepped out of the elevator on the fifth floor, Jasmine didn't have to guess in which direction to walk. It had been years since she heard Kenya's unique high-pitched laugh, but she could still recognize it. Following the laughter to suite 579, Jasmine knocked on the door six times, just as she used to when they were pledging. It was their way of differentiating themselves from their big sisters.

"Jazzy!" Cynthia yelled when the door opened.

Before Jasmine could give Cynthia a hug, she was pulled inside and embraced, receiving a warm reception from all of her line sisters but one. Tionna's welcome was cold, but that was to be expected.

"There's a stroll contest, so we were practicing some old steps. We must keep our winning tradition alive," Kenya informed her.

"I can't remember the last time I hopped around a room. I think I'll need more than an hour to practice," Jasmine joked.

Like old times, J. Amanda gave instructions on how the weekend was going to flow. Since she was the oldest, the girls all respected her natural leadership skills. One would think that would've changed as they matured, but Jasmine found that she was always in need of her oldest line sister's guidance and advice.

After her friendship with Tionna ended, Jasmine worried that her relationships with her other line sisters would end too. Cynthia and Zora had never lost touch with her through the years, but it wasn't until J. Amanda gave her life to Christ that she was able to forgive Jasmine. Making up with Kenya had been a daunting task. She'd reached out to Jasmine only at J. Amanda's request, and for at least two years Kenya tested their sisterhood and friendship. But after that trial period, Kenya relaxed and accepted that Jasmine had changed. All that was left was for Tionna to have a change of heart. But Jasmine feared that day would never materialize.

After the women reminisced and practiced a few steps, they prepared to leave for the party. Jasmine followed Kenya into the bathroom so that she could borrow some of her makeup. Since their complexions matched more than any of the other women, Jasmine knew she could find some colors that complimented her skin tone.

"Remember the great escape?" Kenya asked as she laced her lips with a glittery gloss.

Jasmine laughed. Near the end of their pledge process, she and Kenya were at one of the big sisters' apartments, cleaning the kitchen. Kenya overheard the big sister, who was in the next room, devising a plan to kidnap them. To prevent that from happening, Kenya and Jasmine came up with a plan of their own. "Let's leave now," Kenya urged, and on the count of three, the two girls escaped through the window of the first-floor apartment and charged down the street. As luck would have it, another big sister saw them and chased after them. Kenya and Jasmine knew they were already in trouble, so instead of turning themselves in, they hopped into Jasmine's temperamental Renault Alliance and attempted to drive off. The plan would've worked if Jasmine's car had started.

"That was the worst night ever," Jasmine cried as she relived that day.

"I don't know what made us think that was a good idea."

"Who thinks clearly when they're in the midst of pledging a sorority?" Jasmine said and carefully dabbed at the beads of mascara on her lashes.

"Some things never change." A male voice interrupted their conversation, and Jasmine's heart dropped.

Startled, Kenya turned around and greeted Brian. Jasmine's hands started to shake, so she put the eyeliner in her hand down. She didn't want her fear to be evident.

"Hey, babe. You changed your mind?" she asked nervously. Jasmine had expected Brian to call when he realized she left before he got home. She hadn't expected him to actually show up.

"You look the same," Brian told Kenya, ignoring his wife's question.

"You do too, handsome. Glad you made it out," Kenya replied.

"I don't mean to interrupt your moment, but do you mind if I have a word with Jazz?" Brian said, with eyes as cold as ice focused on Jasmine.

"Uh-oh, girl," Kenya said. "I know that tone. You better go talk to your man."

Jasmine didn't want to go but figured she was safe as long as her sisters were close by. She left the bathroom, and as she passed Tionna on her way out the front door, she wished for a second that they could trade places.

Brian gripped Jasmine's arm and pushed her against the wall once they made it to the end of the hall. He leaned into Jasmine, assuming a fake loving posture so that no one would suspect that he was angry, and moved his lips close to her left ear. "You couldn't wait for me to come home? What was the urgency?" he griped.

"I told the girls I would be here by seven, and when you didn't—"

"How dare you leave the girls with my mother? She's getting too old to watch four kids. How can you be so selfish?"

Brian didn't give Jasmine a chance to respond.

"You must be here for some guy," he continued. "I hear your ex, Orion, is in town."

Jasmine hadn't even given that a thought. She hadn't heard from Orion in at least ten years. Brian had shut down their communication when he listened to an innocent voice mail message. "What are you talking about? I'm here to see my line sisters."

"They're so important that you dump the kids at my mom's?" he snapped.

"The girls are always with your mother, Brian. And Brianna is there to help her."

"My daughter's job isn't to babysit her little sisters."

"Well, what about me?" she wanted to ask but didn't. The moment was intense enough, and she could smell traces of Hennessy on his breath. It was best to play things safe and remain calm.

"Well, I think you need to tell *your line sisters* you're not staying all weekend. We're going to the party, and then we're leaving," Brian stated with force.

Jasmine wanted to cry, but something inside her also made her want to defend herself. "I can't leave, Brian. If you're worried about the girls, your mother already said she would—"

Brian gripped her arm tighter, and Jasmine's body tensed.

Kenya stepped out of the suite, and Brian loosened his grip. "Everything cool?" Kenya called down the hall.

"We're fine," Jasmine replied and wiggled out of Brian's grasp.

With a smirk on her face, Kenya stared at Brian. "We're just about ready to leave," she told Jasmine. "You need anything from inside?"

"No," Jasmine answered. "I'm ready."

For ten seconds, no one moved or said anything. Realizing that Kenya wasn't going back inside the suite, Brian kissed Jasmine on the lips. "I'll see you at the party." Brian strutted down the hall to the elevator, and Jasmine headed back to the suite.

"You sure everything's cool?" Kenya asked.

"Yes," Jasmine replied softly. "He's just a little tipsy."

"Ummm," moaned Kenya. "You know I never liked him in college, and I don't particularly care for him now. Just say the word and we'll handle him Eta style."

Jasmine was about to tear up. "Really, everything is fine. So let's not alarm everyone, okay?"

"I'll try not to, Jazz, but you know we're very protective of one another." Kenya touched the doorknob and then faced Jasmine. "I know there's a lot you're not saying about Brian, but I'll let it go for now. I sure hope you've found Jesus."

"Et tu, Kenya?" Jasmine said with a subtle smile. "It's bad enough J. Amanda's been on my back. Now you too?"

"Hey," Kenya responded, "I know I'm going to heaven. I just want to make sure I see you there."

Jasmine sighed. She was the only one of her line sisters who hadn't given her life to Christ. J. Amanda had been trying to get her to join a church for years, but Jasmine refused. With all the negative things that had happened in her life from childhood, she wasn't sure if there was a God and, if there was, that He really cared about her.

"Just get inside," Jasmine said, and as they walked back into the suite, she hoped that the God her line sisters knew would keep Brian under control all weekend.

~ Chapter 5 ~

J. Amanda

Mitten Hall exploded with applause as J. Amanda and her line sisters finished a modified version of the only step they remembered from their college days. While the other sororities took advantage of their younger alumni members, J. Amanda's crew was determined to prove they still had spunk and stamina in their late thirties. Wearing black cocktail dresses and heels, the women performed for three minutes in front of former classmates and other guests.

As the women exited the stage, Jasmine lingered behind them. Just as she had done when they were in college, Jasmine took the opportunity to show off her flexibility. In those years she would do a back flip and land in a split. Tonight she twirled her limber body and broke out with the latest dance move before carefully lowering herself into a full split. The audience was more than impressed.

The couple of hours they spent rehearsing before the performance had paid off. Although they moved more slowly and their kicks weren't as high, the ladies had pulled off mildly complicated routines without falling or stumbling over the person next to them.

"We've done it again, ladies!" Kenya sang as the women headed to their table.

"We better win," Cynthia huffed as she sat down. "I don't move like that at the gym!"

Kenya stood behind her chair and glanced around the table. Her line sisters were all out of breath. "You're all old ladies," she said, dancing to a remixed version of "Planet Rock," which was playing in the background. "I'm gonna hang with the young folk tonight."

J. Amanda took off her heels and rubbed her aching feet as she watched Kenya wiggle her way to the dance floor. "I feel old tonight," she said.

"Speak for yourself," Jasmine replied and laughed quietly. "I can still do a split."

"You'll be sore tomorrow," teased Zora as she guzzled half a glass of water.

Tionna lifted a half-opened purse from the empty chair in between her and J. Amanda. "Your phone is flashing, Jay. I bet it's David checking up on you."

J. Amanda took her purse from Tionna and reached inside for her phone. She was almost positive it wasn't David. When she left the house for the weekend, David had promised he'd call only if there was an emergency. He wanted J. Amanda to enjoy her time with her sorors.

Without realizing that she was smiling, J. Amanda read the text message on her screen. I'm here.

J. Amanda was expecting to hear from Hunky. He had switched his hours at the telephone company so that he could spend a few hours with her without making his wife suspicious.

With little hesitation, J. Amanda texted back. Can't wait to see you.

"Oooh, somebody's in love," Cynthia chimed in from across the table.

J. Amanda couldn't tell them the truth. At least not tonight. "What gave it away?" she replied.

"You're all red in the face," noted Tionna.

Cynthia put her elbows on the table and rested her head in the palms of her hands. "It's so cute that David still makes you smile," she said lovingly.

"How do you know it's David?" J. Amanda replied jokingly as she looked down at her phone. She had received another text from Hunky. I'm in the car, in front of the law school.

"That better be David, with that cheesy grin on your face," Tionna replied.

As she responded to his text, J. Amanda could feel Jasmine staring at her and stopped smiling. Jasmine was the only person sitting at the table who knew the truth. Give me fifteen minutes, she texted back.

"Who else would it be?" Zora said.

"You all sound as bad as David," J. Amanda told her sorors. "Before I left, I kissed him and joked that I would be a good girl this weekend. He said, 'I know you will.'" J. Amanda put her heels back on and mumbled a little too loudly, "How is he so sure?"

After David made that comment, J. Amanda wondered if her husband was overly confident about their relationship. Did he take for granted that she would never wander? If he knew the truth, his confidence would shatter.

"Sounds like David knows his wife," Cynthia answered.

Humph, J. Amanda thought to herself. *He needs to pay more attention to me.* Trying to contain her excitement, J. Amanda put her phone back inside her purse and zipped it. She hadn't seen Hunky in a week and was looking forward to spending time with him.

"Every time Lawrence goes to the Canada office, he texts or calls me every two to three hours," Cynthia said with a sparkle in her eyes. "When two people are in love, they can't stand to be away from one another. That's real love."

J. Amanda took a sip of her water and thought about what Cynthia had said. Maybe that was why Hunky was back in her life. His reappearance could be a sign that true love always found its way back home.

The day she ran into Hunky, she was with Jasmine at the Whole Foods in Plymouth Meeting. As the two women picked through the organic apples, Jasmine stopped talking and looked over at a man weighing a bunch of grapes. "That's my neighbor," she said.

J. Amanda casually looked in that direction and almost dropped the apples in her hand when she saw him. It had been close to eight years since she'd last seen or heard from Hunky, but she could recognize her high school love anywhere. Since that day, she and Hunky talked on the phone several times a week and met at the same Whole Foods once a month. Over time, Hunky became the solution to the frustrations she felt at home. His conversations were exciting and intense. He made her laugh and gave her something pleasant to look forward to.

J. Amanda glanced at the clock on the wall. In five minutes she needed to head out the door. As she looked away from the clock, she noticed a familiar face standing by the buffet table. "Jazz . . . is that Orion?"

Jasmine turned in her seat and grinned.

Zora leaned close to Jasmine and whispered, "You're beaming, and you better be careful. Brian's been watching you since we sat down."

Jasmine turned around and saw her husband seated three tables behind hers. "I better go keep him company," she sighed.

"Don't be silly," Cynthia responded and nudged Jasmine and Zora out of their chairs. "Orion was everybody's friend before he was your sweetie. Let's go say hello together."

"That's why I left the hubby home," J. Amanda said. "I'd be babysitting him all night."

As her line sisters walked away, J. Amanda watched Brian's eyes follow them. There was something different about him, but she couldn't put her finger on it. Whatever it was, it made her spirit uneasy.

J. Amanda put her hands on the table and faced Tionna. Now that they were alone, she decided this was a good time to tell her about Hunky. Though J. Amanda was close to all of her line sisters, she'd known Tionna the longest and they had become best friends. Tionna was the most guarded of all the women, but also the most mature. While the others had taken detours when it came to their goals, Tionna remained focused. She was driven and accomplished everything she set her mind to do. If only she would release the chains she put around her heart, she'd be able to live her life to the fullest and find the love she secretly craved.

Tionna had aged gracefully through the years. Even with a head full of gray hairs, she glowed with a youthful beauty. J. Amanda envied Tionna's hair. The grays she colored every month were stubborn and annoying. They were few in number but were unflattering for her short, tight-curled hairstyle.

"So . . . we need to talk," J. Amanda began as she quickly checked the time. Hunky had been waiting for more than fifteen minutes, but she thought this conversation was important to have now. She might not get another chance to speak with Tionna alone this weekend. Hunky would understand.

Tionna stopped rocking to the beat of the music and looked at her friend seriously. "Do I need to get a stronger drink for this?"

"Do you remember my high school boyfriend, Hunky?"

"How can I forget him? You only talked about him a million times." Tionna chuckled, then became serious again. "Is he all right?"

J. Amanda nervously played with an unused fork on the table. "I've been talking to him a lot lately."

"What exactly does that mean?" questioned Tionna.

"It means that I am about to go meet him in a few minutes."

"Jennifer Amanda King. Are you having an affair?" Tionna asked, with a look of surprise on her face.

"No, it's nothing serious. It's just that . . . well, David hasn't been real attentive lately, and Hunky's been . . . a good friend," explained J. Amanda.

Tionna exhaled deeply. "Have you talked to David about his behavior?"

"I've tried a few times, but he thinks everything is fine between us," J. Amanda replied. "Do you know I've been spending more time at church and at the market than before? He hasn't even once questioned why. Sometimes I think he's either cheating or doesn't care anymore."

"Or maybe he just trusts his wife, Jay," Tionna pointed out. "That's a possibility too."

J. Amanda didn't believe that.

"So . . . is he married? Does he have any kids?"

J. Amanda briefly shared that Hunky was married and had one stepdaughter. She tried to assure Tionna that she had their friendship under control, but she was unsuccessful. Since she'd been betrayed by Brian, Tionna had a very low tolerance for adultery.

"Oh, J. Amanda," Tionna said disappointedly. "I hope you're sure about what you're doing. Infidelity hurts both women *and* men."

"All we've been doing is talking," insisted J. Amanda. And that was the truth, though she had to admit that their conversations were becoming more intimate.

"You know I deal with this stuff every day. Talking leads to sex in most cases," Tionna informed her. "It's all just a matter of time."

J. Amanda knew Tionna was right, but her words were not going to change her mind tonight. Hunky was waiting for her, and she wanted to see him. She pushed the fork away from her and put her purse on her shoulder. "I should probably go," she said.

Tionna touched J. Amanda's hand, stopping her from getting up out of her seat. "You always taught me that the flesh is weak," Tionna reminded her. "You don't have to meet him. This is supposed to be your bonding time with us."

"I'll be back before you ladies go to bed. We're just going to get a quick bite to eat." J. Amanda stood up, and although she didn't need to tell Tionna, she reminded her not to tell the others.

"Of course I won't," Tionna replied. "And I'm not trying to sound like your mother. I know you're grown and can make your own decisions. I'm just worried. You have a lot of women looking up to you."

"We're just friends," J. Amanda stressed.

"Emotional affairs are damaging too," retorted Tionna. "That's the worst kind of affair, if you ask me. Especially when it's with someone you once had such a strong connection to."

J. Amanda felt like a child. She had preached this sermon several times over the years, and now she was actually living it.

"Go ahead and enjoy your night, Jay," Tionna said. "But just remember why you broke up with him in the first place."

***

As J. Amanda headed out of Mitten Hall, she thought about the week she and Hunky broke up. She was getting ready to leave for college. Since Temple University was only a short drive across the Ben Franklin Bridge, breaking up with him was the last thing on her mind. But a few days before she was set to leave, J. Amanda's oldest sister, Rose, explained how important it was for her to do well in school without unnecessary distractions. Rose never cared for Hunky but hadn't interfered in the relationship.

"At some point," Rose had said, "you and Hunky will argue just because you miss each other, then because he thinks you've changed, and eventually, because you don't come home enough. He may even accuse you of cheating. You don't have time for that. If it's meant for you to be with him, when you graduate, you'll get back together. But for now, let him go so you can enjoy this time in your life *and* make your family proud."

Although Rose hadn't gone to college, she worked hard to put herself through a dental assistant program. J. Amanda knew Rose didn't want her baby sister to face the same kinds of challenges she had overcome. For that reason, she respected her sister's input and let Hunky go.

The only way to move forward was for J. Amanda to keep her distance. When she went to college, she left all the memories of Hunky behind, including pictures, letters, and gifts. The separation was difficult, but she eventually made new friends and started a new life outside of Camden.

Now, after so many years had passed, Hunky had returned.

J. Amanda approached Hunky's car and opened the passenger door. "Hey, Hunky," she said and quickly kissed his bearded cheek. He smelled good and looked even better. The muscles he had as a teen had fully developed and were appealing under his clothes. "Sorry it took me so long."

Hunky shifted the car into drive and then grabbed J. Amanda's hand. "I would've waited all night for you, love," he replied before taking off down the street.

Instead of sitting in a restaurant, Hunky suggested they park near the waterfront walk alongside the Delaware River. Along the way they stopped at a hotdog stand and ordered a couple of hot teas. It wasn't often that J. Amanda had a chance to visit her hometown, and it felt good to be there with someone who actually understood Camden's history. When J. Amanda was growing up, the waterfront was a place she and Hunky would creep off to late at night with friends to fool around. Today it was filled with tourists coming to visit the aquarium, the museums, and the restaurants and to hear outdoor concerts. Of all her current friends, Hunky was the only person who could really appreciate Camden's growth as much as she did.

When J. Amanda and Hunky reached the end of the waterfront, they stopped to take in the full beauty of their surroundings. They both leaned against the railing separating them from the boats.

As J. Amanda leaned against the railing, she admired the scenic city view of Philadelphia on the other side of the river. "Who'd ever think we'd be back here together?" she asked Hunky.

"I sure didn't," he replied and moved so close to J. Amanda that their shoulders touched. "Just like I can't believe that you married someone other than me."

J. Amanda shook her head. "What did you expect to happen when you moved to Atlanta, Hunky? You just disappeared on me."

"I had to," answered Hunky. "I couldn't stand being here without you as my woman. You know, you were the only person that kept my life on track. When we broke up, I lost focus and started doing some pretty dumb things. It was best that I leave Camden for a while."

"I wish you would've contacted me before moving," J. Amanda said. "I'm not sure how that would've changed things, but it would've been nice to keep in touch." J. Amanda took a sip of her tea and then continued. "I wasn't going to be in college forever. Who knows? Maybe we could've picked up where we left off after I graduated. That was the plan when we broke up. Remember that?"

Hunky grabbed J. Amanda's empty cup and stuffed it inside his. "I remember," he said as he threw the cups in the trash can behind them. "But for a man like me, four years was way too long."

"Well, we can't change the hands of time," J. Amanda said, "Besides, you're married now too, and you have a daughter."

"She's my stepdaughter," Hunky replied, correcting her, and leaned back against the railing. "And I've only been married three years." Hunky reached into his pocket and pulled out a thick leather wallet. "She's a good woman," he added as he pulled a family picture from his wallet. "But she's not you."

J. Amanda blushed and then took the picture from Hunky's hand. She was curious to see if the woman he had chosen to marry resembled her. But to her surprise, Hunky's wife appeared to be her complete opposite. Patrice Crawford was at least seven inches taller and a few shades darker than J. Amanda. She had long, thick black hair, a full bosom, and shapely hips. Although J. Amanda's curvy figure was proportionate for her five-foot frame, she wished her bust and hips could fill out her clothes the way Patrice's did.

J. Amanda took her eyes off Patrice and stared at the teenager standing between the married couple, full of smiles. For a moment, she felt guilty for being with him tonight. "You have a very nice-looking family," she complimented and gave the picture back. "How old is your stepdaughter?"

"Kierra is fourteen going on twenty-four," he replied. "I never thought I'd be a father, so she's a blessing to me. Her real father comes around only a couple times a year, so my wife and I have been raising her together." Hunky put the picture away. "You have any pics of your kids?"

J. Amanda reached inside her purse, and as she pulled out her wallet, she hoped she had a picture of her children that didn't include David. She searched through the few pictures she kept and chose one she had taken of Tiffany and David Jr. a few years ago at the zoo. Tiffany was holding her little brother tightly so that he wouldn't fall off the stone turtle they were sitting on. That was a touching moment for J. Amanda. She knew as her children grew older, there would be fewer opportunities to capture the love between siblings on camera.

Hunky quickly glanced at the image in J. Amanda's hand and said, "They're cute, and your daughter looks just like you."

J. Amanda smiled softly and stared at her daughter. Before putting the picture away, she said, "I hope she grows up to be a better woman than me."

Hunky looked confused. "How so?"

"I made lots of mistakes in my youth," J. Amanda explained. "I pray she'll make wiser choices."

"Well, from where I stand . . . I think you turned out pretty good. I mean, you're *Reverend* Jennifer Amanda King."

"That title came with a price," J. Amanda confessed. "I want Tiffany to love God for real while she's young, and not play around with Him like I did."

Hunky placed his arm around her waist. "We all have a path to take. What you experienced was meant to happen. Whether right or wrong, you made out all right. Trust that Tiffany will too."

J. Amanda looked into Hunky's eyes. "That was very mature of you," she replied. "If I didn't know any better, I'd think you'd been going to church." As long as she'd known Hunky, they had never discussed religion.

"My wife goes, so I guess you can say the whole family goes with her too."

J. Amanda knew that not everyone that attended church knew Jesus as their savior, so more out of curiosity, she asked, "Would you say that you have a personal relationship with God? Or do you just go to make your wife happy?"

"I do . . ." Hunky responded as he removed his hand from her waist.

"I hear some hesitation there. Are you sure?"

Hunky stared into the dark sky. "I believe in God, but I have lots of questions," he said. "I mean, how else can you explain the formation of clouds, how airplanes operate, or stunningly beautiful women? But then why would a God that created so many wonderful things allow guns to exist and kill innocent people? Why do babies and children die before they have a chance to fully experience life? How does He decide who should be rich and who should be poor? And why can one thing happen to a person that changes their life forever?" Hunky briefly closed his eyes, and when he reopened them, he faced J. Amanda. "Those questions keep me from committing the way you do."

J. Amanda understood Hunky's concerns, especially now that she was in a weird place with God. Yet she knew her life wouldn't be worth living without having a personal relationship with Christ. "I get everything you've said, Hunky," she responded. "But at the end of the day, I feel comfort in knowing that God loves me and He always has my back. No one is exempt from pain. God uses anything and anyone to teach a lesson. So . . . I have to trust and believe that the lesson, no matter how painful, is meant to bless the world in some way." J. Amanda thought about her marriage and her friendship with Hunky and wondered what lesson God was trying to teach her now. As she fought back her tears, she finished her thoughts. "I have no choice but to trust Him. It's the only way I can make it through this life without going completely insane."

"God comes after us by any means necessary, huh?" Hunky questioned, half joking.

"He does what He has to for his children out of love."

There was a moment of silence before Hunky spoke again. "I'm waiting to understand why we couldn't be parents . . . together."

J. Amanda's heart dropped. They hadn't talked about her first pregnancy since the day she told him she was getting an abortion.

"Do you ever wonder what our kid would've looked like?" Hunky inquired.

"I try not to," J. Amanda mumbled. "That was a difficult decision I had to make."

Difficult wasn't a strong enough word to describe the pain she went through during that time in her life. She'd recently received her acceptance letter to seminary school, and she was about to marry David. Her life had been headed in a positive direction, and she'd refused to let a temporary moment of weakness ruin that.

Had she not run into Belinda, her childhood friend, in Macy's shoe department at the Cherry Hill Mall, she wouldn't have gotten pregnant the night of her friend's wedding. Thrilled that she'd bumped into J. Amanda, Belinda insisted she come to her wedding.

J. Amanda didn't want to go, and there really wasn't a reason to go. Hunky had moved to Atlanta, and she vaguely remembered the names of most of the people from her old neighborhood. In addition, her family had moved out of Camden after she graduated from Temple, so there was no one there for her to visit.

But because Belinda was so excited, J. Amanda didn't want to disappoint her. The plan was to leave right after dinner, but when Hunky walked into the reception hall in a stylish modern-cut gray suit, he easily convinced her to stay.

"I chose a good weekend to visit my mother," said Hunky. "It was only right that I make it to Belinda's wedding."

"Of all the weekends to come back to Camden," J. Amanda said and shook her head. "I had one too many glasses of champagne that night."

"And here I thought you came to the hotel because you missed me."

J. Amanda playfully hit Hunky's arm. "Of course I missed you. That wasn't the problem. The problem was that I was engaged."

"Maybe if I had come back sooner, you'd be my wife."

"You shouldn't have left in the first place."

There was a stretch of silence as a boat sailed into dock. Though he didn't say it, J. Amanda sensed that Hunky was still a little bitter about her decision. He'd been elated when she first told him she was pregnant.

Before J. Amanda had a chance to tell him about her plans to terminate the pregnancy, Hunky shared plans of his own. He wanted to marry her and buy a house in Atlanta for his new family. It broke her heart to crush his dreams, but J. Amanda had to remind him that she was already engaged to another man. And for that reason, she couldn't have the baby. That was the last time she spoke to him until recently.

"You do understand why I had to terminate the pregnancy, right?"

"I didn't then, but I did over time," Hunky replied.

"I don't know what I would've done without my sorors' support," she recalled.

"They are always there for you," said Hunky. "They liked David more than me, even though they didn't know me."

"It wasn't about you, Hunky. They knew I loved you. They just wanted what was best for me," J. Amanda said, trying to assure him. "But let's not dwell on the past. You have a beautiful wife and daughter now."

"Yes, she's the only woman that puts up with me other than you," Hunky shared. "She helped me get my life together. You have no idea how much losing you affected me."

J. Amanda tenderly rubbed his cheek. "I really am sorry for what happened that night. But . . . David and I—"

"You don't have to explain, sweetheart. That night at least told me that you still loved me. I went back to Atlanta a broken man, but I understood."

"If it's any consolation, Hunky, you were my one temptation," she admitted.

"Were?" He chuckled and rubbed her hand.

J. Amanda thought about the chemistry between them and replied, "Let's not go there."

"I apologize," he answered as he moved his hand. "Guess I can't help myself when I'm near you."

J. Amanda knew what he meant. She often found it hard to control her thoughts in his presence. Before their conversation became more intimate, J. Amanda checked her cell phone to get the time. "Though I'm having a great time, it's after midnight. We should probably head back."

Hunky didn't want to leave but didn't pressure her to stay longer. He gently reached for her hand, and as they strolled back down the waterfront, they reminisced about their childhood.

There were too many people in front of the main entrance to the hotel, so Hunky dropped J. Amanda off around the corner. J. Amanda didn't want anyone to get the wrong idea if they saw her getting out of his car at such a late hour.

Before getting out of the car, J. Amanda leaned toward Hunky to give him a good-night kiss on the cheek. Only, instead of his cheek, her lips met his. J. Amanda should've pulled away, but she allowed herself to enjoy the softness of his lips.

When they finally separated, Hunky held her arm so that she couldn't get out of the car. "Why don't I get us a room at the hotel down the street?" he suggested.

J. Amanda felt a warm sensation rush through her body and thought about her conversation with Tionna. As much as her body wanted to say yes, she had to decline. "Good night, Hunky. You know I can't leave the girls hanging."

"Maybe next time," she heard Hunky mumble as she closed the car door. Though she was tempted to get back inside the car, she waved good-bye and headed to the suite to join her line sisters.

As J. Amanda crossed the street, she saw a couple standing in front of a closed Greek bakery on the corner. The couple wasn't standing under the streetlight, so their faces weren't very visible. The man's hands were flying in the air as he spoke, and every time the woman tried to walk away, he yanked her back into place. J. Amanda knew better than to interfere. News headlines were full of people getting hurt or killed for attempting to be the hero in domestic situations. J. Amanda thought that if she was quiet but walked close enough to the couple, perhaps he would leave the woman alone, even if it was only for a few minutes. Those few minutes could possibly save a woman's life.

So she slowed down and headed in that direction, even though it was out of the way. As she approached the couple, she recognized their voices before she actually saw their faces. When the man went to grab the woman again, J. Amanda increased her pace and yelled out the woman's name. "Jasmine!"

Brian quickly lowered his hands as he turned around. "Leave us be, J. Amanda," he urged in a tone she'd never heard from him. "I'm talking to my wife."

J. Amanda stood close to Jasmine and asked, "Are you okay?"

Jasmine lowered her head and stared at the ground.

"She's fine," Brian blurted, and J. Amanda caught a whiff of the heavy alcohol he must've consumed at the party.

J. Amanda touched Jasmine's arm lightly. "I'd like to hear that from Jazz," she snapped. Jasmine flinched, letting J. Amanda know that this was not the first time Brian had physically abused her, and she frowned.

"I said she's fine," Brian stressed, but J. Amanda didn't back away. She refused to leave Jasmine alone with her husband under these conditions. He would have to fight her too if he wanted to take Jasmine away.

"I don't have time for this, Jazz. Let's go!" Brian ordered.

J. Amanda moved so that she stood in between them. "Jazz is staying with her sisters tonight, Brian. And I think you need to find your brothers so you can sleep off that liquor."

Hunky drove up and rolled down the passenger window. "Everything all right, Jay?"

In all the commotion, J. Amanda had forgotten that he was there. She was relieved he hadn't driven away. Before answering, she looked at Brian, who was breathing heavier than normal. She could tell he wanted to say something but realized he was outnumbered.

"Everything's fine, man," Brian grumbled and then angrily eyed his wife.

"Brian may need a ride home," J. Amanda said, and Brian huffed.

"I said everything's cool," Brian fired back, then stumbled to the hotel.

"Thanks, Hunky," J. Amanda said. "Text me when you get home."

Jasmine walked ahead of J. Amanda into the hotel and remained quiet until they got on the elevator. "Please save your comments, Jay," Jasmine begged. "And don't tell any of our line sisters. It's bad enough my neighbor had to see that."

"I wouldn't worry about Hunky," she assured Jasmine. "But I would like to know how long this has been going on."

"I don't think that really matters," Jasmine said with authority. "Besides, I've got this under control."

"That's not the way it looked outside," J. Amanda told her. "This isn't something you can handle by yourself. These kinds of things only get worse over time. Let me help you."

The elevator doors opened, and the women stepped into the hallway. "I don't need your help, J. Amanda!" Jasmine snapped as they headed to the suite.

"This isn't right," J. Amanda replied, and Jasmine stopped walking.

Jasmine stared J. Amanda in the eyes and carefully crafted her words. "Don't talk to me about what's right. I know I'm not perfect, but neither are you, so don't judge me."

Caught off guard by Jasmine's words, J. Amanda watched her line sister walk to their suite. How was she going to respond to that?

Jasmine stood in front of the door and waited for J. Amanda to reach her. Without saying a word, she pulled her room key from her purse and unlocked the door. When Jasmine opened the door, Cynthia was parading around the common area, imitating some of the outrageous dance moves she had seen at the party. Both Jasmine and J. Amanda pretended that all was well and laughed along with the other women.

"Glad you two made it," Kenya announced.

The women were all dressed in their nightclothes and had apparently been snacking on chips, salsa, and mild drinks for some time.

"Hurry up and change," Zora told them. "We've been waiting on you so we can play Taboo."

J. Amanda followed Jasmine into the bedroom she was sharing with Cynthia and Zora. The other women were too busy talking to notice that J. Amanda had shut the door.

"I apologize if I offended you, Jazz. I'm just worried about you," J. Amanda said.

Jasmine knelt on the floor and opened her suitcase. "I know," she replied, and immediately she started to cry. "He said I was a pitiful excuse for a woman, and that's why my real mother didn't want me." Jasmine took a nightgown from the suitcase and then walked to the bed.

J. Amanda sat on the bed next to her line sister and put her arm around her shoulders. "How would he know what your mother thought? Brian just said that to hurt you. Who knows why your mother decided to give you up? But we do know that two great people adopted you. God gave them to you. Do you know how many kids in foster care can't say that?"

Finding her birth mother had always been important to Jasmine, but she was too afraid to take the initiative alone. As she hugged Jasmine, J. Amanda decided it was time for her to help. Somehow, she'd find Jasmine's real mother.

Jasmine used her nightgown to wipe at her tears. "I know," she said and sniffed. "But hearing him say that makes me question why she gave me up and why my husband no longer loves me."

"I don't have all the answers. I'm not perfect," J. Amanda said and chuckled softly. "But God is. All I know to do when I need answers is pray. Do you mind if I pray with you?"

J. Amanda was waiting for her line sister to give her a bunch of excuses, but to her surprise, Jasmine said, "No, I don't mind," then reached for J. Amanda's hand and held it tight.

~ Chapter 6 ~

Jasmine

After a morning social with the undergraduate and alumni sorors of Eta Omicron Pi, Jasmine and her line sisters separated for a few hours. Kenya and Zora decided to get pedicures, while Cynthia helped Jasmine spend the money Brian had given her at Willow Grove Mall.

J. Amanda chose to relax in the suite with Tionna. Jasmine had an inkling that J. Amanda was up to something. Before Jasmine left for the mall, she accidentally opened a Target bag in the closet. Inside the bag were monogrammed white robes, which, she guessed, J. Amanda planned to hand out during their "sister circle" session this evening.

Jasmine couldn't remember the last time she'd been to the Willow Grove Mall, or any mall, for that matter. Wal-Mart, Target, and secondhand stores had become her source for clothes and household goods. Today was a treat, and she intended to spend Brian's money on things that only she could use and enjoy. Thus far she had been in the mall for close to three hours and had purchased a pair of sandals on sale at Nordstrom, a colorful eye shadow pallet, and a tube of lip gloss. Cynthia chose each item for Jasmine carefully, saying that she needed to utilize bright colors to complement her light brown complexion. Since Cynthia was the self-proclaimed fashion guru, Jasmine didn't challenge her judgment.

When she lost the ability to apply the right makeup escaped Jasmine's memory. Somewhere in between being a mother and a third grade teacher, she guessed. Any free time that she had in the morning was spent making breakfast, packing lunch, getting the girls dressed and catching a few extra minutes of sleep.

But this was about to change. Cynthia had given her a few tips on how to apply makeup quickly in the morning. Though Cynthia didn't have nearly as many tasks to do before going to work in the morning, Jasmine figured she'd give her advice a try.

Despite having to listen to Cynthia's continuous ramblings about her fashion expertise and family affairs, Jasmine actually enjoyed spending the day with her. It wasn't often that they had a chance to talk without the others around. It was also hard for Jasmine to sneak away to New York for the weekend now that she was a mother, and Cynthia came to Philly only when Zora brought her for special occasions.

Jasmine chuckled to herself as she rode up the escalator, listening to another story about Lawrence. She remembered the days when she and Tionna mocked Cynthia's bragging monologues about a current boyfriend. More than any of the others, Cynthia was destined to be someone's wife.

Thinking about Tionna saddened Jasmine. She had hoped Tionna would join them on their trip to the mall, but when asked to go, she complained about an upset stomach. No one believed her excuse. The truth was that she was avoiding spending time alone with Jasmine. Though their last encounters were filled with unpleasant memories, the good memories far outnumbered them. Jasmine would've loved it if she and her old friend could have teased Cynthia today, just like old times.

When they were friends, Jasmine and Tionna used to window-shop at the Gallery, Philadelphia's downtown mall, nearly every weekend. Tionna always said she'd be able to buy clothes from the most expensive stores one day. That day had come to pass. Though Jasmine didn't know Tionna's monthly gross, she had been to Tionna's four-bedroom house in Chestnut Hill and had seen the Jaguar sedan she drove. Both were luxuries the average person couldn't afford.

In Jasmine's eyes, Tionna was flawless. Every strand of hair was always in place, and she dressed up a simple pair of jeans better than a runway model could. Compared to Tionna, Jasmine appeared dull and her clothes seemed shabby. This was something to which Brian often cosigned.

"Let's go in one more store before we leave," Cynthia said as she stepped off the escalator.

One more store? Jasmine said to herself. They'd been in the mall most of the afternoon. Her feet ached, and she was hungry. Besides, how much more could Cynthia carry? She had two bags of clothes for her son in her left hand, and the two bags in her right hand were filled with items for her husband and the house they recently remodeled.

"Okay," Jasmine agreed and followed her into Bloomingdale's.

Right away, Jasmine knew she was out of her league. She had only fifteen dollars left from the money Brian gave her, and she'd rather spend that on lunch than a fancy pair of socks with a designer emblem on them.

Barely inside the store, Cynthia removed a fuchsia off-the-shoulder top from a rack. "This would look great on you," she said as she held the top with its single strap against Jasmine's chest.

Jasmine rubbed the soft material and shook her head. She knew better. Brian would have a fit if she attempted to walk out the door wearing something so clingy. "It is cute, but where would I wear it?"

"Anywhere!" Cynthia proclaimed. "Dress it up with pants or down with jeans. Put on a pair of heels or cute sandals and you'll be the hottest woman in the room."

Jasmine looked at the price tag and subtly rolled her eyes. Seventy-five dollars was too much for her to spend on one item. "You must not remember who my husband is," Jasmine replied.

"I do remember . . . and I think he'd like to see his wife in something other than soccer mom clothes."

Jasmine looked down at her loose-fitting jeans, faded brown T-shirt, and Nike sneakers. "I like to be comfy," she lied, then took the shirt from Cynthia and put it back on the rack.

"Just think about it, Jazz," she pleaded and moved on to the next rack. As Cynthia browsed through the new arrivals, she told Jasmine about her plans to visit Canada in the fall.

Jasmine aimlessly looked through the clothes on the racks, silently willing Cynthia to find what she needed so they could leave.

Twenty minutes later, they were still in the same section of the store and Cynthia was still talking about her trip to Canada. When Jasmine's cell phone rang, she jumped at the chance to answer the call.

"I better get this. It's Brian," she whispered and headed out of the store. Jasmine didn't know if he wanted to continue the argument they had last night or if he was just checking on her, but she knew if she didn't answer his call, that would make matters worse when she returned home on Sunday.

"Hey," she said when she answered the phone.

"You need to go get the girls," he barked, and Jasmine rolled her eyes. "My mother can't watch them all weekend."

Jasmine stood in front of the display window with her back facing the store. "Brian, we planned this weekend weeks ago. The kids were supposed to be with you."

"Well, my mother wants to go play bingo, and Brianna wants to go to a movie. You need to go get them," he demanded. "Bring them back to the suite if you have to. Just get over there so my mother and daughter can go out."

"You can't be serious," Jasmine snapped. She was annoyed with her husband. "You told me the kids would be with you, so you go get them. I'll be home tomorrow."

"What about your mother?" suggested Brian.

Jasmine nearly dropped her phone. Her mother lived in Maryland. Did he honestly think she was going to drive two and a half hours just so that her mother could watch the kids overnight? "I'm not calling my mother," she replied adamantly.

Brian huffed. "You should've planned this better."

"I planned this just fine," she remarked. "I just didn't realize taking care of the girls for *one* weekend would be an issue."

"This is ridiculous!" he shouted through the phone. "Those girls haven't cared about you in twelve years. Why are you so pressed to hang with them now?"

People were beginning to stare, and that angered her. "I'm not coming home until tomorrow, so I suggest you figure something out," she responded calmly.

"Oh, so everybody's weekend is ruined because of your poor planning?"

"Look, Brian. I'm not going to get the girls, and I'm tired of talking about it," Jasmine declared. "You need to—" She was cut off by a touch on her arm. When she turned around, Cynthia was standing behind her.

"Everything all right?" Cynthia inquired.

Jasmine nodded and lowered her voice. "Since I'm such a poor planner, you figure out what to do now," she told Brian and quickly disconnected the call. She looked at Cynthia and tried to mask her displeasure. "Brian's upset that he has to watch the kids tonight."

"I understand," Cynthia agreed. "But . . . are you sure that's all that's going on?"

Jasmine wondered how much of the conversation Cynthia had actually heard. "Yes," she lied. "Brian and I are fine. He's just upset that I'm having fun without him."

Cynthia headed to the main entrance to the mall, and Jasmine followed. "Make sure you pray this doesn't become a reoccurring issue," Cynthia said, concerned.

"God doesn't answer my prayers, Cyn," Jasmine nonchalantly replied.

"Why do you say that?"

There were a number of reasons why Jasmine felt that way, but only a few she cared to share with Cynthia. "I prayed that my birth parents would find me when I was young, and they never did. I also prayed that Tionna and I would become friends again. You see that hasn't happened."

Cynthia opened the door leading to the parking lot and followed the signs leading to Jasmine's car. "I'm sorry you feel that way, Jazz. But you shouldn't give up on prayer. Just because those things haven't happened doesn't mean that they won't. And . . . if you never meet your birth parents, or if you and Tionna never make amends, God must have a reason for it."

Jasmine unlocked her car doors, and the two women threw their bags in the backseat before getting inside.

Cynthia continued. "The result of prayer isn't always instant. And you can't give up on God because things don't work the way you want them to. You must have faith that He is working things out for your good, even if you can't see it."

Instead of talking about her family on the drive back to the hotel, Cynthia tried to convince Jasmine that prayer did work. Though Cynthia had the best intentions, Jasmine wasn't easily persuaded.

"Look at that," Cynthia said when they were stopped at a red light.

A young teenage boy had pushed a girl who appeared to be his girlfriend against an old Buick and had commenced yelling at her in front of a small crowd. Unable to watch the scene, Jasmine focused on the streetlight and hoped that it would change soon.

"That's so sad," Cynthia sighed when the light changed to green. "I just don't understand how women let a man abuse them."

Jasmine had forgotten how sensitive Cynthia could be when it came to certain matters. When they were pledging, Cynthia bugged the others with her strong convictions and her desire to please the big sisters. No one understood why Cynthia had been chosen to be a part of the organization, but after spending several hours with the same people for seven weeks, you grew to love them as family whether you cared for them or not. It was difficult learning to love Cynthia in the beginning, but as time passed, the girls discovered that Cynthia had a heart of gold. She was a tough judge, but she would give you her last dime if you needed it.

Cynthia had actually been the first of the line sisters to reach out to her after the affair with Brian was discovered. She hadn't held back when voicing her opinion of the matter, but once she finally said her peace, Cynthia had continued to interact with Jasmine when the others wouldn't even look her way.

"I'm sure that's not the first time he embarrassed her in public," Cynthia continued.

Jasmine tried to keep quiet but felt the need to defend the young girl. There was a time when she didn't understand, either, but now that she was the girl on the corner, she had better insight. "When you love someone, you tolerate a lot more than you should. I think you cling to any bit of hope that things will change," Jasmine responded. "It's a crazy way of thinking, but you can't help who your heart decides to love."

"I give people more credit than that," Cynthia stated. "You know when a relationship has turned sour, and you know when you're being abused."

Mildly aggravated, Jasmine gripped the steering wheel. "I don't think you would understand, Cyn. Your life has always been peachy. You come from a happy two-family home, you married the man of your dreams, you have an adorable son, and you live in a fabulous home in a New York suburb. The women who deal with abuse have real problems."

Before Jasmine could apologize for that last statement, Cynthia had taken offense. "You make it seem like my life is perfect," she retorted. "I may not have a husband that abuses me or parents that struggled to raise me, but that doesn't mean I'm exempt from problems. And it really doesn't matter whether you're rich, poor, from the suburbs, or the hood. Putting your hands on a woman is wrong. There is no excuse that I can accept for domestic violence."

Jasmine regretted her words. She didn't mean for them to come off as judgmental. "I agree, Cyn," she replied in hopes that she could redeem herself. "I only meant that I understand why a woman would linger in that kind of chaos."

Cynthia was quiet for the duration of the ride. When Jasmine parked her car, Cynthia reached in the backseat and dragged a Bloomingdale's bag onto her lap. "I was going to save this for your birthday," Cynthia said, handing Jasmine the fuchsia top from the store, "but I think you can make use of it now."

"I can't accept this from you, Cyn," Jasmine responded. "I don't have any cash on me, but let me write a check—"

"Jazz, I want to do this. I sense that there's something going on with you and Brian, and although this shirt cannot solve your problems, it may brighten your day."

Jasmine took the gift from Cynthia's hand, then dabbed at the tear forming in the corner of her eye. "I really appreciate this," Jasmine said sincerely. "And there's no need for you to worry, Cyn. Brian and I are having problems, but we'll work them out."

Jasmine hugged Cynthia and exhaled. She didn't know how or when things would get better, but it felt good to know that she had two friends praying for her happiness.

As they had planned, Jasmine, Cynthia, Kenya, and Zora met in the lobby at 4:00 P.M. and proceeded to the suite together.

"I hope there are some fine men behind this closed door," Kenya joked as J. Amanda slowly opened the door.

Kenya stepped inside the dimly lit room first and started to dance. "Now, this is what I'm talking about."

Following her line sisters, Jasmine carefully walked on the white rose petals scattered on the carpet and smiled. J. Amanda had outdone herself. Most of the living room furniture had been moved into the bedrooms. In its place were six massage tables positioned in a semicircle in the center of the room. Bowls of fruit, mini waters, and bottles of sparkling cider were neatly arranged on a long table against the farthest wall. Light music and lavender-scented candles added to the spa-like ambience.

"Welcome, my sisters," J. Amanda bellowed from the middle of the room. Dressed in one of the white robes Jasmine had seen earlier, J. Amanda handed each of her line sisters a large gift bag. "Inside your bag, you will find everything you need for our evening massage. Now, go shower and change, and meet me back here in an hour."

An hour later, the women were all dressed in their personalized white robes and white fluffy slippers. As they waited for further instructions, the women enjoyed the light snacks on the table and shared the highlights of their day.

What a perfect ending to a stressful day, Jasmine thought as she listened to Kenya rant about her son's father.

"He wants Tyree to meet his latest girlfriend," Kenya complained. "He moved in with a beauty queen after dating her for three months. I can't have my four-year-old son around that woman. Mack may think he trusts her with our son, but I don't."

"You've got to let him see his father, Kenya," Cynthia commented.

"Mack can see Tyree if he comes to *my* house," Kenya replied. "But he won't have Tyree around any woman that isn't his wife, and *if* he does get married again, I have to like the wife before she gets to know my son."

"If we didn't know you, we'd think you were serious," Zora interjected. "We tried to tell you not to get involved with Mack in the first place, but you didn't listen. Now you have a son with him, so he's going to be around forever. You two need to play nice."

Kenya smirked. "I needed you to say something stronger than 'Leave that old man alone, Kenya.' Y'all know how I am with those old-school rugged and fine men. I needed you to throw up a red flag or some other kind of signal to make me listen."

The women burst into laughter.

"That old, fine, rugged man loves you," Tionna added. "Most men don't leave their wives for the other woman if they don't have real feelings for them."

"I wish he wouldn't have done that," Kenya groaned. "Once you betray me, the thrill is gone. He'll never have me again. I just need him to keep paying that child support."

"All right, ladies!" J. Amanda sang as she surfaced from the bedroom. "Our massage specialists are on their way to the room. Finish up your snacks, take off your robes, and crawl under the white sheets on your table."

Because the tables were arranged in line order, Jasmine was on the end and Tionna was directly to her right. Jasmine had hoped this would force them to speak to one another, but they'd been in the living room for close to an hour, and Tionna hadn't looked her way once.

The women hurriedly threw away their trash before hopping onto their assigned tables. A fork from

Tionna's plate fell on the floor, and Jasmine rushed to get it for her.

"This fell off your plate," Jasmine said as she handed the plastic utensil to Tionna.

In typical Tionna fashion, she took the fork from Jasmine's hand and tossed it in the trash. "Thanks," she said coolly and headed to her table. In that moment, Jasmine gave up hope that anything between them would change.

There was a knock on the door, and Jasmine rushed to get under her sheet. J. Amanda jumped up like a schoolgirl and opened the door. "Awesome women of Eta Omicron Pi, our masseurs for the evening have arrived."

Six tall and exotically attractive men walked into the suite, dressed in all black. A glossy silver imprint on their T-shirts read: TENDER TO THE TOUCH. In each of their hands were baskets of chocolates and a business card.

"J. Amanda," Kenya called out as the men aligned themselves next to a specific table, "I think you've just created heaven for us. Thank you, girl!"

"In talking to each of you over the past few weeks, I thought this was the perfect opportunity for us to pamper ourselves. As women, we have many challenges. We juggle family, work, and this sorority," J. Amanda said as she stood by her table. "Though I don't get the chance to say this often, I hope you all know how much I love you. You are my closest friends. The years have changed, our lives have changed, but what hasn't changed is the love we have for one another." J. Amanda stopped talking to gain control of her emotions.

"Don't worry, Jay," Kenya assured her. "Nothing will ever come between us and harm our friendship. We are line sisters, and that means a lot to *all* of us."

J. Amanda fanned her eyes with her hands and smiled. "Before I have all of us in here crying, let me turn this over to Greg." J. Amanda eased onto the table as a fair-skinned brother strolled to the center of the room.

"Tender to the Touch is a company that was inspired by my wife," Greg explained. "A few years ago she went through what we call in my house 'the change.' She was overwhelmed and was taking care of everybody in and outside of our household. Her needs fell to the background, and as a result, she became sick, grumpy, and short tempered. My kids and I walked around the house on eggshells because we never knew when she was going to explode. Rather than communicate her feelings, my wife kept everything inside because she didn't want anyone to know that she was stressed and in pain. But one day, in the middle of an argument, I shut up and gave her a hug. My wife was speechless. All she could do was cry."

It was hard to pay attention to him as he spoke. Jasmine couldn't take her eyes off the muscles that bulged through his fitted shirt. But she couldn't ignore the sincerity in his tone. The love that he had for his wife brought tears to her eyes.

"I sat her down and massaged her neck and back until I felt the tension slowly release. My wife had been broken. She was tender and just needed a soothing touch to let her know that she was loved and appreciated," Greg revealed. "From that day forward, communication in our house became easier, and over time we were back to normal. She actually came up with the idea for the company. It was her desire to provide a service for other women who were going through tender moments in their lives. So . . . here I am, and I brought a team of trained men with me."

"Now that's a word," Kenya said, and Zora backed her up.

"And God bless your wife," Cynthia commented.

As the men prepared to go to work, Jasmine realized that she was one of those tender women. She needed to release the tension that had built up over the years, but how? She couldn't afford a massage every week, and Brian sure wasn't in a place to read her needs, as Greg had done with his wife. She had to find another way to get rid of her stress. Her daughters were depending on her to be a better example. *Maybe I can start dancing again,* Jasmine thought as tears rolled down the sides of her face. *Yes, that's it! I'm going to dance again.*

With a goal in mind, Jasmine closed her eyes and let her private masseur work his magic.

~ Chapter 7 ~

J. Amanda

It had been years since J. Amanda sat in the pews with the rest of the congregation, but this Sunday was a special occasion. She had reserved the first two rows so that she could sit with her sorority sisters.

David and the kids were in their normal seats in the front row, right across the aisle. J. Amanda smiled as she watched her daughter imitate the choir director. It wouldn't be a surprise if Tiffany one day stood in the director's place. Though she was at such a tender age, music for her was more than something pleasant to listen to. J. Amanda had no idea what David Jr.'s gift in the church would be. Every Sunday he'd rush to his seat and begin solving the Christian-based puzzles in a workbook she'd given him. To anyone observing him, it would appear that he wasn't paying attention to the service. But if you asked him a question, David Jr. could quote, almost exactly, phrases from the sermon of that particular day.

J. Amanda watched her husband mouth the words to the classic hymn being sung by the men's choir and smiled. When Tiffany was her brother's age, she had tapped her father on the shoulder and had told him he was singing too loudly and off-key. After that day, David started mouthing the words to every song, rather than be embarrassed by his daughter.

Looking at her family, she didn't understand how she could feel so empty.

Before guilt set in, J. Amanda turned to her right and leaned toward Jasmine's ear. "Thank you for coming," she whispered. Though Jasmine was in church only to appease her, J. Amanda prayed her line sister would receive something during the service that would help her understand that she needed God, especially at a time when she was so fragile.

Jasmine smirked. "I know how to take one for the team," she replied. "But *if* there is a next time, you better not put me in the *front* row." J. Amanda nudged her playfully, and Jasmine fanned herself with the bulletin as she shook her head and smiled.

A guest soloist moved to the front microphone and began his rendition of "For Every Mountain." As powerful as those lyrics were, J. Amanda's thoughts were in another place. Now that the weekend with her sorors was coming to an end, she realized that she needed to pay more attention to Jasmine. The volatile behavior her husband exhibited on Saturday night was disturbing. She noticed Jasmine's broken spirit months ago but had chalked it up to the overwhelming responsibilities of being a mother, a wife, and a teacher. If only she'd paid more attention to her friend, she would've picked up on the signs of abuse.

Jasmine wasn't the only person that needed more of J. Amanda's attention. She suspected that Zora was in some kind of trouble too. She had purposefully avoided conversations about Reggie. That was unusual. But J. Amanda knew not to push. Zora was a private person and liked to work through her problems before determining if she should share them with her line sisters.

J. Amanda would also be fooling herself if she didn't acknowledge that she and Hunky were dangerously close to having an affair. Though she enjoyed his friendship, the kiss they'd shared was a clear sign that the chemistry they'd once shared had been restored. *Lord, please help me stay in control,* she prayed silently.

With closed eyes, J. Amanda swayed subtly from side to side as the choir assisted the soloist in a beautiful ending to the popular Kurt Carr song. The congregation filled the sanctuary with praise as the singers took their seats. Everyone thought the song was over, but as the band continued to play an instrumental version of it, the liturgical dancers eased their way to the front of the sanctuary.

Already emotionally charged, several people raised their praise to a higher level. Directly behind J. Amanda, Kenya stood to her feet and shouted, "Hallelujah!" several times. J. Amanda didn't have to turn around to check on Tionna. Her praise was always expressed through silent tears and a slow wave of her hand.

As she watched the dancers gracefully move about the floor, something happened to Jasmine that J. Amanda had never seen. Tears were streaming from her eyes as she rocked forward and backward in her seat. When her left leg started to shake, J. Amanda held her hand. It was clear that Jasmine wanted to let loose, but she was fighting the impulse. When the emotion got to be too much, Jasmine grabbed J. Amanda's leg, snagging her sheer stockings with her nails, and cried out loud.

Jasmine leaned to her right and rested her head in Zora's lap. Moved by her actions, Cynthia jumped up and lifted her hands toward heaven. Still holding tight to Jasmine's hand, J. Amanda used her free hand to dab the tears forming in her eyes.

Minutes later, Pastor Olivia appeared at the podium, and the dancers slowly headed to their seats in the back of the church. "This is a perfect time for an altar call," the pastor said.

Feeling the weight of all her line sisters, J. Amanda took a deep breath and slowly stood up. Because her spirit was in an unfamiliar place, she knew someone else needed to cover them in prayer. As she moved toward the pulpit, something remarkable happened. With the exception of Jasmine, all her line sisters followed her to the altar. Wearing the gold-plated pins they received the night they became official members of the sorority, the women joined hands and knelt together.

Before the pastor started to pray, J. Amanda said a quick prayer for Jasmine. Though she wasn't at the altar with the rest of her line sisters today, J. Amanda knew she'd join them one day soon.

Hearing the wheels of their mother's suitcase rolling toward the back door, Tiffany and David Jr. raced to the kitchen to greet her. "Mommy!" they yelled when J. Amanda opened the door.

Though she had seen them in church, she hadn't had a chance to give them her undivided attention. By the time she had conversed with various church members, said good-bye to her sorors, and checked her messages, David had taken the kids out to eat and then driven them home.

J. Amanda set her luggage by the door and then hugged her children. Although she traveled frequently, her children never made her feel like a stranger. Her presence in the house was always missed.

"Where's Daddy?" she asked, and Tiffany pointed to the living room.

If J. Amanda had to guess, David was probably stretched across the sofa, pretending to watch television. It was almost six o' clock, and he'd been with the kids all weekend without any relief. By now, all of his energy had surely been depleted.

J. Amanda walked through the kitchen, looking for something to clean, but as usual, the room was spotless. There wasn't even a cup in the sink. The kitchen and bathrooms were always immaculate. When it came to those rooms, David was anal. He paid attention to the smallest details in those rooms, making sure that everything was neatly placed. J. Amanda wished he'd pay just as much attention to her. Maybe he'd notice they were becoming roommates, instead of growing as husband and wife.

J. Amanda made sure the back door was locked and then headed to the living room with the kids. As she had suspected, half of David's body was hanging off the sofa. The remote was in one hand, and his other hand lay limply on his chest. It was a wonder the room wasn't messier than it was. Whenever she napped around the kids, she awakened to find action figures, dolls, electronic games, and other toys strewn across the floor.

As she approached her husband, J. Amanda grabbed the empty Wendy's bags on the coffee table and gave them to Tiffany to throw in the trash. "Can we play video games?" David Jr. excitedly asked his mother.

"Sure," she answered and eased into the small free space on the sofa. She was tired, too, but rest would have to come later. It was family time.

Subconsciously, J. Amanda rubbed David's arm, and he stirred out of his sleep. "Hey," he moaned and sat up. "How long have you been home?"

J. Amanda moved closer to her husband and then placed his arm around her shoulder. "Not long."

David yawned and squeezed his wife's shoulder. "We missed you this weekend. How did things go?"

J. Amanda wondered if David meant those words, or if they were just something to say to pass the time. If he really had missed her, J. Amanda believed that he would've contacted her at least once. Hunky had. In fact, Hunky had sent several messages throughout the weekend and had come downtown to visit.

"I had a blast," she replied, "but it feels good to be home."

Thinking about the kiss she'd shared with Hunky, J. Amanda tilted David's face toward her. *This is how you show someone you missed them,* she thought as she kissed him passionately.

David responded with half her intensity and then pulled away slowly. "Wow! What was that for?" he asked, confused.

J. Amanda sat back and shrugged her shoulders. "I haven't seen you in a few days. I wanted to kiss my husband."

David didn't respond, and for the next five minutes they watched their children play a video game on the television. J. Amanda's eyes started getting heavy, and she laid her head on David's chest as her hand gently rubbed the side of his leg. It felt good lying down with him, but for some reason, David moved her hand from his leg and held it still.

Perplexed, J. Amanda sat up. "What's wrong?"

"Nothing, babe," he whispered. "Just not in front of the kids."

What? J. Amanda questioned silently. What was wrong with rubbing his leg in front of the kids? Were they not allowed to see their parents make small gestures of love?

Feeling rejected, J. Amanda stood up. That was the last time she was going to initiate any kind of affection with her husband. "Guess I'll turn you away when you tap me on the shoulder at four A.M.," she said and headed to her bedroom to change.

On her way upstairs, she wondered how that scene would've played out if Hunky were her husband instead of David.

~ Chapter 8 ~

Tionna

Tionna listened to Kenya snore as she drove through West Philadelphia. After the massage last night, Kenya's masseur invited her out for drinks in the lobby. Only Kenya could walk into a room full of strangers and leave with at least one date.

With such an outgoing and bubbly personality, it was hard to believe that she was still single. Kenya loved people. Coming from a large family, she had learned how to adapt to various personalities, speak her mind, and care for others. Qualities that had helped her rise to the position of director for a social services agency.

Her strengths when dealing with people became her weaknesses when it came to men. When a female friend or a relative betrayed Kenya, he or she had to work extra hard to rebuild Kenya's trust. Men weren't given the same chances. Kenya would never admit it, but the fact that her father divorced her mother without warning when she was eight years old played a major role in the way she interacted with men.

Getting pregnant by a man over ten years her senior was a shock to everyone. Kenya wasn't the settling down type, but when Mack came around, he treated her like a princess. As he spoiled her with gifts and dinners, Kenya found herself spending more and more time with him. At some point, she realized that the admiration she felt for Mack was really misplaced love, love that she was missing from her father. She tried to distance herself from Mack, but it was too late. He had fallen in love with her, and she had gotten pregnant. Marriage was on the table, but that scared her. Eventually, Mack grew tired of Kenya's coldness and decided to move on.

Tionna's and Kenya's struggles with the opposite sex were what had connected them as friends over the years. Neither believed she was wife material, but each had faith that the other would one day find true love. It would be tough, though. They both kept brick walls around their hearts.

At least Kenya did go out on dates. She hadn't been intimate with any of the men she'd dated since her son, Tyree, was born, though many people thought otherwise. But Kenya didn't care what people thought. Having a child out of wedlock had opened her eyes, and she had vowed to wait on God. She would often joke, "God has until I'm forty to prepare me. I'm not gonna be celibate in the prime years of my life."

Tionna was the complete opposite. She didn't have the time, the patience, or the desire to entertain a bunch of men. Since Brian had scarred her in college, she'd been in a serious relationship with only one other man. When that didn't work out, because she was "emotionally detached," Tionna gave up on men altogether.

Meeting Casey was an accident. One Sunday morning she opened the patio door to water her plants before going to church, and the alarm system had gone off. She tried to input her code, but the system didn't recognize it. Minutes later Casey and another policeman appeared at her front door.

It took an hour to clear up the confusion, but that was all the time Casey needed. Before leaving the house, he asked her out to dinner, but Tionna refused. "I'm flattered, sweetie, but I think I have a daughter your age," she told him. Casey assured her that he was older than he looked, but that still wasn't old enough for Tionna. But Casey didn't give up. For the next three weeks he drove by her house, leaving a small token on her porch each time. The only way he was going to stop was if she accompanied him to dinner. That was six months ago.

Music from a nearby car broke Kenya's sleep, and she mumbled as she perked up. "You're in deep thought," she said to Tionna and then turned the air conditioner down a notch.

"Does Brian seem different to you?" Tionna inquired.

"No, he's still the same nut he was in college," Kenya replied. "Why do you ask?"

"No reason," she said as she turned onto Lancaster Avenue. "When he came to the party, we had a chance to talk. I see him all the time, but something that night seemed different."

"He's drinking more. That I can see," Kenya commented.

"Jasmine's driving him to the bottle, huh?" Tionna joked, but Kenya didn't find that statement funny.

"Everything isn't always Jasmine's fault," retorted Kenya. "Brian's no idiot. He just chooses to be one at times."

Hearing the truth about Brian always struck a chord. For years Tionna blamed Jasmine for the affair, but the reality was that they both had played an equal role in the betrayal. The fact that he was drinking more than normal was a serious concern, but whatever he was going through wasn't her problem unless it related to their daughter.

Tionna knew for a fact that Brian and Jasmine were dealing with some marital challenges. Weeks ago Brianna mentioned that her father and Jasmine had argued over money one weekend while she was there. That, coupled with the tears Tionna witnessed Jasmine shed during the massage and at church, confirmed in her mind that something between them had gone awry.

The only reason Tionna maintained a friendship with Brian was out of the love she had for his mother. From the very beginning, Mrs. Dorothy accepted her as an adopted daughter. That relationship had strengthened when Tionna's mother passed away two years ago. His mother was also the reason that she forgave Brian when they were still in college. If she hadn't been pregnant at that time, she wouldn't have given him a second chance.

Looking back, she wished she had ended the relationship then. The years they spent trying to get things back to the way they were, were pointless. After Brianna was born, Tionna and Brian got an apartment together, and although he came home every night, she woke up every day suspicious of his actions. Every time he talked to a female friend or stared at another woman for more than two seconds, Tionna questioned his intentions. Eventually, her frequent inquisitions led to arguments. When the arguments started to affect their daughter, Tionna ended the relationship.

The night of the party Tionna was reminded of how charming Brian used to be. They had sat alone at the table for an hour, reminiscing about the pleasant parts of their past. But then Jasmine appeared, reminding them of the present—a present that Tionna wanted to avoid every time Jasmine came around. The pain Jasmine caused had cut deep, and it had cut even deeper when Jasmine started dating Brian a year after he moved out. When they got married, Tionna became numb to the pain, which only affected her future relationships with men.

In Tionna's eyes, there was no reason for her and Jasmine to be friends again. A real friend wouldn't marry the man you thought was the "one." So no matter what her other line sisters believed, Tionna wasn't interested in making amends. This was made clear at Brianna's first birthday party, when Tionna snapped on Jasmine and Brian, and it was confirmed the day of their wedding, when Tionna refused to let Brianna participate.

"Enough about Brian," Kenya said. "I think Zora and Reggie are having problems because she doesn't want kids."

"She *still* doesn't want children?" Tionna asked. "They've been talking about that for years."

"She says she wants to wait until her book is done, but . . . I don't think she wants kids at all."

"You think she can't have kids?"

"No, I really think she's happy being an aunt. Between her and Reggie, they've got, like, ten nieces and nephews."

"That's not the same, Kenya, and you know it," Tionna stated. "Zora better be careful. Lots of couples get divorced over this issue."

"I hope Reggie's not foolish enough to let her go because she doesn't want children," Kenya remarked. "They've been together too long and should come to a compromise."

"What kind of compromise is there?" Tionna retorted. "Either you get over wanting kids or you don't. I just hope Zora isn't being selfish. I mean . . . Reggie's one of the good guys. I'd make the sacrifice for a husband that's been good to me for *most* of our marriage."

"I disagree. Just because Reggie's a good husband doesn't mean Zora should be forced into having his kid," Kenya replied. "And who says he's going to be a good father? He does travel a lot. Zora would be, like, a single parent."

Tionna could tell Kenya was getting upset, so she didn't try to prove her point any further. "Looks like Zora has a lot to think about."

"Yup," Kenya agreed. "I'm glad I'm not in her shoes."

Tionna turned onto Overbrook Avenue and saw Brianna playing jump rope with Sasha and a neighbor. Watching the girls take turns jumping and turning the rope, Tionna wished that she'd given her daughter a sibling. Though she did her best to entertain Brianna as she grew up, there were some experiences best shared with a borther or sister.

"I'll only be a minute," Tionna told Kenya when she parked her car.

Kenya rolled down her window and waved to Mrs. Dorothy, who was sitting on her porch, tending to her youngest granddaughters. Before Tionna headed to the porch, she looked at Brianna jump double Dutch. She had no clue her daughter was such a good jumper.

When Brianna's turn to jump ended, Sasha faced Tionna. "Do you wanna jump?"

"No thank you," Tionna responded blandly.

"C'mon, Mom. I know you can still jump," Brianna begged.

"Not in these heels, sweetie," Tionna answered. "Maybe next time. Besides, we need to go. Kenya's in the car."

Tionna felt bad as she walked up the steps leading to the porch. If anyone but Jasmine's daughter had asked her to jump rope, she might have tried. But she hadn't developed a relationship with Jasmine's children on purpose and wanted it to stay that way.

"Hey, daughter," Mrs. Dorothy said, as if she hadn't seen Tionna in years. "You have fun with the girls?"

"I sure did," Tionna said and bent down to kiss her cheek. Tionna felt something wet near her right ankle and looked down. Glaring back up at her was Jasmine's daughter Gabrielle. She knew from pictures that Gabrielle sucked her thumb, so she figured the baby had touched her with that thumb. Tionna stepped to the side, away from Gabrielle, and leaned against the iron railing. "Let's go, Brianna!" she called, praying her bags were already packed.

Gabrielle crawled closer to Tionna, and she tried to ignore her.

"Looks like you made a new friend," Mrs. Dorothy said. She knew Tionna was uncomfortable, so she picked Gabrielle up and sat her on the chair next to her sister. "You and Amber sit still," she told them.

Relieved, Tionna changed the subject. "How was your weekend?"

"We were stuck with the kids all weekend," Brianna interjected as she walked up the steps.

Tionna looked at Mrs. Dorothy, confused. "You didn't miss bingo night at the firehouse, did you?" she asked, but she didn't need an answer. The expression on Mrs. Dorothy's face said it all.

"I haven't heard from that son of mine since Saturday morning, and Jasmine's been MIA since she dropped my babies off on Friday," Mrs. Dorothy complained.

"Daddy said Jasmine was supposed to come yesterday, but she didn't," Brianna confirmed. "I had to cancel my date so I could help Grandmom with the girls."

"You'll have to talk to your father about that," Tionna told her daughter. "Now, hurry and get your things."

Tionna waited for Brianna to go inside the house and then continued to speak. "Brianna could've watched the girls for you, Mom. You didn't have to miss bingo."

Bingo and monthly trips to Atlantic City were two events in Mrs. Dorothy's life that she looked forward to since she retired last year.

"Nonsense! I wasn't going to leave that burden on her," Mrs. Dorothy replied. "Bingo happens every Friday. I'm sure those old folks were glad I wasn't there, anyway. I always win the good prizes."

Tionna laughed and looked toward the street. Jasmine had pulled up behind her car.

Gabrielle snatched a stuffed giraffe from her sister's lap and threw it to the ground. Mrs. Dorothy softly popped her hand. "So . . . how did things go between you two?" she asked Tionna.

"Same as always."

"So you two didn't talk," Mrs. Dorothy said and laughed as she handed Gabrielle the stuffed bear she'd thrown on the ground.

Jasmine jumped out of her car, ran up the steps, and said a quick hello to Tionna. "I'm sorry, Mom," she said, out of breath. "Brian was supposed to get the kids."

"C'mon in and help me get their things together," Mrs. Dorothy replied. "My grandkids are always welcome here, but I don't want you to take advantage of me."

Brianna came out of the house with her duffel bag as her grandmother was going inside. *Perfect,* Tionna thought. Now she didn't have to make up small talk to pass the time.

"We're gonna hit the road, Mom," Tionna said before Mrs. Dorothy walked into the house. "It's getting late, and I still need to take Kenya home."

"No!" Gabrielle cried, and everyone turned in her direction.

Shocked, Jasmine lifted her daughter from the chair. "What's wrong, Gabby?"

"Isn't that cute?" Mrs. Dorothy cooed. "She's taken a liking to Tionna."

Instead of ignoring her, this time Tionna waved good-bye and smiled. For a brief moment, she considered having another child. *I must be going crazy!* she thought. She was close to forty, and Brianna was going to college in a few months.

"No bye-bye," Gabrielle whimpered as she reached for Tionna with both hands.

Warmed by the baby's gesture, Tionna couldn't help herself. On her way off the porch, she gently pinched Gabrielle's chubby legs. The look on Jasmine's face was priceless. "She's adorable," Tionna said. "She reminds me of Brianna at that age."

"Wait till you see the pictures we took during Easter," Jasmine mentioned. "They could pass for twins."

Tionna wasn't interested in seeing those pictures, nor was she interested in talking to Jasmine as if they were friends. She waved again to Gabrielle, who was silently sobbing on her mother's shoulder, then said good-bye. "I'll call you tomorrow, Mom," she yelled and headed to her car.

On the way to her house, Kenya gave Brianna highlights of the weekend. Brianna was amused by the stories. She couldn't wait to see the video of the step competition. She hadn't seen her mother dance, let alone step, in several years.

"Did Daddy step too?" inquired Brianna.

Kenya faced Brianna in the backseat and smirked. "Now, that would've been a sight worth seeing. Your father couldn't step when we were in our twenties."

"My dad has skills, Auntie." Brianna chuckled. "So give him some credit."

"You wouldn't say that if you ever saw him step. He may be good at some things, but having rhythm is not one of them," Tionna said, and Kenya confirmed that it was true.

"Well, I hope he talks to his wife about sticking me with the kids this weekend. That wasn't right," Brianna charged.

"Hold on, Bri," Kenya interjected. "Your father promised he'd watch the kids this weekend. He wasn't supposed to go to the reunion."

"That's not what he told me and Grandmom," Brianna replied. "And this isn't the first time this has happened. I don't know how Daddy does it."

"Does what?" Kenya questioned and stared at Tionna. "Your child thinks Brian's a saint, huh?"

"Mommy knows I'm right," Brianna added.

"Just because you're almost eighteen doesn't mean that you can bad talk Jazz," schooled Kenya. "Whether you like it or not, Jazz is family, and family respects one another."

"She doesn't respect my mother or my grandmother," Brianna shot back.

"All right, Brianna," Tionna said, cutting in.

"Girl, you better handle your child. Jazz cannot be blamed for everything, and Brianna should know that," Kenya said and then looked out the window.

Tionna sighed. Since Brianna was an only child, there were times when Tionna treated her more like a friend than a daughter. The feelings Brianna had toward Jasmine were Tionna's fault, and unfortunately, those feelings had been instilled in Brianna at such a young age that it was too late for Tionna to change them.

"Despite how I feel, Brianna, Jasmine's been nice to you," Tionna said in an effort to change her daughter's point of view. "And I know I taught you to respect adults."

"Yes, I am respectful, but I don't like what she did to you," Brianna mumbled.

"I understand," Kenya said, butting in, "but one day, you and your mother will finally give Jazz a second chance. Everybody else has."

Tionna was glad when they reached Kenya's condominium development in Chestnut Hill. She'd heard enough about Jasmine and how much she had changed. While Brianna helped Kenya take her bags inside, Tionna called Casey. After being with the girls all weekend, she needed to hear his voice.

"Hey, baby," Casey answered. "You home?"

"Not yet. I just dropped Kenya off. Are you busy tonight?"

"You must've missed me." Casey chuckled.

Tionna blushed. "A little."

"I'll take that," he said. "I'll come by around nine."

Tionna hung up, then leaned back into her seat. It had been only six months, but Casey made her feel wanted and loved. She really wanted to show him the same kind of affection that he gave her, but Tionna was afraid he'd abuse her love once her guard was down.

As she waited for Brianna to come back to the car, Tionna prayed that God would show her how to love again and when.

~ Chapter 9 ~

Jasmine

"What do you mean, you didn't get the girls?" Jasmine shouted into the phone. "You were supposed to get them last night."

"I got sidetracked," Brian said smugly. "And now I'm at work, so you have to do it."

Jasmine hung up the phone and turned her car around at the next intersection and jumped back on Route 76. She was almost home, but now she had to drive back to West Philly to get her daughters. *I can only imagine what his mother is saying about me,* she thought as she sped along the highway. After such a powerful church service, Jasmine had expected to return home with a new mind-set, one where she didn't react to Brian's nonsense. It was amazing how easily annoyed she'd become by the sound of his voice.

As Jasmine flew past the Sunday drivers, she tried to refocus and thought about things that made her happy. Dancing was high on her list. Thinking about the liturgical dancers at church, Jasmine couldn't believe how a simple dance could evoke such emotion. As she'd watched the dancers create art with their bodies, Jasmine remembered how peaceful and free she felt when she danced. She wanted to feel that peace and freedom again.

In record time, Jasmine made it to the Overbrook section of West Philly, and when she turned onto her mother-in-law's street, she rolled her eyes. "Great," she uttered at the sight of Tionna's car. Quickly, she parked in the space behind Tionna's car and then went to get her children.

Right away, she explained why she was late—something Jasmine hated to do in front of Tionna. Mrs. Dorothy was the only person Brian felt comfortable leaving the girls with, and Jasmine didn't want her to stop watching the girls because Brian had messed up.

"We're gonna hit the road, Mom," Tionna said, and Jasmine cringed. It bugged her that Tionna referred to *her* mother-in-law in that way. Especially when Tionna rarely parted her lips to speak to her. The distance Tionna put between them had also rubbed off on her daughter. Brianna used to hold conversations with Jasmine, but in the past couple years, she said the bare minimum. As much as Jasmine wanted their relationship to change, she couldn't do it alone. Tionna had to want it too. After the weekend, Jasmine had come to the conclusion that her line sister didn't want it.

Gabrielle hollered as Tionna headed to the steps, and Jasmine looked confused. She was stunned when Tionna touched her baby's leg. For a second, Jasmine thought Gabrielle had opened a door for them to break the tension, but that was immediately squashed. Tionna politely waved to her daughter and then, without saying good-bye to Jasmine, headed to her car.

I'm done, Jasmine said to herself, but deep inside she didn't believe her own words.

Jasmine walked into her house and immediately wanted to turn back around. There were empty pizza boxes and beer cans scattered throughout the living room, and the kitchen looked like a tornado had gone through it.

"Did Daddy have a party or something?" Sasha asked.

Jasmine asked herself the same thing, though she didn't know when Brian could've had time to entertain when he was supposed to be with his line brothers all weekend. But the mess in the house did explain why he had to leave the girls with his mother. "Take your sisters upstairs, Sasha," Jasmine demanded as she started to move the furniture back in its place. She needed them out of her way while she tried to restore order in the house.

Sasha did as she was told, but returned minutes later. "Want me to start washing the dishes?" she asked.

Frustrated, Jasmine gathered the trash in the living room and stuffed it all into a large garbage bag. "Thanks, sweetheart. I'll be in to help as soon as I'm done in here."

"Okay," Sasha replied, but she didn't go into the kitchen. "Mom, can I ask you a question?"

"What is it?" Jasmine muttered, trying not to take her disgust out on her daughter.

"How come you and Ms. Tionna aren't friends?"

Jasmine exhaled as she continued to work. She wasn't in the mood to talk about this. "Why are you asking, Sasha?"

"Brianna said that Daddy was Ms. Tionna's boyfriend until you broke them up."

Jasmine slammed a stack of coasters on an end table and stared at her daughter. "Your father and Tionna *were* a couple in college," she snapped. "That's all you need to know."

"But Brianna said Ms. Tionna was pregnant when you broke them up."

"Why are you asking me these questions, Sasha?" Jasmine asked, highly annoyed. It wasn't Brianna's place to share that information with her younger half sister.

Sasha caught an attitude as well. "I wanted to know why Ms. Tionna didn't like me and my sisters. We didn't do anything to her."

"Well, you should've asked me. Next time you want to know something about me and your father, or Tionna and your father, come to me. Do you understand?" Jasmine stated, furious.

Sasha stormed into the kitchen, and Jasmine fell into one of the living room chairs. As she tried to calm her nerves, Brian walked through the front door, carrying a case of beer.

"I thought we agreed not to keep alcohol in the house," she barked.

Brian sat the case by the sofa and sat down before addressing his wife. "I just walked in the door, Jazz. Don't start your mess."

Jasmine stared at his unshaven face and dirty sweats and wondered if Brian had showered at all today. She got up and threw the garbage bag in her hand by his feet. "I'm not your maid, Brian. The least you could've done was clean up after your company left."

Ignoring her, Brian turned the television on and kicked off his boots. Outraged by his rudeness, Jasmine snatched the remote from his hand and hit the power button.

Brian looked up and stared into Jasmine's eyes. "What's wrong with you?"

"While you were partying with your friends in our house, your oldest daughter felt the need to tell Sasha that I stole you from her mother," she answered and threw the remote in his lap. His red eyes were evidence that he'd been drinking.

Brian smirked. "Well . . . isn't that what happened?"

"I don't think that's funny, and no, Brian, that's not what happened and you're missing my point."

"Well, get to the point, Jazz. The game's about to come on."

"I don't care about some dumb game, Brian. We need to talk."

Brian turned the television back on. "I don't feel like hearing all that, Jazz. Whatever's on your mind, get it out so we can be done with this conversation."

"Since you've been so friendly with Tionna lately," she began, referring to the party Friday night, "you need to talk to her and Brianna. Brianna has no right sharing information about our past without permission."

"Don't make this bigger than what it is," Brian grumbled. "I'll talk to Sasha after the game and clear things up."

Jasmine didn't like his reply. "No, Brian. You need to talk to your precious Tionna. It's her fault Brianna knows so much, anyway. What happened in college is none of Brianna's business. But, if you won't say anything, maybe I—"

Before Jasmine got out her last words, Brian leaped off the sofa and firmly grabbed her arm. "Don't tell me what to do with my daughter, and if I hear that you approached Tionna with this foolishness, you'll be sorry."

Jasmine yanked her arm away from her husband's grasp and walked into the kitchen. There was more she wanted to say, but getting into an argument with him wasn't the way she wanted to spend the evening.

"You okay, Mommy?" Sasha asked as her mother headed to the table.

"She's fine," Brian replied from the living room.

Jasmine dropped her head to the kitchen table. "I can't do this anymore," she whispered.

"What? You're crying now?" Brian yelled.

Jasmine lifted her head and looked at her husband, who was standing by the kitchen door. "I'm tired, Brian," she told him.

"Tired?" he responded. "What do you have to be tired about?"

Jasmine knew what was coming next and asked Sasha to get her sisters and go next door. Brian was in the mood to fight, and she didn't want the girls to be subjected to his ranting.

"Yeah," Brian agreed. "I need to have a word with your mother."

Sasha put the dishrag in her hand on the counter and eyed her mother as she left the kitchen. As best she could, Jasmine nodded to assure her daughter that she'd be okay.

"I don't want you contaminating my daughters with your crazy thoughts," Brian said.

"Nobody's doing anything to your kids, Brian. You need to be concerned about what they think of you."

Without warning, Brian snatched Jasmine from the chair and threw her up against the wall. "If they have a problem with me, it's all your fault," he charged.

In pain, Jasmine didn't want to say anything until she was sure the girls were out of the house. She remained still as Brian accused her of trying to turn the girls against him. That was far from the truth, but whenever Brian had been drinking, there was no telling what thoughts raced through his head.

As Brian pinned her to the wall, Jasmine tuned him out and pictured her line sisters at the altar today in church. She had considered joining them but had feared her disbelief would somehow block their blessings. Listening to the chaos surrounding her, Jasmine wished she had gotten up from her seat. Maybe today was the day that God would've listened to her cry. But she had let the opportunity pass her by, so she'd never know.

When Jasmine heard the front door close, she used her strength to push Brian away. He stumbled backward, and before he caught his balance, Jasmine ran upstairs to their bedroom. Quickly, she locked the door and then fell to the floor. She was tired of Brian and embarrassed that she didn't put up more of a fight in front of her daughters. Jasmine wanted to be a better role model for them, but she didn't know how. *I've got to do better,* she told herself. *Things have got to change.*

Later that night, Jasmine put the girls to sleep and then got ready for bed. Brian had been calm for several hours, and Jasmine made sure she and the girls stayed out of his way. Whenever Brian was in a rage for no reason, Sasha chose to sleep in the same room as her sisters. Though Sasha was full of attitude, she was extremely protective and smart for a child her age. "I don't like the way Daddy treats you," Sasha told Jasmine when the girls came back from the neighbor's house. That had broken Jasmine's heart. All she could think to say was, "Things will get better. So don't you worry." Sasha didn't believe that any more than Jasmine did.

Jasmine turned off her night-light and settled under the sheets. She had a great weekend with J. Amanda and the other women, but that high had worn off the minute she left their presence. As she closed her eyes, Jasmine imagined being back at the hotel with the masseur. As he tenderly touched her body in her dream, Jasmine fell into a deep sleep.

***

"Jasmine," Brian called and tapped her shoulder. "Jasmine, baby, wake up."

Startled, Jasmine opened her eyes and saw Brian kneeling by the side of the bed. "Everything okay?" she asked.

"Baby," Brian moaned, "baby . . . I'm sorry I yelled at you today."

"Go to bed, Brian," Jasmine sighed and turned her back to him. She was used to his temporary apologies. They were often followed by his need to make love to her, but tonight she didn't want to follow that script.

"I mean it, baby," Brian said as he wiggled his way into the bed, pushing Jasmine over to his side. "I love you so much. If you want me to tell Tionna she was wrong, I'll do that for you, okay?"

"You don't have to," Jasmine said nonchalantly.

Brian eased his hand around her waist and pulled her close to him. "I'll do it if you want me to. I love you," he insisted as his hands roamed her body.

Jasmine felt his warm breath on her neck and started to get out of the bed, but Brian pushed himself firmly against her and was ready to do his business. "I think we should try for a son."

"A son?" she muttered. *This man is crazy!* Jasmine thought.

"Yes, I think that's what's wrong with me."

No, you're nuts! Jasmine said to herself. *That's what's wrong with you.*

"C'mon, Jazz," he moaned and climbed on top of her. "Let's make another baby."

Rather than argue, Jasmine let Brian have his way. And as he made love to her, she was glad she hadn't missed any of her birth control pills this month.

~ Chapter 10 ~

Zora

"What did Orion want?" Zora asked Cynthia as she helped load bags into Cynthia's car.

"He wants Jasmine to teach a few dance classes at his studio," replied Cynthia.

There was barely room in the trunk for all the bags she accumulated in Philly, but they stuffed the bags in between the boxes of supplies Cynthia kept handy for the many organizations she participated in. Zora flattened the last bag and pushed it between two boxes. "That'll be good. She used to be a gifted dancer," she said and closed the trunk.

Cynthia walked to the driver's side of her car and opened the door. "I just hope Brian won't have a problem with it."

"I know," Zora agreed. "He was weird at the party. Is he all right?"

"Something's going on. He was kind of harsh with her while we were shopping yesterday," Cynthia said. "And Kenya mentioned that he was a little aggressive with her at the hotel on Friday."

"That doesn't sound good."

"Tell me about it," Cynthia replied. "I just have this bad feeling about them."

Zora lifted the handle of the suitcase next to her. Her issues with Reggie suddenly seemed miniscule compared to what Jasmine might be going through. "I'll pray for her," she said, concerned.

"I'm praying for both of you. Now stop stalling and go work things out with your husband," Cynthia said as she got into her car.

Zora stood on the sidewalk, gripping the handle of her suitcase and clinging to her computer bag and purse, looking like she had just lost her best friend. She waited until Cynthia's car turned the corner, then made her way into the house.

Inside, she heard familiar voices over the television coming from the dining room. Those voices belonged to her in-laws. Zora sighed as she walked down the hallway. It wasn't unusual for them to stop by uninvited. They drove to New York a few times a month from their southern New Jersey home to catch a play or other social event. She wasn't upset that they were there. They were a close-knit family. She was upset that Reggie might have shared their disagreement with his parents before they had a chance to straighten things out.

No one heard her come in. Zora could tell by the huge smiles and the warm welcome she received from her in-laws when she entered the room. It was also possible that Reggie hadn't mentioned Valencia or the issue about children to his parents.

"Put your bags down and have a seat," said Renee, Reggie's mother, as she pulled out a chair at the table. "Jerome and I bought a large pizza."

"I have to pass this time, Mom. Cynthia and I grabbed something on the drive back," answered Zora. "And as much as I'd love to chat with you and Pop, I really need to get some work done."

Reggie looked disappointed but didn't challenge Zora. "It was a girls' weekend, Mom. You know what that's like."

"It's been years since Renee's had a girls' weekend. I'm her only friend now," Jerome joked.

"He *thinks* he's my only friend," Renee teased, then kissed her husband's cheek. "I'm just kidding, love. You know you're all I need."

Zora was touched by the love her in-laws shared. They had been married since they were eighteen years old, had struggled through an affair and career choices, had dealt with a child Jerome conceived during the marriage, and had come close to getting a divorce, and yet somehow their love was strong enough to survive it all.

Though Zora and Reggie had been together since junior high school, they hadn't experienced half of what his parents did. It was clear that they loved one another, but Zora was beginning to question if they'd survive without having children.

"I thought I'd have a chance to work, but my sorors kept me busy the whole time," explained Zora. "I've got a ton of papers to grade before my afternoon class tomorrow."

"Reggie," Jerome said, "you married a woman just as driven as your mother. Good job, son. She's a keeper."

"I know," Reggie replied, and Zora forced a smile. She hoped he'd remember that the next time he was tempted to visit Valencia in the middle of the night.

"Well, I'll be upstairs if anyone needs me," Zora said and walked out of the room.

Zora changed into more comfortable clothes and then separated the clothes in her suitcase. Clothes that she didn't wear were placed back in her closet, and dirty clothes were put either in the hamper or in a basket of clothes designated for the cleaners.

While she moved around her room, Zora considered the comparison made between her and Renee. Though it was a compliment, she wasn't sure she could be as forgiving as Renee had been when it came to her husband.

They were both women who were passionate about their careers. Renee had climbed the corporate ladder in a large hotel chain within a short time frame, while maintaining a life at home with a husband and children. Zora was still reaching for the goals she'd set for herself, and she didn't want to juggle teaching, writing, being a wife, and being a mother. One of those areas would suffer, and at this point in her life, she didn't want that to be her career.

Jerome had also cheated on Renee during the time of her multiple promotions. To make matters worse, a child was conceived with his lover. After witnessing her in-laws deal with life during and after the affair, Zora knew that she couldn't tolerate infidelity in her marriage. If Reggie was involved with Valencia, it would be difficult to let him go, but that was what she'd have to do.

Now Renee was the owner of an event-planning firm, but she still made time for family. Though she had grandchildren from her middle son, she wanted more Especially since her youngest son died in a car accident before he graduated from high school. With him gone, the pressure was on Reggie to expand the family name.

As Zora rolled her suitcase under the bed, there was a knock at the bedroom door. When she stood up, she saw that Renee had already invited herself into the room.

"Got a minute?" she asked and leaned against the tall dresser next to the bed.

Zora felt her stomach drop. Something in Renee's tone suggested that this wasn't going to be a pleasant conversation. "Sure," she answered and sat on the edge of the chaise on the other side of the dresser. "What's up?"

Not one to beat around the bush, Renee jumped straight to the point of her visit. "I asked Reggie if you were okay. You didn't seem like yourself," she began. "He mentioned that you didn't want to have kids."

Zora exhaled. "That's not what I told him," she said and made the correction. "I want to wait until my book has been published. Is that so hard for him to accept?"

"I think he can," Renee responded gently. "But I know he's afraid you'll find another reason to wait after that. Should he be concerned about that?"

"I can't honestly answer that right now. All I can honestly tell you is that I'm not ready right now," Zora stated and prayed her answer would be enough.

Renee sat next to Zora and stared at the Persian rug beneath her feet. "I know I can lay pressure on thick," she admitted. "But that's my son. I know he wants children, and all I want is for him to be happy." Renee paused, and when Zora didn't speak, she continued. "You and I have always been open with each other, but I can understand why you wouldn't want to share this with me. My boys mean the world to me, but Zora . . . I love you too. You've been with this family for a *long* time and have seen us at our worst. You were there for me when things hit rock bottom, so I don't want you to feel like you have to hide your feelings from me."

Zora held back her tears as she remembered Renee's struggles. There wasn't much she could do to ease her hurt, but she was around to offer encouragement. That was exactly what she needed now. "I followed Reggie for so many years," she confessed. "I moved to Chicago because he wanted to go to college there. I moved to New York because it was a great opportunity for his career. Now that he's a little more settled, I want to pursue what I love."

Renee held Zora's hand. "Sometimes being a woman seems unfair. We give up so much of ourselves for our husbands and sacrifice our own happiness. I refused to be that woman, so I worked extra hard to succeed at home and at work. But look where that got me." Renee chuckled. "I can't say that I'm proud of everything I did, but I'm happy I tried to balance it all. I love running a business . . . but I love my family more. Now, I'm not telling you to be like me," Renee said and smiled, "but I am telling you to find your balance. If you want your marriage to last, sometimes you have to fight through what hurts and make sacrifices to keep you both happy."

"I understand what you're saying, but . . . I don't want to bring a child into our home if Reggie is always traveling and I'm on a book tour. I don't want a nanny to raise my baby, so I'm stuck. And I'm afraid that it would be me giving up something once again."

"You're fortunate enough to have a husband that adores you and a family that supports you," Renee explained. "Tell Reggie how you feel. If he really wants a child, he'll need to make some changes too. And you know Jerome and I would be overprotective grandparents. If you needed to go on tour, the baby could stay with us or I could tag along and take care of the baby's needs. I'm sure your mother would do the same."

Zora hadn't considered that. "I guess," she replied.

"I still hear hesitation. What else is wrong?"

Zora almost brought up Valencia but felt that was something Reggie should share with his mother before she brought it up. "I'm afraid I'll be a bad parent."

"What parent isn't afraid, baby? There's no manual you can read that'll make you a perfect parent. Whether you have one child or eight children, you're going to make mistakes. I made *plenty,* and somehow my kids turned out all right. You've got to trust that God will provide all that you need to raise your kids," Renee advised. "*And* that He'll cover them and you when you mess up. Remember how bad Reggie was in school?"

That made Zora laugh. When they were young, Reggie was lazy. He rarely did his schoolwork, barely played basketball, although he was gifted, and followed behind the wrong crowd. Getting into college was short of a miracle, but once admitted, Reggie turned a new leaf and worked diligently to become a sports doctor.

"Thanks for talking to me, Mom," Zora said.

Renee hugged her daughter-in-law and then stood up. "Pray about it, but know that I'm here for you." Renee headed to the door and stopped before entering the hallway. "One more thing," she said and faced Zora. "Reggie told me about that ballplayer."

Zora looked surprised.

"Yeah, he told me," she repeated. "I know her kind well. Some women tend to go after what they want no matter what. I didn't handle Taylor well, but you're different from me. Don't let that woman interfere with what you've spent years building. You understand me?" Zora nodded yes. "I told Reggie if her name comes up again, after I knock sense into him, I'm going down to that arena to do the same to her."

Zora shook her head when Renee went back downstairs. She knew her mother-in-law wasn't kidding, because she'd seen her in action many times. Taylor, Jerome's former lover, didn't stand a chance once Renee chose to fight for her marriage.

Zora gathered her computer bag and slid into comfortable slippers. *I hope things won't get that deep,* she thought as she headed to her office on the third floor. *I feel sorry for Valencia if they do.*

***

It was after midnight when Zora finished grading papers. She hadn't expected to be in her office for more than an hour, but once she got started, she lost track of time. When she walked into the bedroom, she thought Reggie would be asleep. The Knicks had a game in Boston, and he had to catch an early flight to meet them there.

"You're still up?" Zora said as she headed to the vanity.

"I was waiting for you. Is it too late to talk?" Reggie asked.

Zora grabbed a few bobby pins from a porcelain tray and pinned her locks. "It is late, but we shouldn't go to bed without saying what's on our minds."

Reggie lowered the volume on the television and sat up tall in bed. "I just want you to know that I didn't sleep with Valencia."

"Then why were you there?" Zora asked as she wrapped a scarf around her locks.

"You were mad at me that day, and I knew she was having a party, so I went over there to be around the team. I didn't plan to stay that late, but we started talking, and the next thing I know, it was light outside," explained Reggie. "I know this isn't a good reason, but it's the truth."

Zora changed into one of Reggie's old T-shirts and crawled into bed. "So . . . you're gonna turn to Valencia or whoever's available every time we disagree on something?"

"Of course not—"

"Don't say that, Reggie, because I'm not going to change my mind about having a baby anytime soon. So every time you get upset about that, I'm gonna wonder if you're with someone else."

Reggie fell back into his pillow and threw his arm across his forehead. "I don't want anyone but you, Zora. But I have to be honest. . . . You're not helping me understand why you don't want kids."

"Stop saying that," Zora responded. "For the billionth time, I don't want to raise a child by myself. You travel more than half of the year, and I would be left to be Mommy *and* Daddy."

"You know our parents would help," Reggie reminded her.

"Our child will be *our* responsibility. I don't want to put that burden on our family."

"Nothing I say is a good compromise for you," Reggie said and turned on his side. "That's why I believe you're dragging this out until you won't be able to have kids at all."

Zora turned in bed to face her husband. "Everything about my life will change, Reggie. What kind of changes are *you* willing to make?"

"You want me to get a new job?" Reggie questioned and lay on his back. "That's ridiculous. We do need money to raise a kid and pay the bills."

"I don't want you to switch careers or anything, but maybe you can cut back on traveling or something—"

"I think you're being unfair," Reggie snapped and turned off the light.

Zora sighed and turned her back to her husband. She loved Reggie but didn't see how they were going to get past this.

"I just want you to be honest with me," continued Reggie. "If you know you don't want children, tell me now so that I—"

"So that you can what?" she interrupted. "Leave me? Is that what you were about to say?"

"You're overreacting, Zora."

"Then tell me what you were about to say."

"This is crazy," he said and got out of bed. "I know it's your body that will carry a child, but I think it's unfair that what I feel doesn't get any consideration." Reggie headed to the door as he continued to speak. "You're not the only person that needs to adjust to the decision you'll make."

"I just need time," Zora remarked again.

Reggie stopped at the door. "One year? Five years? Twenty?" he retorted. "You do know there are a number of risks and complications a woman faces when she waits too long."

Feeling pressured, Zora rolled on her stomach. Reggie wasn't the only person needing a break from the conversation. "Sarah and Abraham made out all right in their old age," she snapped.

"So you want to wait until you're eighty?" Reggie replied sarcastically, and then marched downstairs. His wife's comparisons to the biblical icons were not helping her case at all.

An hour later, Reggie returned to the bedroom. Though Zora was tired, she couldn't sleep. Reggie got into bed and put his hand on her back. "It's been over a month since we've been intimate, Zora. Are we gonna let this come between that too?"

Zora rolled her eyes. Of course she wanted to make love to him. It was just hard to switch emotional gears as quickly as he could.

"I miss my wife."

Don't let that woman interfere with what you've spent years building, Zora recalled her mother-in-law saying. If Reggie was being honest about Valencia, she couldn't continue to withhold sex. If she did, there was a chance Reggie would fulfill his needs in another woman's bed.

Zora took a breath and moved closer to her husband. "I'm sorry, honey," she said and lightly rubbed his chest. Reggie lifted her hand to his lips and kissed it. "I let stress take over, but I do want you," she continued.

"Then let's stop arguing tonight and just enjoy one another."

"You and Reggie must've made up. I haven't heard from you all week," Cynthia told Zora as they walked to the ladies' room in Mount Vernon Baptist Church.

Zora blushed. "We're getting there," she said. "We decided not to discuss kids until next year, so everything's cool right now."

"Wonderful! I told you prayer works. What about a certain basketball star?" inquired Cynthia.

"He said nothing happened, so . . ." Zora pushed the bathroom door open and stopped walking. Valencia was standing in front of the mirror, putting on mascara. Zora knew that Valencia attended the same church, but Mount Vernon was a mega-church. Unless you sat in the same section every week, there was no guarantee you'd see the same faces each Sunday.

Valencia flung her natural brown weave to the right and pushed one side of her hair behind her ear. Seeing Zora standing at the door, she grinned and said, "Good morning, Zora."

Zora wanted to correct her by saying, "It's Mrs. Thomas to you," but Cynthia nudged her past the sinks and into a bathroom stall. As she took a deep breath, Zora recalled the conversation she had with her mother-in-law, focusing again on the comment that had registered with her the most. "Don't let that woman interfere with what you've spent years building," Renee had told her.

Feeling Renee's take-charge spirit, Zora walked out of the stall and strolled toward the sinks, where Valencia was still applying makeup. Carefully studying the woman who had kept Reggie out all night, Zora paused by the last sink. The way Valencia seductively applied her lipstick irritated her. *She's probably exaggerating because she knows I'm looking,* Zora thought.

With only three sinks separating them, Zora had to give Valencia some credit. She really was a beautiful woman. But she seemed to be the opposite of the kind of woman Reggie liked. He preferred down-to-earth women who were proud of their natural beauty and who didn't paint their faces with makeup or wear outrageously long weaves. As Zora approached Valencia, she could feel her mother-in-law's presence.

"You okay?" Valencia inquired as she eyed Zora in the mirror.

"I know about the night Reggie stayed at your house," Zora said with authority. "I want you to know that he is *my* husband and we're happily married."

Valencia rubbed her lips together, then put her gloss inside a small makeup case.

As she stuffed the case inside an oversized Gucci bag, she looked Zora directly in the eyes and smirked. "If that's what you want to believe."

"Excuse me?" Zora replied, shocked at her boldness.

Cynthia rushed from her stall and pulled Zora back down the aisle.

"God won't bless what you're doing," Zora blurted.

Valencia stood in the aisle so that Zora could see her as Cynthia held her line sister's arm tight. "What exactly am I doing, Zora? Reggie's my friend. But you . . . you're supposed to be his wife. Do you think God will bless what you're doing, or *not* doing, to your husband?" Valencia remarked with a sly grin.

Zora's jaw dropped. How dare she speak those words to her! She thought about what her mother-in-law would've done and tried to free herself from Cynthia's grip. A good slap was what Valencia needed, and Zora was prepared to deliver it. Only, Cynthia wouldn't let her get close enough to touch the foul woman.

"That's enough, ladies. We're in church," Cynthia reminded them.

"Stay away from my husband," Zora declared sternly.

Valencia brushed her off with a nonchalant shrug. "You need to ask yourself why *your* husband is seeking a friend like me."

"Valencia!" Cynthia barked, annoyed. "Please, just get your bag and leave."

With an air of confidence, Valencia checked her hair in the mirror one last time. "Enjoy the service," she said smugly before leaving.

When she was gone, Zora covered her face with her hands. "What just happened?" she cried.

Cynthia walked to the sink and cleaned her hands. She was in shock too. "I've never seen anything like that. My mother would call her a vixen," Cynthia said in an attempt to make Zora laugh, but it didn't work. "Listen, what you and Reggie have is special. Everyone can see that. There's something between you two that a lot of couples will never experience. Valencia sees that love, and she wants it for herself. But she can't have it, because God gave Reggie to you."

Barely listening, Zora tried to decipher Valencia's words. What did she know about her marriage? Did Reggie discuss their problems with her? Wasn't there someone else he could confide in?

Hoping that her words were getting through to Zora, Cynthia stood next to her and continued. "Reggie made a *stupid* mistake. I think he knows that. But *you* have to recognize that having children is important to him. The fact that you're on the fence with starting a family is not easy to accept. Most women *want* to have kids with their husbands. But that woman has *nothing* on you. Reggie loves you, and I know God is going to see both of you through this."

An older woman walked into the bathroom, and Zora pulled herself together. She went back into the stall and stared at the dispenser on the wall. Though she felt like an idiot for approaching Valencia, she was glad the incident happened. At least now she knew the kind of woman she was dealing with.

~ Chapter 11 ~

Tionna

Tionna had never been inside an actual police precinct. When Casey asked her to stop by on her way to work, she'd imagined a scene similar to what was shown on one of the cop shows on television, where the holding cells were in the same room as the policemen's desks. In Casey's office, there were no holding cells or criminals waiting to be processed. There were private offices with huge see-through windows along one of the walls and a series of desks with computers on them for each officer and detective.

As instructed by the receptionist, Tionna stood by a tall artificial plant and waited for Casey. She surveyed the large open-spaced room, trying to figure out which desk belonged to him. She'd been to his bachelor-pad apartment a few times, and although his place smelled pleasant and things were in order, it could still use a woman's touch. Tionna imagined that his desk would need some feminine attention too.

A door opened at the end of the hallway, and Tionna redirected her attention. Casey was in the private office with a small group of policemen, some dressed in uniform, others in street clothes, like Casey. As he pointed to images on a screen, Tionna felt proud. He'd been a cop for only seven years and a detective for less than three months. She pictured him running the office by the time he turned forty.

When he ended the meeting, everyone piled out of the room and returned to their desks. Casey was too busy talking to recognize Tionna standing by the front door. Her eyes followed him as he sat at a corner desk near a slightly opened window and put away the folders that were in his hand.

Suddenly, a woman close to Casey's age appeared and sat close to him on the edge of his desk. By the way she giggled and tapped his arm whenever he said something funny, knew they weren't discussing business. Tionna's left brow rose suspiciously. *Who is that woman? And why is she so comfortable with my man?*

The receptionist noticed the flustered look on Tionna's face and stood up to draw Casey's attention in her direction. At the sight of his woman, Casey jumped up from his seat and strolled toward her, beaming with pride.

"Hey, babe," Casey greeted and unexpectedly kissed Tionna on the lips.

Standing tall at six feet four inches, Casey was the perfect height. Because she was taller than the average woman and loved to wear heels, it felt good to look up and into his eyes. Unless she wore flats with the guy she was dating, Tionna was usually the one bending down for a kiss.

For the next ten minutes Casey escorted Tionna around the office, introducing her to his colleagues. Some names Tionna recognized, and quite a few she forgot the minute she left the person's presence.

"I know who this is," the mystery woman said, gloating, as they approached her desk, which was positioned next to Casey's. "You have to be Dr. Tionna Jenkins. I've heard so many wonderful things about you." The woman gave Tionna a friendly hug.

"Wish I could say the same about you," Tionna remarked and limply returned the embrace.

Casey grabbed Tionna's hand. "This is my partner, Lee. LeAnn Davis," he said, as if that would jog her memory. "I told you about her."

Yes, Casey had mentioned his partner several times. But he never mentioned the fact that *Lee* was short for *LeAnn*.

Trying not to twist her face, Tionna remained polite. "Nice to meet you."

"What brings you by?" asked Lee.

"I promised Casey I'd bring him lunch on my way to work," Tionna replied.

"My baby makes the best chicken marsala I've ever tasted," bragged Casey.

Lee sat on Casey's desk again and grinned. "So that's how you got him. I better take a few lessons, or I'll be single forever. You free on Wednesday nights?" she kidded, but Tionna didn't find her remarks funny.

"I only cook about five dishes really well," she answered.

"Tionna's so modest," Casey said and squeezed her hand. "She can throw down in a kitchen."

Casey and Lee talked about their favorite foods and restaurants Tionna had never heard of. Tionna felt like a stranger as she listened to them compare notes, and suddenly she felt old. Lee was much shorter than she was, and had muscular arms, full hips, and perky breasts. Tionna also couldn't overlook the fact that Lee's long, silky ponytail was jet-black. When she compared herself to Lee, she didn't understand why Casey was so attracted to a tall, slender, and gray-haired old lady.

"I hate to leave," Tionna interrupted, "but I have a class in an hour. I should probably head out."

"Okay," Lee said with an upbeat tone. "It was such a pleasure to finally meet you. I hope you come back soon so we can get to know each other."

"That would be nice," Tionna said, just to be polite.

"Let me walk you outside," Casey said as Lee finally returned to her own desk.

"I'll be okay. You stay here and enjoy your food."

"Thanks again, babe," he said and kissed her. "If I'm not here too late, I'll stop by your place tonight."

Tionna let go of Casey's hand and waved to a few friendly faces as she headed out of the precinct. Casey didn't give her a reason to be suspicious or jealous, but it bugged her that his partner was a woman. Now she had another reason to stay guarded.

Every seat in the classroom at the clinic was filled with people suffering from some type of sexually related problem. The majority of the attendees were her patients, but there was a growing number of people coming to sessions who were patients of other doctors in the clinic. If enrollment continued to rise, she would have to recruit another doctor to teach the same class or cut back on the hours she spent treating patients.

Tionna had had no idea that the classes she offered would become a vital addition to the clinic. The information and support she provided in each eight-week session had become one of the reasons people chose to visit her facility. With so much success the first year, Tionna had enrolled in a two-year counseling program at Temple so that she would be well educated and qualified to lead the groups. This was now the fourth year she had offered the classes.

Today was the beginning of a new session that would help people deal with the leftover scars from former relationships. It was ironic that Tionna led such a class.

She hadn't been delivered herself from the relationship with Brian. In some ways, the discussions in class served as therapy for her as well. Each time she coached someone through their problems, she pretended she was talking to herself. Many of her friends couldn't see the change that had taken place in Tionna's heart, but the classes had softened her heart . . . just a bit. For years she ignored signs of interest from men enthralled by her beauty and intellect, but a year after teaching classes, Tionna occasionally entertained a friendly lunch or a brief conversation over coffee. Now, three years later, she was in a relationship.

The first day of each session was not as intense as the weeks that followed. The entire hour was spent engaging in interactive exercises to help participants get to know one another. It was important for each member of the midsize group to feel comfortable sharing sensitive information.

By the end of class, people were more relaxed and willing to share their story. Tionna sat among the group with a notepad in hand, ready to take notes. In order for her to address each person's specific issue, she needed to record important details about him or her. One would think Tionna would be numb to the various stories shared in her classes. Many of the stories were similar at their root and thus were the same issue, just different players. But that was far from the truth. She listened to each testimony with fresh ears and a heart filled with concern.

Today a woman in her late twenties told the group that she contracted a disease that would one day claim her life. The man she'd been involved with had been her best friend for more than ten years. When the friendship transitioned into a relationship, she didn't think twice about using protection. Now she was paying the price for trusting a man she had once loved. A middle-aged man admitted that he had abused several women intimately and emotionally because his wife left him for another man. He was unable to have a decent relationship because he still blamed his wife for ruining his life. The last gentleman who shared his story brought the group to tears. He had spent several years in prison for a rape he didn't commit. While he was in prison, his family alienated him and he was violated by another inmate in the worst way. Although he'd been a free man for many years, anger dwelled in his heart, keeping him from moving forward with a happy and emotionally healthy life.

Listening to each story, Tionna thought about J. Amanda. What she was doing was risky. She hadn't seen Hunky in almost a decade, yet she was willing to put her marriage in danger. Tionna said a prayer for her friend. At this point, no matter what J. Amanda decided, someone was going to get hurt.

Tionna ended the session with prayer and then headed back to her office. She had a few patients to see and patient records to update. Before digging into her work, Tionna checked her cell phone for messages. She was expecting a call from Brianna.

The first message came from Kenya. "You may need to come bail me out of jail tonight. Mack took Tyree to Chuck E. Cheese's with his new woman without my permission. He's on his way here, and my box cutter's in my hand."

Tionna laughed aloud. Kenya should've been a comedian.

Brianna left the next message. "Q and I are going to the movies tonight. I should be back before midnight."

Quentin, or Q, as he preferred to be called, was Brianna's boyfriend. He wasn't the guy Tionna wanted her daughter to date, but she knew better than to force

Brianna to date someone else. Quentin was smart. He attended Central High School and had been accepted into the University of Pennsylvania, but he had a know-it-all air about him, something the girls his age found attractive. Brianna could've chosen a less desirable young man as her boyfriend, so Tionna tried not to complain. Though she did pray college would expose them to new interests.

The last message came from Casey. He had called to tell her that his colleagues were jealous. It wasn't every day that a beautiful woman came to the office to deliver a home-cooked lunch. "Lee wants you to make her a plate next time," he said and laughed.

Tionna deleted the message and then responded to each of them via text. She told Kenya she'd see to it that Mack and the woman raised Tyree if she went to jail. That should be enough incentive for Kenya to behave when Mack arrived. She told Brianna to make sure Q brought her home on time, and she told Casey that she looked forward to seeing him tonight. She didn't respond to what Lee had said. Until she understood their relationship, Tionna wasn't going to prepare lunch for her or invite her over for cooking lessons.

Tionna put her phone in her pocket and grabbed the folder of her next patient. Before going into the waiting room, she scanned his medical history and jotted down a few notes. Tionna hadn't seen a new patient in months, but she was doing a colleague a favor and the patient was a member of a current group. When she finished writing down information that she had learned in today's session, Tionna tucked the manila folder under her arm and headed to the waiting room.

"William," Tionna called, and the man looked up from the magazine he was reading. "C'mon back to my office."

***

The house phone rang at 9:35 P.M., as Tionna was sitting at the kitchen table and reading the notes she'd collected in today's group session. She looked down at the cordless phone next to her arm and smiled when she saw Casey's name on the caller ID. "Hey," she said. "Are you on your way?"

"Can I get a rain check?" Casey asked, and Tionna frowned. "Lee and I made a huge bust tonight. We have a few more people to interview and paperwork to turn in."

"I suppose I have to accept that," she replied, unaware of the shift in her tone.

"Is my baby upset?" Casey asked playfully. "I can still come by, but it'll be closer to midnight. I wasn't sure if you'd still be up."

Though Tionna had never given him a curfew, she had insisted that they shy away from spending the night together. She hadn't been intimate with a man since her last boyfriend several years ago. After their breakup, Tionna decided she didn't want to share her body with another man until she was married. This was often an issue for the few men she had briefly dated. But not for Casey. He was raised by a Christian mother, and although his job prevented him from going to church as often as he liked, he understood and respected Tionna's decision to remain celibate.

"It's really okay, Casey. I'm working tonight, anyway," she said.

"No, I can tell you're upset. I promise I'll make it up to you."

There was no reason for Tionna to be upset. Casey worked late many nights. That was part of his job, and she understood that. Still, the thought of him working late hours with Lee bothered her. Maybe her feelings would be different if Lee had been his partner for more than three months, but that wasn't the case. "Go ahead and finish working with your partner. If you and *Lee* don't have plans for tomorrow, maybe we can catch up."

"So . . . is that what you're upset about?" Casey questioned. "Babe, you know you have absolutely nothing to worry about. I only have eyes for you."

Tionna wanted to believe him. She even told herself that she was acting like a child, but she couldn't control the words that came out of her mouth. "I'm not naive, Casey. I see the way she looks at you," she answered, careful of her tone. She and Casey had never had a major disagreement, and she didn't want Lee to be the reason they had one tonight.

Still in a pleasant mood, Casey chuckled softly. "It doesn't matter who looks at me, Tionna. You're the only woman I'm crazy about."

"Can you honestly tell me you haven't had intimate thoughts about her? I mean, you haven't been with me, and we've been together six months," Tionna replied. "Not many men can hold out that long."

"They can if they really respect a woman," Casey stated with more bass in his voice. "It's not just about sex with you and me."

"You're definitely in the minority with that thinking."

"Well, I'm not the average man," Casey replied in a serious manner. "I thought you knew that about me."

Tionna suddenly felt bad and tried to turn the conversation around. "I'm sorry, Casey. I guess I got nervous when I saw how young and beautiful Lee is."

"One day you'll understand that your age is more important to you than it is to me. I'm not out to hurt you. I've never been that kind of guy."

For fear of saying the wrong thing, Tionna felt they needed to say good-bye for the evening. "Well, we both have work to do, so let's—"

"It's getting too hot for you, huh?" Casey remarked. "You know, not all men are dogs, Tionna, and every man won't do what Brian did to you. I'm going to let you go, but . . . I think you need to figure out whether or not you want to pursue a relationship with me. I'm not a man to play games, and I don't want to spend all my energy trying to make you believe how much I care about you. So when you're certain you want to have a real and honest relationship with me, give me a call."

Astonished, Tionna swallowed hard and stared at the phone. The lump in her throat prevented her from responding, and it was probably for the best, because she was clueless. What should she say?

"I know I've said a lot, so I'll let you go," Casey continued after a brief silence. "I do hope I hear from you," he said and then wished her a good night.

Tionna stared at the phone for at least fifteen minutes after Casey hung up. In her mind she replayed the conversation several times, and each time she pointed out a different reason why it had ended poorly. She wanted to call him back and apologize for her immaturity, but she was embarrassed by her behavior. Plus, she wasn't sure that she was ready for a man like Casey. It was clear that her heart was still too fragile.

"Guess I messed up again, God," Tionna whispered and leaned back in her chair. Before she called Casey back, she was going to take his advice. The last thing she wanted to do was hurt him, so Tionna decided to pray for direction. She wouldn't make another move where Casey was concerned until God answered her prayer.

~ Chapter 12 ~

J. Amanda

Women's season was the busiest time of the year for J. Amanda. As the minister over the women's ministry, she was responsible for all activities and events. This year was extra special. In honor of the ministry's ten-year anniversary, Pastor Olivia suggested the church host all the main events. That included the women's prayer breakfast, the evening gospel gala, and the weekend conference.

Hosting all of the main anniversary events at the church was great. It was less expensive and more convenient for the members. On the flip side, J. Amanda had twice as many committees to oversee and even more planning meetings to attend. Many nights she wished they had booked a hotel to host the special events, as they had done for the last five years. Utilizing hotel space was costly, but the services they provided were well worth the money, and committee members weren't completely burned out by the day of the event. Nevertheless, J. Amanda made a commitment to her pastor, and she was going to work overtime to make sure women's season was spectacular.

With so many added responsibilities to an already packed schedule, J. Amanda had little time to catch up with her line sisters. Every day there was something to do at the church, and evenings were spent with her children. Quality time with David had also been reduced. When she finally got home, she helped Tiffany with homework while David cooked dinner. After dinner, she either read a story or played a game with the kids while David cleaned the kitchen. And while he prepped the kids for bed, she prepared for the next day and made phone calls to check on various members of the church.

David didn't complain about J. Amanda's hectic schedule. He knew once the season was over, their life would go back to normal. But his laid-back attitude didn't do much to soothe J. Amanda. Rather than view his behavior as support, she saw it as another form of detachment.

In the midst of everything, J. Amanda's relationship with Hunky was the only thing that remained consistent. Understanding that her schedule had changed, he sent her two messages every day, one to say good morning and another to say good night. Those messages lifted her spirits on the most chaotic days. Though their actual phone conversations occurred only on Tuesday nights, J. Amanda and Hunky never missed the opportunity to meet at Whole Foods on Saturdays.

Today was one of the rare moments when she completed all the tasks on her daily list before 5:00 P.M. Once she finished a draft letter for the publicity committee to approve, she planned to spend some time with Jasmine. The last message Jasmine had left on her phone concerned her.

J. Amanda toyed with different ways to write a sentence and was distracted by the vibration of her cell phone on the desk. Surprised to see Hunky's name on the screen, she looked away. The letter was due by the end of the day, and she wanted to get it done while her thoughts were flowing. If his call was important, he would send her a text.

J. Amanda continued to write, and a few seconds later her cell phone vibrated again. It was Hunky again. *That's odd,* J. Amanda thought and dropped her pen. Hunky had never called back within seconds before. Just as she went to answer the call, Pastor Olivia entered her office.

"I've been watching you work, Reverend King," Pastor Olivia said as she walked over to J. Amanda's desk. "I like what I see and what I've been hearing."

J. Amanda wasn't aware that the pastor was keeping tabs on her actions, but she was thrilled to hear the good report. "Thank you," she humbly replied.

"Listen, I have another suggestion," Pastor Olivia said, and J. Amanda got nervous. She was already in over her head. Anything else the pastor wanted would probably send her over the edge. "I want you to kick off women's season on my television segment."

"Sure," J. Amanda said. "I think it'll be great to let your viewers know what's happening this year."

"Oh no, my dear. I want you to deliver a word for the kickoff."

J. Amanda was speechless. Pastor Olivia's segment aired on the cable network in areas across the country. It was rare that an invitation was extended to preachers who hadn't already made a worldwide name for themselves. J. Amanda was a local name, so she knew God had shown her favor. The opportunity to appear in the pastor's place could take her ministry to a higher level. "I'm . . . I'm—"

Pastor Olivia smiled. "I hope you're trying to tell me you accept."

J. Amanda got up and hugged her mentor in ministry. "Of course," she cried. "This is such an honor. Thanks so much for inviting me."

"You've been a part of this ministry since it began, and sometimes I think you preach better than me," Pastor Olivia joked. "You have a heart for women, more than any other minister on staff. So I know God will use you to deliver a powerful word to set off the season. This one may be the best yet."

"It will," J. Amanda confirmed as she wiped her tears of joy.

Pastor Olivia patted J. Amanda on the back and then left the office. Though J. Amanda had another assignment to fulfill, she felt energized and ready to take on the challenge.

Still excited from the pastor's invitation to appear on television, J. Amanda parked in front of Jasmine's house, eager to share the news. When she turned off the car, she faced Hunky's house, and it dawned on her that she'd forgotten to call him back. She glanced inside his house from her car and caught a glimpse of a woman sewing in the living room. She figured the woman was his wife.

J. Amanda got out of the car and walked toward Jasmine's house. As many times as she'd been in the neighborhood, she hadn't run into Hunky or his wife. In case they should ever come face-to-face, J. Amanda rehearsed her greeting to be sure nothing came across as suspicious.

"Aunt Manda's here," Amber shouted from an open window upstairs.

J. Amanda looked up and smiled. "One day you'll say my name right," she teased. "Tell your mom to come open the door."

J. Amanda heard Jasmine dragging her feet toward the door. When the door opened, J. Amanda could tell her friend had had a rough day. Her hair was pulled back in a ponytail, and her sweats looked more than a day old.

"Hey," Jasmine said somberly and then walked over to the sofa.

J. Amanda closed the door behind her and slowly stepped inside the house. "Where are the kids?" she asked and stood behind the sofa.

"Gabby's asleep, and Amber should be watching a movie. Danielle should be on her way home from school."

"I'm guessing you didn't go to work today. Is everything okay?" J. Amanda asked as she stared at a cracked framed picture near the bottom of the stairs. On her way to pick up the picture, she noticed a lamp lying on its side near the opening to the kitchen. Afraid to investigate further, she left the picture in its place and sat next to Jasmine, who was staring at an invisible spot on the floor.

"What happened, Jazz?" J. Amanda said and sighed. "You have to tell me sooner or later. Might as well be now."

"I feel like I'm being repaid for all the bad things I've done in my life," Jasmine said coldly. "Once again, I went to church and tried to connect. I was determined to be different, but I didn't even make it home before Brian started his mess."

"What is he angry about this time?"

"Cynthia told me about Orion's studio in South Philly. He wants me to teach a class, so I called him to discuss the details," Jasmine explained. "I was so excited that I didn't hear Brian come in the house." Jasmine started crying. "I'm going to dance, Jay. I've got to."

Fighting back tears, J. Amanda turned to her friend. "I don't know why Brian's so angry, but we'll figure a way out of this. I won't stop praying until things change."

"I don't know why he hates me so much. I've been a good wife to him," Jasmine continued. "But nothing I do now is right. A few weeks ago Brianna shared inappropriate information with Sasha. When I asked him to talk to Tionna about it, he flipped on me."

J. Amanda didn't want to choose sides, so she remained neutral in her response. "Perhaps things are out of order because you and Tionna aren't getting along. There's no reason you and Brian should be at odds because of her. It may be best for you two to find some middle ground. Maybe then things in that area will change."

J. Amanda's cell phone rang, and she pulled it out of her bag. Hunky was calling again, but this wasn't a good time to talk. She hit the IGNORE button and then asked Jasmine a series of questions. "Has Brian hit the girls? Is he staying out late and getting drunk all the time? Where is he now?"

Jasmine wiped her eyes. "I feel like I'm in an interrogation room," she said, trying to joke. "But no, he hasn't touched the girls. He's starting to drink and stay out more than usual, and he should be at work."

J. Amanda's phone rang again, and this time she sent Hunky a text. "I hope Hunky's all right," she told Jasmine. "He's been calling me all day."

"He probably wants to tell you about the noise coming from my house last night. The girls had to spend the night over there," Jasmine replied. "His wife has been good to my girls during all this."

Hearing that, J. Amanda felt some relief. Maybe she could convince Hunky to look out for Jasmine and keep her informed. It would also help if he had a few words with Brian. There was a chance that Brian just needed a good male friend to help him change.

Hunky replied to J. Amanda's text, letting her know he was all right. He explained that he had been near her church earlier and wanted to take her to lunch.

As J. Amanda responded, Jasmine stared at her and shook her head. "If only you could see your face," she said. "Does he know you're here?"

"He saw my car out front," J. Amanda said and put her phone away. "He told me I was a good friend."

"That you are, but . . . how good of a friend are you to him?"

"Let's not make this about me," J. Amanda insisted, though she wanted to share her good news. "I want to make sure you're going to be okay."

"As long as you're praying for me, I know everything will be fine," Jasmine answered. "But I want you to think about this thing with Hunky. I don't want you to mess up what you have with David. He's a good guy. You could've ended up with a husband like mine. Don't take that for granted."

"Where did all this wisdom come from?" teased J. Amanda.

Jasmine shrugged her shoulders. "Maybe you're rubbing off on me."

For the next hour, J. Amanda helped Jasmine identify ways to protect herself and the girls when Brian was in one of his moods. In the end, she made Jasmine promise to call the police if the situation was more than she could handle. Jasmine also promised to leave Brian if he refused to get help or change by the end of the school year. J. Amanda didn't like that part of the plan but understood Jasmine needed the time to make other arrangements.

Jasmine prepared her girls a small snack and then walked J. Amanda to her car. Outside, Hunky stood in his driveway in a white tee and cargo shorts, trimming the hedges. When he saw J. Amanda, he waved and subtly blew her a kiss.

"I saw that," Jasmine acknowledged, and J. Amanda blushed. "Remember what I said earlier. Count your blessings." Jasmine stood on the sidewalk as J. Amanda walked to the driver's side of her car. "By the way," she called, "thanks for coming by. It really meant a lot."

"You're my sister, Jazz. If you hurt, so do I. Remember that," J. Amanda answered, glad that she had given her friend a glimmer of hope.

J. Amanda got into the car and checked her watch. It was time to get back on schedule. David should've picked up the children, and he was probably on his way home. Before pulling off, she had an idea. She pulled out her phone and sent out a text to all her line sisters, inviting them to a Mother's Day brunch in the park. At that event she would share her exciting news with everyone at the same time.

Tiffany was sitting at her desk in the family room when J. Amanda got home. She had already started her homework, and David was almost finished frying chicken. There wasn't much time to change before dinner, so J. Amanda sat down next to her daughter and watched her work.

"I'm ready when you are," David yelled from the kitchen.

"Go get your brother and get ready for dinner," J. Amanda instructed, and as Tiffany charged up the stairs, she headed to the kitchen. She couldn't wait to tell her family about the invitation to appear on television.

"I got your text," David remarked as he placed a bowl of rice on the table. "I wasn't sure you wanted to go out for Mother's Day, but brunch works for me."

J. Amanda was confused. How did he know about the brunch? "You got a text from me?"

David laughed. "Yes. You don't remember sending it? You must've been really busy today."

J. Amanda went back into the next room and checked her cell phone. She navigated through the different functions until she was able to view the last text she'd sent. She wasn't used to the new touch screens, so there was a chance she had sent the message to David, instead of to her friends. J. Amanda tapped the screen and the recipients of the message she'd sent appeared. As clear as day, David's name was included on the text.

"I didn't mean to send that to you," she told David when she went back into the kitchen.

"Okay," David responded and continued to make himself a cup of tea.

J. Amanda sat down and suddenly became annoyed. Not that she wanted to explain herself, but she felt that David should've asked her a few questions. "Sooo . . . do you care who the text was for? Or do you just not care?"

"What are you talking about?" David asked and leaned against the counter. "You said it was a mistake. So I figured it was meant for someone at church. Should I be concerned?"

"Yes, David, you should be. Why do you just *assume* it was for someone at church?" she snapped. "I had a great day at work, and I was ready to share it with my family, but then I come home to a husband who continues to give me nothing."

"Nothing?" David repeated, confused. "What are you talking about?"

"I'm talking about the attention you don't give me anymore. The kisses I don't get. The conversations we don't have. The dates we don't have. Maybe you don't feel a change, but I'm starting to feel like your room-mate and not your wife."

"You've got to help me here, babe. You've been busy with work, and I thought I was doing the right thing by giving you space. Is that not what you want?"

J. Amanda sighed. "Of course I want support, David. But I also want to know that my husband still desires me."

"What makes you think I don't?"

"David," J. Amanda grumbled, "the only time I feel desired is when you tap me on the shoulder at four in the morning."

"When we come home, the priority is always the kids. Four in the morning is the only time we have to ourselves," David argued.

"Just forget I said anything," J. Amanda replied. "You don't get what I'm trying to say."

David stood at the counter, staring at his wife. Tiffany and David Jr. slowly entered the kitchen while there was silence and eased into chairs around the table. They weren't used to hearing their parents dis-agree.

David put the plates on the table and stood behind his chair. After saying a quick blessing over the food, he doctored his tea and then joined his family at the table. He had no clue why his wife was agitated.

"Well," J. Amanda began once everyone had food on their plates, "Pastor Olivia wants me to preach on her television segment for women's season."

"You're gonna be on TV?" David Jr. asked with the excitement his mother should've felt.

"That's so awesome," Tiffany said and beamed.

"Congratulations, babe. I'm proud of you," David said without looking up from his plate.

David Jr. barraged his mother with questions. He wanted to know when she was going to be on television, on which station, and at what time. He asked her what she was going to say and if she was going to be a movie star. J. Amanda entertained her son's inquisition, secretly waiting for her husband to match David Jr.'s enthusiasm, but it was clear that wasn't going to happen tonight.

Disappointed, she sprinkled a little pepper on her rice and wondered how long her husband was going to pretend there was nothing wrong with their marriage.

~ Chapter 13 ~

Zora

Zora sat on her patio, wiping tears from her eyes with a crumbled tissue. Just when she thought her problems were great, Cynthia had shared information with her that made her problems seem insignificant. Hearing that her best friend had breast cancer frightened her. Cancer was an illness that had taken her father's life, so she knew the fears Cynthia faced. Zora had cared for her father through chemotherapy and had taken him to every doctor's appointment. It was a tiring and emotionally draining process, but she was ready to endure it again if Cynthia needed her to.

"You've got to stop crying," Cynthia sobbed from across the patio table. "I need you to be strong for me."

Zora balled up the tissue in her hand and sat it on the table. "Do you know what stage it's in?"

"Stage one," Cynthia said. "I'll need a lumpectomy and radiation therapy."

Zora closed her eyes to keep from crying again. Stage one wasn't as invasive as stage five, but there was always a chance the cancerous cells would return after a lumpectomy. "Have you scheduled the surgery?"

Cynthia dabbed the corner of her eye. "It's all set for a week from tomorrow. Lawrence is going with me, but . . . I want my sister by my side."

"Of course I'll be there," Zora assured her friend and reached across the table and held her hand. "I'll be with you until it's all over."

"I'm scared, Zora," Cynthia confessed. "I keep thinking about Lawrence and my son. What's going to happen if—"

"Don't talk that way. All we can do is pray and take things one day at a time. Don't worry about anyone else—not even your son and husband—right now. Concentrate on staying healthy so you can fight this thing."

Cynthia took another tissue from a box on the table and wiped her eyes again. "Life is full of surprises. I was just in Philly, enjoying a massage with my sorors," Cynthia uttered. "Who knew this would be waiting for me when I came home? Can you believe I have breast cancer?"

"You always tell us to be rooted in faith. This may have come as a shock, but now that it's here," Zora said, "you've got to pull on those roots to get through this. God has been in your life for a long time. He's not gonna abandon you now."

"When did you get so smart?" Cynthia sniffed. "I know you're right. I guess I'm just having a moment."

"I'd say in this case you're allowed."

Cynthia smiled and took another tissue from the box and held it tight in her hand. "I forgot to mention that I'm going to Philly for the surgery and treatments. Lawrence has a good friend at the cancer center in Fox Chase, so he'll be performing the procedure."

"Now I know you'll be all right," Zora remarked. "God knew I'd be done with the semester, so I can just pack my bags and hang in Philly for a while."

Cynthia tightened her lips, willing her tears to cease. She was so filled with emotion that "Thank you" was all she had the strength to say.

It was difficult watching her best friend in this state. Cynthia was the person she leaned on for encouragement. But now the tables had turned, and Zora had to be Cynthia's source of strength.

Zora reached for both of Cynthia's hands, now damp from wiping her tears, and she prayed with her friend until she felt her spirit lift.

Unable to work, Zora turned off her computer and rolled her chair close to the window. Since Cynthia had told her about the breast cancer, it had been hard to focus on writing a book. The news caused her to focus on her own life, and it had given her a new perspective.

Life was not promised to anyone. Knowing that, she realized that asking Reggie to be patient about parenthood was a little unfair. Life for either of them could end tomorrow, and his dream of having a child with his wife would never be realized. These were truths Zora had no control over, yet she couldn't deny her reasons for wanting to wait. Did God want her to put her dreams on hold? Did He want her to wait? Zora didn't know the answers to those questions.

Zora heard the lock on the front door click, and she looked at the clock on the wall. Reggie had come home early from work. Hearing him walk up the steps, Zora headed for the hallway.

"Hey, you," Reggie said when he saw her.

Zora didn't speak. At the sight of her husband, she thought about Cynthia and the arguments she had had with him over children, and started to cry.

Without knowing why she was upset, Reggie immediately dropped his briefcase and ran to his wife. He wrapped her in his arms and kissed the top of her head.

Feeling comforted and safe, Zora laid her head on his chest and wept like a baby.

"What's going on?" Reggie asked when Zora's moans subsided.

"Cynthia has breast cancer," she cried softly.

Reggie squeezed her tighter. This was the second person she loved who had been diagnosed with cancer. Her father's battle had stretched across two years before he died. He knew Zora was afraid the same would happen to her best friend. "Don't worry, babe. She's gonna be okay."

Zora wiped her face on Reggie's cotton shirt and shared all the information with him. She also told him about her promise to be with Cynthia during the process. Although he didn't want to be away from his wife for six weeks, he knew she had to go. "Whatever you need to do," he said, "I'll support it. I'll even come to Philly on the weekends if you want me to."

Zora tilted her head back and looked up at her husband, teary eyed. "I love you," she said affectionately. "And I'm sorry for being selfish."

"Selfish?"

"I know we agreed not to talk about kids, but in light of—"

Reggie placed his index finger over Zora's lips. "We agreed to wait until your book is published, and that's what we're gonna do."

"I love that you're being so understanding, but something Valencia said to me on Sunday keeps popping into my head."

Reggie looked confused. "You spoke to her?"

Zora pulled away from her husband. "I didn't tell you, partly because I was wrong and partly because I wanted her to know I wasn't going to just hand you overe to her. Your mother told me to fight for my husband, so—"

"I'm not sure my mother is the best person to take advice from when it comes to this matter," Reggie joked. "But . . . what did Valencia say that's been on your mind?"

"I know you shared things with her about us," Zora began, "and although I hate that you did, I guess I understand."

"What did I tell her that would make you upset?" Reggie asked.

"She suggested she knew I wasn't ready for children."

Reggie rubbed his chin as he shook his head. "Zora, she asked me why we didn't have children, and I told her that I was waiting on my wife. That's it. If she got anything else from that, it came from her head, not my lips."

Zora was relieved to know that Reggie hadn't confided his innermost feelings to another woman. "She seems like the type," Zora remarked.

Reggie pulled Zora to him and placed his hands on her cheeks. "I'm sorry for staying over there that night. It was wrong. I love you and only you. Don't ever question that."

As Zora stared into Reggie's eyes, she thanked God for her husband and prayed their love for one another would never change.

In honor of Mother's Day, Reggie arranged for his brother's family to come to New York for the weekend. They were going to surprise Renee in church on Sunday. Though Junior, his wife, and three children flew into town on Friday night, Reggie wanted to keep them hidden until Sunday. If Renee knew they were in New York, she wouldn't give the brothers any time alone together.

Zora stood on the basement patio, watching the steaks Reggie had cooking on the grill. While he was inside the house, gathering the condiments, Zora was in charge of the grill. Grace, Junior's wife, sat at the table, eating a bowl of edamame. Zora didn't know how her sister-in-law survived on nothing but fruits and vegetables. Though she didn't eat lots of meat, every once in a while her system craved it. She couldn't remember how long Grace had been a vegan, but she could whip up a substitute for any meal you presented her. The meals were usually tasty, but there was nothing like the taste of a tender, juicy steak.

There was room on the grill for the kebabs Zora spent hours putting together, so she took a few from a bowl on the table and laid them along the edges. As she covered the bowl with foil, Reggie's cell phone rang. Zora looked down to see if it was someone from work and was surprised to see Valencia's name.

Zora started to answer his phone, but it stopped ringing before she could wipe her hands clean. As she turned away from the table, the phone made a buzzing sound, indicating Reggie had either a voice message or a text message. Zora looked down at the phone and put her hand on her hip. Valencia had sent him a text.

"Are you okay?" Grace asked.

"Would I be terribly wrong if I read Reggie's message?"

Grace swallowed the salty soybeans in her mouth. "If it's gonna start an argument the day before Mother's Day, I'm not sure I would." She popped a few more soybeans in her mouth. "It's not Valencia, is it?"

Zora rolled her eyes. "How'd you guess?"

"Maybe it's work related," suggested Grace.

"Somehow I doubt that," Zora said and looked back to check on the food. She didn't want to break her husband's trust, but she was curious to know why Valencia was calling his cell phone. Against her better judgment, Zora picked up the phone, and Grace shook her head in disagreement.

Right on time, Reggie and Junior stepped onto the patio, carrying the condiments and bags of salad. Reggie took one look at his wife and knew something was wrong.

"Are you serious, Reggie?" Zora asked and waved the phone in the air.

"Uh-oh." Junior laughed. "What did my brother do?"

Grace eyed her husband and stood up. "Maybe we should go check on the kids."

"Don't do that," Zora replied. "I'm sure Reggie has an excellent reason for why Valencia is calling him."

Reggie sighed and put the plastic bottles in his hands on the table. "I have no idea," he said and took the phone from Zora's hand. With all eyes on him, he read the message and looked relieved. "See? It's nothing. She wants me to wish Mom a happy Mother's Day."

Junior and Grace giggled softly and lowered their heads.

Zora took the phone from Reggie's hand to verify the contents of the text. "First thing," Zora stated, "Mother's Day is tomorrow. Second thing . . . why does she feel the need to wish your mother a special day?" Reggie started to speak, but Zora wasn't done. "Why are you *still* talking to her?"

"I am her physical therapist," Reggie reminded her.

"This isn't good," Junior commented in the background, and Grace motioned for him to keep quiet.

"She needs to lose your number," Zora demanded.

Grace mumbled, "Amen" under her breath, and Junior laughed.

Reggie checked the steaks on the grill, and Zora stood right beside him. This was an emotional period in her life, and she was about to leave the city for a month. She didn't need Valencia making any subtle moves on her husband.

"I'm serious, Reggie. Can't she call your assistant if there's an emergency?" she asked.

"It's really not that deep, babe. I've learned my lesson," Reggie answered.

"I think you need to delete the number, bro," Junior interjected with his wife's approval.

Reggie eyed his brother as he looked through his phone. "If that will ease your mind, Zora, consider it done."

When Valencia's number was deleted, Reggie kissed his wife. "Are we good now?"

Zora took the phone from Reggie's hand. "Not quite," she said and went through his call log. Seeing that Valencia's number still appeared in the log, she pushed a few more keys, then gave the phone back to Reggie. "Her number needs to be blocked too."

"That's my girl," Grace cheered and got up from the table to give Zora a high five. "You handled that well."

Zora grabbed Reggie from behind and stood on the tips of her toes. "I hope that's the last time we have to discuss Valencia," she said and kissed the side of his neck.

"Valencia who?" he playfully replied.

"He's such a good husband," Zora cooed.

~ Chapter 14 ~

J. Amanda

After a long day in the park with two of her line sisters and the kids, J. Amanda should've been exhausted. It was Mother's Day, so she'd been up since 5:00 A.M. preparing for one of the busiest services of the year. It was her Sunday to preach, but Pastor Olivia had invited a guest preacher to deliver the message. J. Amanda was relieved when she received word of that, because she had little free time to prepare a sermon herself.

After church, she took the kids to a quiet park in the Northeast to share the day with Kenya and Tionna. J. Amanda expected all her line sisters to be there, but Jasmine declined because Brian made plans to have dinner at their home, and of course she had to do all of the cooking. Zora and Cynthia had called at the last minute to cancel because of other family commitments. In return for their absence, each soror had promised that she'd be in attendance the day J. Amanda preached on television.

J. Amanda dropped the picnic basket on the kitchen counter and placed the soiled dishes in the sink. "Happy Mother's Day, Mommy!" she heard from behind and turned around. Tiffany and David Jr. walked in, along with their father, who carried a beautifully wrapped gift in his hands. J. Amanda glanced at the time on the microwave. She had one hour to make it to Plymouth Meeting in time to meet Hunky for dinner.

"Happy Mother's Day, Jay," David said and barely kissed her cheek. Since their argument a few days ago, they had had little to say to one another. J. Amanda had refused to bring it up, and David didn't want to discuss the conflict. It was easier for him to wait it out and pray that things would change for the better.

David didn't plan anything special for Mother's Day, at her request. This year she decided that she wanted to spend the day with her friends and children, rather than sit around with David's family and pretend everything was good between them. So while she was at the park, he went to visit his side of the family in Delaware.

J. Amanda smiled and took the large gift from her husband. "Thanks," she said and sat it on the table. As she complimented the creativity of the childlike wrapping, David Jr. jumped up and down.

"Do you like it, Mommy?" Tiffany asked before the gift was fully unwrapped.

J. Amanda hugged the pedicure spa kit after peeling off the gift wrap. "I love it," she squealed.

"We picked it out all by ourselves," David Jr. said proudly. "We know you stand on your feet a lot."

"It's perfect," she told them and covered their faces with kisses. J. Amanda was thankful her son paid attention to details. She only prayed he'd remain that way as an adult.

Pleased by her reaction, Tiffany and David Jr. zoomed out of the kitchen to play video games before it was time for bed.

J. Amanda put the ripped gift wrap in the trash and then headed to the bedroom to shower and change. She had to hurry, or Redstone would give her dinner reservations with Hunky to someone else.

***

When J. Amanda stepped out of the shower, David was waiting for her in the bedroom. She prayed this wasn't the one time he wanted to show affection. There was no time for that tonight.

"I got something for you too," David said and pointed to a small velvet box on her pillow.

In silence, J. Amanda walked to her side of the bed and sat down. She took a deep breath and slowly opened the box. David knew she didn't wear a lot of accessories, so it was odd that jewelry was his gift of choice. *Maybe he forgot,* she thought. *Maybe he thinks this will make up for the months he's been distant.* Either way, J. Amanda told herself to be grateful. Jewelry wasn't a bad gift idea for most women, and . . . at least he'd tried.

Expecting to see a pair of earrings or a ring, J. Amanda was shocked to find a beautifully engraved gold cross. "Wow!" she exclaimed. She grazed the top of the pendant lightly with her finger. A sterling-silver cross was the one piece of jewelry she wore every day. Her grandmother had given it to her the day she was ordained.

A few years ago, while shopping for Christmas gifts, she and David stopped at a jewelry counter. "I really need a gold cross," J. Amanda had said. Now, after a number of years had passed, J. Amanda finally got her gold cross. More than anything, she was touched that David had remembered.

"I'm speechless," she said.

David stood in front of her and smiled. "I hope this lets you know that I do pay attention to you. I'm sorry if I seem distant, but believe me, it's not intentional."

"Thank you," she said and placed the box on the nightstand. "This really means a lot."

"I hope you know that I love you."

J. Amanda held the towel wrapped around her in place. "I know you love me, David. I just want to feel that love again."

"I hear you," David said and leaned down to kiss her cheek. "Well, I don't want to hold you up. I know you have plans with your girls, so I'll get out of here so you can get dressed."

When David left the room, J. Amanda looked at her gift one more time. For months she complained about David's inattentiveness, becoming angrier as each day passed. Then, in a matter of minutes, he had given her a present that challenged what she'd been feeling.

J. Amanda almost felt guilty for going to dinner with Hunky tonight, but she needed to get out of the house and clear her head.

The traffic was heavier than J. Amanda had anticipated. By the time she made it to Plymouth Meeting, it was 8:45 P.M. Their reservations were for 8:00 P.M. J. Amanda had called Hunky when she realized that she was going to be late, and he suggested they go to the restaurant in the Doubletree Hotel across from Redstone.

J. Amanda strolled through the parking lot carefully. It wasn't every day that she wore stilettos, but tonight she wanted to wear something out of the ordinary. As she approached the main entrance, she pulled a sheer baby blue shawl over her shoulders. Though her mid-length dress covered most of her upper arms, she still felt naked.

David should've suspected something when she left the house, but he just smiled and told her she looked lovely. Rather than argue, J. Amanda said, "Thank you" and left. Was David really that trusting of her? That was a question she'd asked herself all the way to the hotel. If the situation had been reversed, she would've known the names of the friends he was going to meet, as well as the name and the location of the restaurant.

Inside the Doubletree, J. Amanda sauntered past the front desk and into the restaurant behind the open bar area. Hunky was standing by the door when she arrived. As she drew near, she felt his eyes studying her body from head to toe and then resting on the space at the top of her dress that showed a small amount of cleavage.

"Hey, beautiful," he said, and her insides tingled.

Hunky was handsome in his chocolate khakis and matching shirt. Instinctively, she hugged him and gripped the tight muscles in his back, which reminded her why she'd given him the name Hunky. For a moment she pretended they were back in high school and were going on their first date. *We're just friends, oho* reminded herself and withdrew from his embrace.

Inside the restaurant, Hunky escorted her to a small table in the middle of the room that he'd secured before she arrived. There was a bouquet of roses positioned in the center of the table, as if it were the centerpiece. But when J. Amanda sat down, she noticed a card leaning against the glass vase and glanced around the room. None of the other tables had roses on them. "Are these for me, Hunky?"

J. Amanda felt special tonight. The last time she enjoyed an intimate dinner with David, she was three months pregnant with her son. J. Amanda picked up the card, and as she read the words she blushed.

After all these years you're still the only woman that holds the key to my heart.

"You really didn't have to do this," J. Amanda said, wondering where she was going to showcase her roses. Though David probably wouldn't say anything, she didn't want to disrespect him by bringing them home. The office was also out of the question. Someone at church would think they were from David, and she didn't want to be in a position where she had to lie.

"I had to," he replied. "I wanted to see that wonderful smile."

J. Amanda and Hunky lost track of time as they nibbled on their meals. The topics of conversation seemed to transition smoothly from one to another, making it easy for them to forget that they both had spouses to return to. All night Hunky complimented her strengths and applauded her accomplishments. He fed the part of her spirit that craved a connection with another human being.

The lights in the restaurant dimmed, causing J. Amanda to pay attention to the time. She almost choked on her water when she saw the hour illuminated on her cell phone. "It's almost midnight, Hunky. We've got to go!" she exclaimed and checked her phone for any missed calls. There were several, but none from David.

After Hunky paid for dinner, they both stopped in the lobby to make calls. J. Amanda guessed Hunky called his wife, while she chose to contact Kenya. She would've called Tionna, but she wasn't in the mood for a lecture. Besides, Kenya was the only friend J. Amanda could count on to be awake at this hour on a Sunday night. She only prayed Kenya was actually in the house.

Luck was on her side tonight. Kenya answered her cell phone on the second ring. In less than five minutes, J. Amanda gave Kenya an update on her interactions with Hunky and then asked if David had called. He hadn't, and J. Amanda was a little disappointed. "He thinks I'm with you," she offered, though Kenya hadn't asked a question.

"I understand that no one wants a loveless marriage, but I have to agree with Tionna on this one, Jay. You need to go home," Kenya said. "If David thinks you're with me, then you're in the clear *this* time. But . . . are you sure he doesn't know about Hunky?"

"I'm pretty sure," she replied.

"So he thinks you're out serving the Lord all the time, huh? I wish my man would—"

"Kenya, don't make me feel bad. I just had *dinner* with an old boyfriend."

"A *dinner* you didn't tell your husband about and an old friend you talk to regularly. But I'm not gonna judge you, darling. God has that under control," Kenya informed her, "Just go home to your family."

J. Amanda hung up the phone and walked nervously over to Hunky. "Ready?"

Hunky gave her a mischievous look, one she recognized from their youth. "My wife thinks I'm working overtime. I can get us a room for the night. It's really too late for you to drive home. Besides, with your schedule, I may not get quality time like this with you until next month."

J. Amanda had been driving home at odd hours for several years. Not once had she encountered trouble. She should've said no, but Hunky's cologne had taken control of her senses. She hesitantly agreed and stood by the glass elevators until he returned from the front desk. J. Amanda knew what she was about to do, and yet she couldn't convince herself to turn around.

She should've called David as she waited, but she feared this would be the one time he questioned her whereabouts. J. Amanda closed her eyes and tried to pray, but she couldn't find the right words to say. *How do you ask God to cover you when you know you're about to do wrong?* she thought.

J. Amanda glanced at the front desk and sighed. Why did Hunky have to move away when they were young? This scenario wouldn't have happened if he had waited for her to graduate. He could've been her husband, and they could've been living the fairy-tale life most people desire.

J. Amanda's cell phone rang, and her heart raced. What if it was David? She reached into her clutch and was relieved when she saw Tionna's name. "I know Kenya called you," she said when she answered. There was no other reason why Tionna would call at this hour.

"I'm glad she did," Tionna responded. "Have you lost your mind? Do you want David to find out about Hunky?"

"Of course not, Tionna. I lost track of time, that's all."

"What if someone recognizes you?" Tionna said. "How would you explain being with another man at this time of night?"

J. Amanda vaguely thought that through. "I wouldn't worry. We're way outside of the city. If anyone sees me, they're probably creeping too."

"This is not the time to be funny, Jay."

"I know," J. Amanda moaned.

"Well, I hope you're on your way home."

Hunky was headed in her direction, grinning like he'd just hit the lottery. He really filled out his khakis well. J. Amanda quickly turned her head and willed the romantic thoughts in her mind to leave.

"I know you heard me, Jay. You're on your way home, right?"

Hunky hit the elevator button and then grabbed J. Amanda's hand. As hard as she tried to free her mind from intimate thoughts, feeling his skin against hers created a sensation she hadn't experienced in months.

"J. Amanda," Tionna called.

"I'm here," she answered and entered the elevator. "Let me call you in the morning."

"You can walk away right now," Tionna urged, but she could tell her words were moot.

"I know," J. Amanda said softly as Hunky nibbled on her ear. "We'll talk about it in the morning."

Without saying good-bye, J. Amanda disconnected the call and kissed Hunky on the lips. "I hope you have condoms," she said.

Hunky kissed her gently along her neck and moaned, "Yes, love. I came prepared."

At 5:00 A.M. J. Amanda stood at her bedroom door, contemplating whether or not she wanted to get in bed with her husband after being with another man. Before leaving the hotel, she had made sure her tight curls were in place and all traces of Hunky's scent had been removed.

The night with Hunky was as she had remembered. And though that moment in time was pleasurable, those feelings disappeared the minute she stepped off of the hotel grounds.

J. Amanda caught a glimpse of the cross David had bought her, still on the night table, and took a deep breath. *What have I done?* she asked God as a tear rolled down her cheek.

David stirred in bed and barely opened his eyes. "Is that you, Jay?"

J. Amanda quickly wiped her eyes. "I'm sorry. I was trying not to wake you."

"It's all right," David said groggily. "Did you and your sorors have fun?"

J. Amanda covered her face with her hand in shame. "Yes," she lied.

"You coming to bed?"

J. Amanda walked up to the bed and stared at her husband, but images of Hunky came to mind. "I have an early day at church," she lied again. "I might as well shower now, while I'm up."

With his eyes still closed, David smiled. "I'm glad you enjoyed Mother's Day."

Guilt hit J. Amanda hard in the pit of her stomach. Before she burst into tears, she walked briskly into the bathroom and closed the door. She'd already taken one shower, but another one wouldn't hurt.

She turned the water pressure on high and muffled her cries with her hands as she fell to her knees. J. Amanda knew she had messed up, and prayed for forgiveness. She didn't know how people could cheat. The pain her heart felt wasn't worth the temporary satisfaction to her flesh. As she thought about Hunky, she wondered if he was going through a similar emotional breakdown.

J. Amanda prayed for guidance, but she feared that it wouldn't be easy to stop what she had started.

~ Chapter 15 ~

Jasmine

With Gabrielle on her hip, Jasmine walked downstairs in a hurry. Today she was going to Orion's studio to teach her first jazz and hip-hop classes. "Let's go, Sasha!" she yelled as she went into the family room to gather the lunches and snacks she'd prepared late last night. All three of her children were enrolled in classes too, so she had prepared enough food to last until two o'clock.

Brian lay on the sofa, dressed for work, watching Jasmine struggle to leave the house. He was supposed to be gone by now, but he had told his boss that he would be in late. There was nothing wrong with him, and he was awake and dressed by 7:00 A.M., so Jasmine knew he was still there to be nosy. Brian didn't like that Jasmine had found something fun for her and the girls to do on Saturdays.

It hadn't been easy to convince Brian that dance classes would be good for the girls. She had to stroke his ego for days before he agreed. Agreeing to try for another baby was also a part of the compromise. Brian had tried to use money as an excuse, but Jasmine had been ready. "I get a huge discount for the girls because I'm teaching classes. I can cover whatever the balance is," she'd told him. Brian stared at her that day, desperately trying to come up with another excuse. When he found none, he'd walked away, mumbling under his breath.

Jasmine shifted Gabrielle to her other hip and walked to the dining room. "Sasha!" Jasmine called again as she searched for her car keys in a purse on the table.

"Give me another minute, Mom! I'm curling my hair!" Sasha yelled from her bathroom.

Jasmine put Gabrielle down and held her hand tight so she wouldn't take off running through the house. "That's why I woke *you* up first," Jasmine groaned.

"She's stalling because she doesn't want to go," Brian snidely remarked. "Don't make her go if she doesn't want to."

"She wants to," Jasmine replied.

"I can't tell," he fired back. "Dancing isn't for everyone. You never did anything with it."

Jasmine took a deep breath and put her dance bag on her shoulder. Brian was ornery this morning, but Jasmine wasn't going to let him make her lose her cool. Dancing was great in his eyes when they were dating, and he could never get enough of the special performances she gave when they were newlyweds. Everyone knew Jasmine was gifted. The only reason she didn't "make it" was that she kept having his kids.

"Why don't you see if she can stay next door until you come back?" Brian added.

"Kierra is going too," Jasmine retorted and stood at the bottom of the stairs. "Your one minute is up, Sasha! Get your sister and come on!"

"You're getting everyone in on this, huh?" Brian responded. "I don't know why you bother."

"It's my passion. I may decide to open my own studio one day," she replied to amuse him.

"Ha!" Brian chuckled. "You're too old for that dream."

You need a dream, she mouthed and yelled upstairs one last time. "Move it, Sasha!"

With an attitude, Sasha stomped downstairs behind her sister. Jasmine didn't know why she had spent a half hour curling her hair. Once she started dancing, her curls would fall out from sweating.

"You and Amber, go get the bags of food from the kitchen. I'll meet you at the car," Jasmine ordered and unlocked the front door."Oh, call Kierra and tell her we're ready."

"Can you order some balloons for next Friday? Something real nice," Brian said as Jasmine opened the door.

"For what?" she questioned, annoyed.

"We're going to my mom's house for Brianna. My baby girl is going to her senior prom," he gloated.

Jasmine frowned. If Sasha didn't adore her half sister, she would've come up with an excuse not to go. "We'll be back by dinnertime," she said and walked out the door.

While Jasmine secured Gabrielle in her car seat, she saw Hunky heading toward her from the corner of her eye. She tugged on the buckle to make sure her daughter couldn't wiggle her way out of the seat and then closed the door.

"Hey, Jazz," Hunky said. "Kierra went to the store with her mother. I'll bring her to the studio when she gets back. They should've been back by now, but you know how Patrice is. She probably made four other stops."

Amber ran to the car, while Sasha took her time. Jasmine rolled her eyes and opened the door. "That's cool. It's only the first day."

As she hopped into her car, Hunky grabbed her arm. Seeing the startled looked on Jasmine's face, Hunky apologized. "Can I have a word with you before you leave?"

Jasmine glanced at her house to see if Brian was watching, and then stepped away from the car. She hoped Brian hadn't said anything to upset her neighbors. They were the only people on the block she spoke to, and Kierra was Sasha's best friend. In addition, Hunky and his wife cared for her children when Brian was in a rage. She hoped nothing had happened to ruin their relationship. "What's going on?"

"It's nothing, really. . . . I wanted to check with you to see how things were going at home."

Jasmine looked toward her house again. Even if she wanted to share details with him, now wasn't the time. Brian was home, and she had two classes to teach in less than an hour. "We're all fine," she said. "Why? Did you hear something?"

"No," Hunky said. "I haven't talked to you or J. Amanda in a while. I just wanted to catch up. Have you spoken to her?"

Becoming aggravated, Jasmine blinked her eyes a few times to keep from twisting her lips or saying something inappropriate. "Have I spoken to J. Amanda?" she asked, and Hunky nodded eagerly. "Of course I have, but I really—"

Hunky chuckled softly. "You two are so close. All of you are."

Something about the way he had said that troubled her. Of course they were close. They were line sisters. "J. Amanda's been super busy with women's season," she replied and made a mental note to call her friend. "I haven't spoken to her in a couple days. But I better get moving. The highway gets backed up after nine o'clock on Saturday mornings."

Jasmine backed away as Hunky kept talking. "The sorority taught you to be very close. I bet you ladies have secrets you've never told anyone."

Jasmine touched the car door and looked at him. He was acting weird. "What do you mean?" she inquired. "Secrets aren't meant to be shared with everyone."

Hunky shook his head slowly. "I guess you're right."

"Jazz," Brian yelled from the front door. "Y'all okay?"

Jasmine slowly took her eyes off Hunky and faced her husband. "We're fine. He's just telling me that Kierra doesn't need a ride." Brian didn't respond, but Jasmine knew she better leave before he made his way out of the house. "I better go," she told Hunky and got into the car.

Unnerved by his presence, Jasmine called J. Amanda on her cell phone and attempted to have a conversation with her, but J. Amanda reminded her that it was dangerous to drive and talk on the phone. Though she'd done it many times, Jasmine put her phone away. She'd have to call her between classes.

Jasmine stood in front of the mirrors in her classroom, applying foundation to an old bruise on her right arm. While demonstrating a simple step for her students, she had noticed the mark she received from a hard fall on the kitchen floor.

"Hey, Jazzy," Orion said as he entered the room. "I peeked in on your jazz class this morning. You still got it, girl."

Jasmine threw the foundation in her dance bag on the floor and smiled. Orion hadn't changed much since college. He was still the tall, lanky man she met in Comp 101 her freshman year. Never outrageously outspoken or dramatic, Jasmine and Orion had connected because of their love for the arts. Always a pleasure to be around, Orion was loved by everyone he knew. And though he was a great guy, after a few months of dating, they both came to the conclusion that they were better friends than lovers.

"Thank you, Orion," Jasmine told him. "You're a lifesaver."

Orion leaned against the wide mirror and reached out to touch the bruise on Jasmine's arm. Though the bruise was more than three weeks old, the area was still sensitive and she jumped.

"I was nervous, but once I got used to it. I felt at home," Jasmine continued, to take attention away from her arm.

"You never should've stopped," Orion noted as he subtly examined the rest of Jasmine's body.

Uneasy, Jasmine attempted to add more space between them, but Orion stopped her. With concern in his eyes, he gently rubbed a faint scar camouflaged by a few hairs in her left eyebrow. Jasmine had received that wound from Brian months ago, when she bad-mouthed Tionna. "Is Brian doing this to you?" Orion whispered as he rubbed the side of her cheek.

Jasmine looked down at her feet. "Everything's fine, Orion. Really, it is," she said, trying to convince him.

There was a cough from the double doors at the front of the room, and Orion and Jasmine separated. "I didn't mean to interrupt," Hunky said as he strolled closer to them. "I just dropped off my daughter and wanted to give Jasmine a check for the class."

"This is Mr. Crawford, my neighbor," Jasmine said nervously, afraid Hunky would get the wrong idea.

"Mr. Orion, something's wrong with the soda machine," a student called from the hallway. Orion excused himself and told Jasmine they'd finish their discussion later.

"Thanks," Jasmine said and attached the check to Kierra's application in a folder on her desk. Hunky remained silent as she wrote out a receipt and handed it to him. "Do you need me to drop Kierra off?"

"If you don't mind," he answered with cold eyes.

"Is something wrong?" Jasmine asked, spooked by his glare.

"I'm sorry, Jazz. I don't mean to be in your business," he told her, "and I'm probably out of line, but . . . it would be a terrible thing if Brian saw another man touch you the way that man did."

"I don't know what you saw," Jasmine stated, "but I have a class in about a minute. I'll see to it that Kierra gets home."

Hunky smirked and slid out of the room. When he was gone, Jasmine called J. Amanda. Her instincts could've been wrong, but just in case, she wanted J. Amanda to know that there was something strange going on with her friend.

"No wonder he's going crazy," Jasmine said as she listened to J. Amanda tell her what had happened on Mother's Day. "You can't turn him out and then not call him every day, like you used to."

Sitting on her mother-in-law's porch, Jasmine kept an eye on her youngest daughters, who were running around on the sidewalk. Though Brian was with them, he was too busy entertaining relatives and taking pictures of Brianna's prom date.

"I don't know what came over me," J. Amanda said quietly.

"You made a mistake," Jasmine said. "It happens. I should know. But don't let your mistake turn your life around the way mine has."

"I'm actually glad I'm so busy at church. It takes my mind off what I did," J. Amanda replied.

"That may be true, but you know you can't run from it. You can't hide from God," teased Jasmine. "And please call him so he can stop acting weird."

As they talked, Tionna pulled up in her freshly cleaned Jaguar. Kenya and two other people got out of her car and unloaded the trunk. Carrying bags of ice and trays of catered food, Tionna led the group up the stairs.

"Need some help?" J. Amanda asked and stood up.

"I think we're good," answered Tionna, and before she went into the house, she thanked Jasmine for the collage of balloons she'd purchased for Brianna's prom.

"That was nice of her," J. Amanda said when Tionna was no longer visible. "Maybe I can get you two to join me for dinner one night."

"I wouldn't rush things," Jasmine said. J. Amanda had no idea how much she and Brian had argued over those balloons. "But tell me. What's up with you and David?"

"We're not back to normal, but I can say that he is trying," J. Amanda informed her. "He actually made plans for us to spend a week in Myrtle Beach after Women's Day. I was shocked." J. Amanda lifted the gold cross around her neck. "And look at this," she said. "You like my Mother's Day gift?"

"It fits you," Jasmine responded. She couldn't remember the last time Brian had brought her a cup of coffee, let alone a piece of jewelry. "Though considering your latest actions . . ."

J. Amanda smacked Jasmine's knee lightly. "I'm gonna make this right. I don't know how," she said, "but I will."

The front door flew open, and Sasha charged onto the porch. "She's ready!" she shouted.

Everyone outside made their way inside the house and positioned themselves so they could get a better view of Brianna when she came downstairs. Jasmine stayed in a corner and out of the way. As she waited for the young woman of the hour to make her debut, Jasmine studied the tables full of food and seventies-style decorations around the room. That had to be Tionna and Brian's idea, she thought as she stared at the glittery disco ball hanging from the ceiling. Times had changed since she went to her prom. There was no party at her mother's house, only a few friends to help her get dressed.

Mrs. Dorothy's high-pitched laughs caught Jasmine's attention. Close to the staircase, she was standing in between Tionna and Brian as they posed for pictures. Relatives on both sides of the family shouted out specific poses: Mrs. Dorothy and Brian, Mrs. Dorothy and Tionna, and Brian and Tionna. The photos of Brian and Tionna shouldn't have bothered her, but seeing them together dug under her skin the wrong way.

It wouldn't have been so bad if Mrs. Dorothy hadn't cooed over Tionna. "Tionna's a great mom." "Tionna's gonna run that clinic in a few years." "Tionna this. Tionna that." It made Jasmine's stomach turn.

One of Brian's aunts realized that Jasmine was hiding and pulled her through the crowd to the staircase. "C'mon, Brian," the aunt said. "Let's get some pictures with your wife."

In rare form, Brian pulled Jasmine close and kissed or hugged her in every picture. She wanted to take this opportunity to show the family the physical scars he had left on her body or to tell them about his abusive behavior. Instead, she smiled at the phony acts of love he performed.

After the pictures, Stevie Wonder's "Isn't She Lovely" came from the speakers in an upstairs bedroom. Eyes were glued to the stairs as a stunning Brianna made her way down the steps. Totally contradicting the seventies theme of her party, her free-flowing peach gown was classic. Sophisticated like her mother, Brianna glowed as she proceeded to her date, pausing intermittently to have her picture taken.

Watching the family shower Brianna with attention, Jasmine tried to control her emotions. She understood this was a proud moment for Brian and Tionna, but she wished circumstances were different so they could all enjoy this moment as a family.

Before walking outside, Brian stood in front of the door, with Tionna crying by his side. He gave a long-winded speech about watching Brianna grow from a beautiful baby into an intelligent and strong young adult. "And . . . we know your birthday isn't until next week, but because you're such a great role model for your three sisters . . . your mother and I decided to give you an early birthday present."

Brian opened the front door and led everyone to the sidewalk, stopping at a shiny silver Honda Accord. Jasmine saw Brian's mouth moving, but she couldn't believe the words coming out of his mouth. But when Brianna took a set of car keys from his hand, Jasmine knew what she thought was true. He had helped Tionna purchase a car for their daughter.

Jasmine almost fell backward. "Where did he get money for a new car, when we struggle to pay bills each month? Why didn't he tell me? Why wasn't I included in the decision?" she mumbled to herself.

More pictures followed the presentation of Brianna's gift, and then came a lecture to her date about driving her car. If Kenya hadn't pulled him away, Brian would've shoved the date out of the car and driven them to the prom himself.

As people formed a line to say their good-byes and offer well wishes, an unmarked police car stopped in front of the house. A tall, handsome officer emerged from the car and headed toward Tionna. They exchanged a few quick words and then walked to the passenger side of Brianna's new car. He handed Brianna an envelope and then waved to Kenya and J. Amanda before returning to his car. From the sour look on Brian's face, Jasmine suspected the officer was a good friend of Tionna's.

Ready to leave, J. Amanda gathered everyone close to Brianna's new car and led a prayer. As she asked God to cover them in their travels, Jasmine stared at her husband, full of rage. Feeling disrespected, she eased out of the prayer gathering and went into the house. She couldn't stand to be in Brian's presence any longer.

Jasmine walked to the dining room and searched for her purse in the hall closet. That was where Mrs Dorothy said she had placed it, but Jasmine had a difficult time locating it through her tears. She mumbled to herself as she tossed bags around, and jerked when she felt a tap on her shoulder.

"Do you need some help?" Tionna asked and then realized Jasmine was crying. "Are you okay? J. Amanda wanted to get a picture of the four us by Brianna's car before she drove away."

Jasmine rubbed her eyes and continued to search for her purse. "I'm fine." At the moment she wasn't the least bit interested in having her picture taken with her line sisters.

"Did something happen that you want to talk about?" inquired Tionna.

Jasmine found her purse and threw it on her shoulder. "As a matter of fact," she said and looked at Tionna, "there's a lot I want to talk about, but now may not be the best time."

Tionna twisted her face the same way she used to when they were pledging. That expression meant that she was trying to bite her tongue. "Jasmine, before everyone comes back inside, if there's something you want to say—"

"I'm tired of being compared to you," Jasmine snapped. "There you have it. Better now?" Tionna closed her eyes and poked out her lips. Before she could respond, Jasmine continued to rant. "I'm not perfect, but that doesn't mean I'm not a good parent or a good person. I hate that most of this family can't see that. I hate that *my husband* can buy his daughter a car without consulting me. I hate that Brianna can tell *my daughters* about what I did in college, and that *my husband* gets upset because I said his child was wrong. And I'm tired of—"

Tionna cut her off. "Leave my daughter out of your mess, Jazz. If you're having problems with Brian, it's not because of my child."

J. Amanda walked up behind Tionna and gently nudged her aside. "People are starting to come back in, Jazz. Let's talk about this later. Don't let your girls see you this way."

Tionna headed out of the room as Brian walked in with Gabrielle. "You need to handle your affairs," she told him as they passed one another.

Brian took one look at Jasmine and frowned. "What did you do now?"

People started walking into the room, and Jasmine realized that she needed to leave. "I'm going home," she said and gave Gabrielle a kiss. "I'm sure someone can give you a lift home."

Jasmine saw the fire in her husband's eyes, but she kept moving. If she didn't escape, there was no telling what could happen next.

"Can I go?" Sasha asked, and it pained Jasmine to tell her no.

Jasmine needed to be alone, and she needed to be in a place where she could be free to release her frustrations. That place was the studio, and that was where she was headed.

After spending two hours in the studio, Jasmine was ready to face her husband. Though tired from dancing, she drove home and dragged herself into the house. Brian was in his usual spot on the sofa, but this time Amber was under his arm and Gabrielle was asleep on his chest, sucking her thumb.

"Where did you go?" he asked.

Jasmine put her purse in the dining room and joined them on the sofa. "To the studio."

Brian huffed softly. "Just like old times. Do you feel better?"

Amber moved from her father's arm to her mother's and put her finger inside her mouth. Jasmine didn't know where her daughters got that habit from. "I always feel better after a good workout."

"You wanna talk about what happened?"

Jasmine was glad Brian was calm. Maybe tonight they could have a rational conversation without the rage. "Why didn't you tell me about the car?"

"I probably should have," admitted Brian, "but I wanted to avoid an argument. Tionna wanted to get her a car, and as Brianna's father, I wanted to help."

"I understand that, Brian, but Tionna can afford to pay another car note. We can't. I'm sure she would've understood that."

"Maybe . . . but we promised to do things together."

"If you say so, Brian. Just try to remember that *I'm* your wife. If you're not going to consult me on major decisions when it comes to Brianna, you should at least tell me about them."

Brian didn't respond. Instead, he questioned the reasons why she had left his mother's house. "You had my family thinking I did something to you."

Jasmine almost laughed aloud. Of course he was the reason she'd left. Why couldn't he see that? "I felt like an outsider," she sighed.

"So you were jealous?"

"No . . . I felt disrespected," she said carefully. "At some point what *I* feel should matter when it comes to you and Tionna. Right now everything I say about her is wrong. My thoughts and opinions are never appreciated or considered."

"I thought you two made up at the reunion," Brian remarked sarcastically. "That sorority and fraternity stuff is a joke. That's why I don't hang around those guys anymore."

Jasmine knew that was a lie, but kept quiet. "We're working on things in our own way . . . slowly. But the sorority has nothing to do with our marriage. This is about you respecting me. You still refuse to let me say when Tionna or Brianna is wrong about something."

"All right, Jazz, I hear you," Brian responded. "I'll try to be more understanding."

Jasmine was shocked. She and Brian hadn't resolved their issues this calmly in a long time. She almost wanted to kiss him. "Well," she said, "I better get the girls ready for bed. We have a full day at dance tomorrow."

"Why don't you take Amber up?" Brian suggested. "I'll bring Gabby when a commercial comes on."

Jasmine tugged on Amber's arms and legs until she opened her eyes. "C'mon, baby. You're too big for Mommy to carry."

Amber moaned, but after a few seconds she got up and went upstairs as she was told.

Jasmine stopped by Sasha's room before going to bed. As usual, she was on the phone, talking to Kierra. "Don't forget I'm waking you up first tomorrow. Don't stay up too late." Sasha huffed and then turned her back to the door. Jasmine couldn't wait for this adolescent stage to pass. Sasha had too much attitude for her taste.

Inside the bedroom, Jasmine pushed a laundry basket of clean clothes to the center of the room. Before taking a shower, she wanted to fold and put away the clothes. She heard Brian walk upstairs and then into Gabrielle's bedroom. *He sure is in a good mood,* she thought as she kicked off her shoes. *I wonder why the sudden change?*

Before Jasmine could come up with reasons for his calm demeanor, Brian came into the room and pushed her so hard, she rolled across their queen-size bed and landed hard on the floor. She scrambled to get to her feet before Brian reached her.

"Not tonight, Brian," she said with force and hopped on the bed. "I've been through too much today, and I have class in the morning."

Brian attempted to jump on the bed too but tripped over the laundry basket in his way. "The next time you embarrass me in front of my family, you'll feel more than a push," he grumbled.

"Give it a rest, Brian," Jasmine said nonchalantly, and he lunged forward again. This time he made it on the bed.

As he tried to grab hold of Jasmine, she darted off the bed and ran down the hall to her daughters' bathroom. Jasmine quickly locked the door and then sat on the toilet. *I don't know how much longer I can do this,* she told herself.

"Mommy," Jasmine heard outside the door, and she sighed.

More than the abuse, Jasmine hated that Sasha knew what was happening. "Yes?" she replied, trying not to sound annoyed.

"Are you okay?"

That seemed to be the question on everybody's mind when it came to her. "Yes, sweetheart, I'm fine. Go on back to bed. You have to get up early tomorrow."

~ Chapter 16 ~

J. Amanda

J. Amanda's cell phone rang at 2:23 A.M., and she jolted awake. With half-opened eyes, she stretched her hand to the nightstand and picked up her phone. Though her vision was blurry, she could see Hunky's number on the screen.

David lifted his hand from around her waist and turned on his side. "The church is calling, babe," he muttered and almost immediately drifted back to sleep.

J. Amanda eased out of the bed and rushed into the bathroom. It had been weeks since she talked to Hunky at this hour, and she'd forgotten to turn off the ringer before bed. But now that he had called, she had to answer, because David thought it was a church emergency.

J. Amanda's heart beat fast as she hit the call button. "Hey, Hunky. What's up?"

"Can you talk?"

"Of course I can't talk," she wanted to tell him. Instead, she simply said, "No. Is something wrong, or can I call you on my way to work?"

"I haven't heard from you, love. I miss you," Hunky whined.

J. Amanda blamed herself for cutting him off cold turkey and realized she needed to have a heart-to-heart with him. It was the right thing to do. Hunky meant more to her than her actions showed. "I've been really busy, but I should've called. I'm sorry about that, but can we catch up tomorrow?"

Hunky perked up. "That would be great! Can you make it to the Doubletree tomorrow? You choose the time. I have the day off."

Going to the Doubletree sounded too tempting, so J. Amanda proposed an alternate plan. "I'm supposed to meet with our travel agent tomorrow. Can we meet at the Panera on Route 30 for lunch?"

"Are you going on vacation?" he asked.

"David and I want to take the kids to Disney."

Flustered, Hunky replied, "You and *David?*"

"Yes, Hunky. He is their father. It's not unusual for us to vacation together," she explained, then caught herself. Why was she explaining herself? "It's late, Hunky. I'll give you a call tomorrow."

"I really need to see you, Jay," Hunky pleaded. "Please try to come to the hotel. I just want to talk. Nothing else. I promise."

To get him off the phone, J. Amanda agreed. "I can make it after three," she replied and said good night.

J. Amanda tiptoed back into the bedroom and slid under the covers. She made sure the ringer on her cell phone was off, then tried to get comfortable. David lifted his head to check the time and then cuddled next to his wife.

"Somebody needed prayer?" he asked.

When J. Amanda wanted David to question her actions, he didn't. She closed her eyes and uttered, "Yes."

"What's all this?" J. Amanda asked when she entered the hotel.

The room Hunky had reserved this time was even fancier than the last. It had a lounging area, a kitchenette, and a separate work space. He had apparently cooked an early dinner. The table was set for two and was covered in rose petals.

"I want you to know how much I miss you," he said and handed her a single rose.

"Hunky, I couldn't keep the bouquet of roses you gave me last time," J. Amanda said. "I can't accept this one, either. I think we need to talk, sweetie."

"Let me go first," he begged and escorted J. Amanda to the couch. "I know I've been acting a little strange lately, but that's the effect you have on me. Being with you that night made me remember just how much I love you."

J. Amanda sat the rose on the coffee table. "I love you too, Hunky. But let's not forget that we're both married."

"I know this sounds bad, but I'd leave her if it meant we'd spend the rest of our lives together."

"Hunky . . . I'm not gonna leave David. We're having problems, but I can't just transport my kids out of one home and into another. We probably should've talked more before we were intimate," J. Amanda said. "But we have such a strong chemistry that we let our emotions cloud our reality."

Hunky put her hand in his. "Our love is all that matters, Jay. If you love me, I can wait this time for as long as you want. Everything will fall into place if you want me."

J. Amanda eased her hand from under his. "Of course I love you, but I think we need to start over. We moved way too fast, and I take the blame for my part in what's happened," J. Amanda stated. "We've always been friends, and that's what I'd like us to focus on."

"You and I both know we're more than friends," Hunky said and moved in for a kiss.

J. Amanda jumped up and moved away from the couch. "God wouldn't want me to handle things this way, Hunky. I didn't listen to Him before, and look at what that's done. Please . . . just try to understand what I'm saying."

"Why can't you see that God wants us to be together?" Hunky was reaching for ways to get his point across. "Out of all the people in the world to have as a neighbor, He put me in a house next to Jasmine. Can't you see that this is fate?"

"If God wanted us to be together, Hunky, He'd make a way without confusion," explained J. Amanda. "We're *both* married now. That's not the way God would join us together. You don't have to believe it, but I do. And I'm sorry, but friendship is all I have to offer right now."

"Friendship wouldn't work. At some point, I'd want to kiss you, and not the kind of kiss I give my daughter." As Hunky talked, someone knocked on the door, and he went over to the window. He pulled the curtain back and grunted.

"I know you're in there," a woman said. "And I know she's with you."

J. Amanda rolled her eyes. Though she knew who it was, she asked, anyway. "Is that your wife?"

Hunky snatched the door open. ""What are you doing here, Patrice?"

If there was a back door, J. Amanda would've snuck out of the room. "Why don't I leave you two alone to talk?" she said and started walking, but Patrice blocked her path.

"No, Reverend King. Stay a while," she said and walked by Hunky. "Stay and tell me why you're here with my husband. Or . . . is that a silly question to ask?"

J. Amanda fell on the couch and buried her head in her hands. *What have I done?*

"Don't pray now, preacher woman," Patrice remarked.

"Let's not start a scene here, Patrice," Hunky urged. "This isn't what you're thinking."

"I'm not slow, honey. I've been onto you and preacher girl for a month," Patrice confessed. "I don't get it," she said to J. Amanda. "This man is *my* husband. Why would you want to destroy my family?"

Patrice moved closer to J. Amanda, and she didn't know whether to run out the door or prepare to fight. Hunky's wife wasn't a large woman. In fact, her upper body made her appear heavier than she actually was. Still, she was a solid woman, and J. Amanda feared her anger would give her the strength to knock her out cold in one shot.

J. Amanda looked Patrice in the eyes and connected with her pain. She deserved whatever words Patrice spewed her way. "I should really leave," she said and stood up.

Hunky rushed to block the door. "J. Amanda is my friend, Patrice. I can't let her leave until we all have an understanding."

"Your friend?" Patrice asked, slightly amused by his statement. "You have intimate relations with all your friends? Do you sneak to hotels, cook dinner, and buy roses for all your friends? Do you sneak off to grocery stores and hide in the basement to talk to your friends?"

Filled with guilt, J. Amanda stared at the floor. This was more than she could handle. "I'm sorry, Patrice."

"Don't tell me you're sorry, because you're not. If you were, you wouldn't be here with my husband."

J. Amanda touched the handle on the door, and as she lifted it, Patrice said, "If you're really sorry, you'll leave him alone."

J. Amanda eyed Hunky as she opened the door. "This is too much confusion," she said before leaving.

As J. Amanda drove back to Faith Tabernacle, she replayed the saddened look in Patrice's eyes. She couldn't help imagining that David would wear that same look if he found out about Hunky too. This was all her fault. How could she be so weak? She knew better than this!

And . . . if she'd paid attention, she would've realized that there was a pattern to Hunky's return visits. Every time they reconnected, there was an unfortunate outcome. This time it was adultery. The last time it was an abortion.

A stout and friendly-faced nurse escorted J. Amanda into a slightly chilled room. At the sight of the equipment around the room, J. Amanda halted her steps. Four chairs, separated by a curtain for privacy, were positioned in each corner. Though she was the only patient in the room, she wondered how many other women had stood where her feet were planted.

The nurse held J. Amanda's shaking hand and tried to ease her fears. "I'm gonna be with you the entire time. Try to relax."

J. Amanda followed her to the chair where her procedure would be performed and sat down. The nurse helped her adjust herself in the leather chair.

"You won't be in here more than five minutes," she told J. Amanda as she lifted her feet into the stirrups.

If that was supposed to erase the guilt she felt, the nurse would have to come up with a different line. Only five minutes to take away a life, J. Amanda thought. A life that is growing inside of me because I used poor judgment. *Somehow what she was doing didn't seem fair to the embryo inside her.*

A middle-aged doctor entered the room and walked straight to the machine near J. Amanda's feet. Without looking at her, he said hello as he counted the objects on a metal tray beside her chair. "Just relax," he said coldly as he touched the inside of her knees.

J. Amanda's legs shook uncontrollably, and the nurse rubbed her hand. "You'll be fine, honey. But you have to open your legs wide."

J. Amanda knew she had to be strong, so she opened her legs as wide as they could go and held her breath.

The doctor turned on a vacuum-like machine, and she closed her legs clenching them, on impulse. "I can't get in there if you don't open your legs," the doctor stated, causing her legs to shake more.

"It's okay, sweetie," the nurse said and lightly pushed down on J. Amanda's left leg. "It'll be over before you feel a thing."

J. Amanda closed her eyes and tried to relax as she lowered both of her legs. What if this is my only chance to become a mother? *she thought as the doctor widened her legs. Then, before J. Amanda could get used to his touch, he inserted a cold metal speculum inside her. She squeezed the nurse's hand tight as it slid into her. With her free hand she held her stomach and repeated, "God, forgive me," over and over.*

"You're doing great," the nurse said. "Squeeze as hard as you need to, baby doll. I can take it."

J. Amanda cracked a tiny smile and said, "Thank you."

Once the speculum was in place, the doctor pulled on a long tube attached to the loud machine, and as he approached her, she flinched. She could feel the suction before the tube touched her.

*"Wait a minute!" she cried. "I need another min-
ute . . . please."*

Visiting that abortion clinic was one of J. Amanda's
worst experiences. As a young adult, it's difficult to
understand why God designed intimate relations for
marriage. The effects were often damaging. For years,
every time she heard a vacuum or saw a long tube, she
shuddered.

When Tiffany was born, J. Amanda vowed to teach
her early on the importance of celibacy before marriage. Her only education about sex came from an old
health book in high school and conversations she overheard between her older sisters. J. Amanda was going
to provide a better sex education for her daughter so
that she'd be equipped to fight against her flesh. And so
that she'd never have to visit an abortion clinic or be a
willing participant in an affair.

~ Chapter 17 ~

Tionna

Alone again on a Saturday night, Tionna lay awake in bed, watching old movies and munching on baked potato chips. Tonight's BET movie choices started with *Mo' Better Blues,* and right after that was *Jason's Lyric.* Staring at Allen Payne and a young Jada Pinckett float down a scenic bayou in a canoe, in love, Tionna hoped this wouldn't be the blueprint of her weekends once Brianna moved into the dorms.

Since Brianna's prom a week ago, Tionna had been running around, preparing for graduation and the leadership program Temple had recommended Brianna attend before the semester officially began. Though Tionna was thrilled her alma mater had recognized Brianna's abilities, she wanted to spend the summer with her daughter before she became an official college freshman. Tionna knew that once the semester began, she'd have to compete with Brianna's friends for her daughter's time during holidays and summers.

After leaving the clinic, Tionna rushed home in hopes of treating Brianna to dinner at Seasons 52, her favorite restaurant in Cherry Hill. But Tionna was disappointed when she pulled into the garage and discovered that Brianna's car wasn't there. Inside the house she discovered that Brianna left a note on the refrigerator saying that she'd be spending the weekend with her cousins in New Jersey.

Now that Brianna had her own car, she'd been traveling across state lines to visit relatives and friends. She no longer depended on Tionna or her boyfriend to take her where she needed to be. Tionna was beginning to regret buying that car in more ways than one. If she had known Brianna's car would stir up ill feelings for Jasmine, she wouldn't have let Brian assume part of the cost. It was her plan to purchase the vehicle on her own, but when she told Brian her plans, he insisted he could help. Tionna assumed he had discussed the matter with Jasmine, so she accepted his five-thousand-dollar down payment and his offer to pay Brianna's insurance.

Though Tionna believed Jasmine should be upset with Brian, she didn't agree with the timing of her outburst. Nothing Jasmine had said was Tionna's fault, and she took offense at being Jasmine's verbal punching bag. It wasn't her fault that Brian and his family treated her as one of their own. And it wasn't her fault that most of the family viewed Jasmine as the reason Tionna would never become an official in-law. No, none of what Jasmine felt was her fault. Jasmine had brought those attitudes and feelings on herself. And to think that Tionna had actually tried to reach out to Jasmine that day, despite her feelings about her.

Not even Jasmine could ruin Brianna's prom day, or change the fact that Casey had shown up. *That* had been a complete surprise. She had no idea that Casey had remembered the actual prom date or that he had contacted Brianna for details.

Tionna sighed. She was certain Casey would've called her by now, given the way he looked into her eyes that day and the fact that he'd told her that he missed her.

Thinking of Casey warmed her heart. He had, in so many words, given her an ultimatum weeks ago. Yet, despite the fact that she *still* hadn't called him, he had made a point to be a blessing to her daughter.

Watching the movies and thinking about Casey stirred up a feeling Tionna hadn't felt in years. Remembering the trinkets she'd purchased at one of Kenya's home parties, Tionna got out of bed and walked to her dresser. She pulled out the middle drawer and pushed her underwear to the side until she felt her adult toys. She took one out and pushed the on button, praying the batteries were still good. The toy vibrated in her hand, and Tionna turned it off and headed back to her bed. As she sat at the bottom of her bed, staring at the object in her hand, she wondered if the silicone toy would be her intimacy companion for the rest of her life.

She called out to God. *What am I doing wrong? What's wrong with me that I can't let go of the past? I want to love again. . . . I just don't know how.*

One thing was for sure. Love wasn't in the toy in her hand. If she really wanted to find love again, she'd have to lose the chains protecting her heart and allow love to come in.

Tionna tossed the toy back inside her drawer and then picked up the receiver on her phone. *I hope I'm not too late,* she prayed.

Her heart felt a release when Casey answered after the first ring. It was now or never, she told herself. "Hey . . . are you free for dinner tomorrow?"

After church Tionna rushed to the grocery store to pick up a few ingredients for the chicken cordon bleu she planned to make for dinner. To her surprise, Casey was on vacation and was heading to Hawaii in the morning with some of his friends from the academy. Since he would be away for a week, she wanted to make tonight special. She was ready to open up her heart and prayed he was still willing to do the same.

The doorbell rang at exactly 6:00 P.M., and Tionna was ready. Dinner was warming in the oven, the table was set, and the wine was chilled. When she opened the door, Casey was grinning from ear to ear. Without hesitation, he stepped inside and gave Tionna a hug. As he squeezed her tight, Tionna wrapped her arms around his waist and held him just as tight. She wanted him to know that she had missed him too.

"Where should I begin?" she asked when they released one another.

Casey lightly kissed her lips and said, "How about we start at the beginning?"

Over dinner, Tionna spent two hours talking about her fears and her desire to let go of her past so that she could move forward with him.

"I'm gonna make you a believer," Casey promised. "I'm gonna prove to you that good men still exist."

"I like the sound of that," Tionna said and beamed. She couldn't remember the last time she had felt so at ease with a man.

Casey glanced at his watch. "It's almost ten," he said. "Why don't I clean the dishes before I leave?"

After tonight Tionna felt confident enough to relax her late-night guest rules a little. "I can take care of the dishes later. You'll be gone for a whole week, so let's just enjoy the time we have left before you head to Hawaii."

"I like the sound of that," Casey agreed. "I'm already packed, so what do you have in mind?"

Tionna got up from the table and walked over to Casey. "We could play Scrabble," she began and pulled him up from his chair. "Or . . . we could watch a movie . . . in my room."

"Wait a minute," Casey said, as if he hadn't heard her correctly. "Are you talking about your *bedroom*?"

Tionna nodded and led him through the dining room to the stairs.

Casey paused before climbing the stairs. "Are you sure about this? It is past your curfew," he teased.

"I'm asking you to watch a movie with me, Casey. That's all," she answered and tugged on his arm.

Casey slowly marched up the steps. "Okay, but if you wanted to do something more . . ."

"Just a movie," Tionna stressed and led him into her bedroom.

"I had to ask," he replied nervously. This was the first time Casey had been inside her bedroom.

"I'm still holding out for my husband," she reminded him.

"Well, you better play your cards right." He laughed. "You could have a ring by Christmas."

Hours later, Tionna lay in bed next to Casey, listening to him breathe. They'd watched a romantic comedy together, adding their own narration to every scene. Tonight she didn't feel like an old woman with a young man. Tonight she was just a woman in love. And as they lay together in each other's arms for the rest of the night, she believed in her heart that Casey was the "one."

~ Chapter 18 ~

Zora

For the past hour Zora had been staring out the cafeteria window, watching people walk in and out of the main entrance. Her laptop was open, but she hadn't touched the keys since she sat down for lunch. She had sat in the same seat for the past three weeks, while she waited for Cynthia to finish her treatment, and for the most part, she'd been able to pour out the words to her story. But today she had writer's block.

Cynthia had been in high spirits during the first stretch of radiation treatments. But this morning she awoke in tears. Traveling to and from the hospital every day with tightly bound breasts and thin tubes hanging from one of them was draining. Only halfway through the process, Cynthia was trying her best to appear strong, but the light in her eyes had dimmed.

It was hard for Zora to be in Philly without letting her line sisters know, but that was Cynthia's request. Cynthia was staying with Lawrence's parents and didn't want the heavy traffic of visitors coming in and out of their home. Zora had chosen to stay with her mother, but after a long day at the hospital, she desperately wanted to spend time with her girls.

If Cynthia was feeling up to it, after treatment they were going to go to Faith Tabernacle for Bible study.

Cynthia needed to hear a Word to keep her encouraged, and Zora felt it was time to let J. Amanda know about her line sister's condition.

Rumblings in the area behind her caught Zora's attention, and she turned her head in that direction. A few people were voicing their opinions about a player who had been injured in a charity basketball game yesterday afternoon.

Zora turned her chair to listen to the news on the flat-screen television mounted on the far wall. Reggie had flown out to Arizona the other day to accompany some of the Knicks players at the event. To her surprise, it wasn't a male player who had been injured. It was a female. Valencia Lambert. As clips of the injury were replayed, Zora spotted Reggie running out on the court and rolled her eyes. The accident was unfortunate, but she prayed Reggie wouldn't have to spend months helping Valencia recuperate.

"Do you mind if I sit here?" a gentleman asked.

Eager to shift gears, Zora turned slightly and removed her computer bag from the long table. She figured the man wanted to get close enough to hear the sports news on the television. "Sure," she said. "There's plenty of room."

Zora put her fingers on the computer keys and typed the thoughts that entered her mind, in hopes that most of them made sense. Editing was her least favorite part of the writing process.

"College student?" the man asked, and Zora stopped typing.

"Teacher and writer," she answered, trying to regain her groove.

"Is that right?" the man continued. "I should write a book. My life is a best seller."

Zora made sure her wedding ring was visible in case he was flirting. She wasn't knowledgeable when it came to pickup lines and gestures. "Everyone has a story inside them," Zora politely remarked.

"Some stories are more thrilling than others," he said. "Is writing hard?"

"I'd say so," she answered. "I've been at this off and on for a few years. But these days, you can hire someone to write a story for you."

The man paused to listen to a different news feature and then resumed his conversation. "I hope your husband supports you."

Zora beamed as she thought about their journey. "As a matter of fact, for the last twelve years he has, just as I have supported him."

"You're lucky," the man responded. "You can't find too many couples these days that are willing to do that for their mate."

"It hasn't always been easy, but when you respect one another, you can get through anything," Zora shared as she thought about Valencia.

"My woman left me before I had a chance to show my support," he replied with saddened eyes. "I guess it was for the best."

"Well, whatever her reason for leaving, look at it as her loss."

The man smiled and stood up. "Say . . . if you're around tomorrow, I'll be back during my lunch break," he said excitedly. "If I try my hand at writing tonight, would you read it and tell me what you think?"

"Sure," Zora said. She had rarely missed an opportunity to help a budding writer with their ideas.

"It was nice to have met you," he said and walked away.

***

Zora held Cynthia's hand as she told J. Amanda about the breast cancer.

Always the pillar of strength, J. Amanda firmly stated, "We're gonna get through this."

"Can you tell the other girls for me?" Cynthia asked. "I'm really not up for any visitors yet."

"Of course I will, but . . . you know we all want to be there for you, Cyn," J. Amanda replied.

"I know. I just need a little more time."

Zora was glad Cynthia had made it out to church tonight. Every time she left the hospital or her mother's house, she ran the risk of running into one of her line sisters. Now that Cynthia had given her permission to share the news, Zora looked forward to seeing them.

"Well," Zora said, "I've been out of the loop for too long. What's been going on with everyone? Anything exciting?"

J. Amanda leaned back in her leather chair and exhaled. "You have no idea."

"Do tell," Cynthia urged, and Zora agreed. "I need to focus on someone other than myself."

"You're gonna make me late for Bible study," J. Amanda joked. "Cyn, you were the timekeeper when we pledged. Make sure we're at that door at six forty-five."

On the edge of their seats, Zora and Cynthia listened intently as J. Amanda gave them an update of each line sister.

"So . . . let me get this straight," Zora said when J. Amanda finished talking. "Jazz snapped on Tionna because Brian bought Brianna a new car."

"At her prom party. You can't forget that part," Cynthia added and laughed.

Zora nodded and continued. "Tionna flipped out because Casey's partner is an attractive woman—"

"An attractive *young* woman," Cynthia interrupted.

"Yes, but they made up and are in love now," Zora said. "And Kenya tried to run Mack over in a parking lot because he was with his new girlfriend."

"The beauty queen girlfriend," Cynthia commented, and the women laughed in unison. "He knew he was wrong. Kenya shops at the same Target every Tuesday night."

Zora inhaled deeply and stared at J. Amanda. "And you . . . you've been sneaking around with Hunky? That's a name I haven't heard in a long time."

"I hope it's nothing too serious," Cynthia interjected.

"Is it time to go yet?" J. Amanda uttered and dropped her head on her desk.

"I feel like we're in college again," Zora commented. "Please don't say you're having an affair."

J. Amanda admitted that she had slipped up one time and had been praying for forgiveness since that day. The confession hit too close to home with Zora. After what had happened with Valencia in the women's bathroom at church, she despised any woman who slept with a married man. *The flesh is not that weak,* she thought as she listened to J. Amanda plead her case.

"I'm not sure we should be talking about this in church," Cynthia said, full of concern, "but I really hope it's over between you and Hunky."

Zora took the opportunity to share her input. "Please don't think I'm judging you, but you're a dynamic minister and an inspiration to so many women. What you're doing can't go unpunished. If you don't stop . . . you could risk losing everything God has given you."

J. Amanda looked as if she wanted to cry. "You're not telling me anything I don't tell myself every day.

I'm trying to make this right, but Hunky doesn't seem to understand."

"You can't make this right, Jay, but God can," Cynthia replied. "Let God take care of Hunky. He knows how to reach him better than you do."

Zora thought about the massages they had received during the reunion weekend. It dawned on her that all her closest friends were going through what the owner of the massage company would call "a tender moment." Zora reminded Cynthia and J. Amanda about that massage session and tried to encourage herself and her line sisters. "Let's not let our tender moments catch us off guard and destroy the great things going on in our lives."

"On that note," J. Amanda said, "I think this is the perfect time to pray. We have about ten minutes left before I have to be in the sanctuary."

The three women stood in a circle and held hands and took turns saying a prayer for one another and for their friends.

~ Chapter 19 ~

J. Amanda

J. Amanda sat in a rotating chair, waiting for the makeup artist to finish preparing her for today's live taping. She was nervous, but she was ready for her television debut. Family, friends, and women that had followed her through the years had come out to support another J. Amanda milestone. As they anxiously awaited her appearance on the set, J. Amanda arranged for the choir to sing a few selections.

One of the station's interns rolled a cart of flowers into the room and unloaded them in the space designated for J. Amanda. "These came in for you this morning," the young assistant informed her. "Sorry we didn't set them up before you arrived."

J. Amanda glanced at the floral arrangements on the table. The beautiful summer colors added warmth to the room.

"Here you go," the assistant said as she handed J. Amanda the cards from the flowers. "Someone will be by to escort you up front in about thirty minutes."

Time was moving quickly, but J. Amanda didn't mind. She was eager to share the message on her heart. She opened each of the cards in her hand. Various members and a few ministries in the church had sent words of encouragement and inspiration. There was also a card from David and the kids, one from her line sisters, and another from other members of her sorority. There was even a card from Hunky. It read: *I'm so proud of you. I'll always be in your corner. Nothing will ever change that. You're stuck with me forever. . . .*

J. Amanda tucked the cards in the thin space between her hip and the chair and sighed. No matter what she said, Hunky refused to give their friendship some space. Every day he made sure to reach out to her. If she didn't answer the phone, he would leave a voice message. If she didn't respond to the message within a few hours, he was sure to send a text. This kind of persistence was something J. Amanda had never seen, and to appease him, she made sure she answered one call or one text each day. If she didn't reply to him at all, she feared Hunky would call at two in the morning again.

"Don't you look lovely," Pastor Olivia remarked as she entered the room. "I see somebody's trying to show me up."

"I can't compete with the main star," J. Amanda humbly replied.

Pastor Olivia pulled a random chair close to J. Amanda and shared key points to remember as she waited for the makeup artist to leave the room. When she asked the makeup artist to close the door behind her, J. Amanda thought her mentor was about to give her a private teaching moment, as she'd done many times in the past.

Like an apt student, J. Amanda prepared to take mental notes.

"Ministry is hard work, but if your heart is in the right place with God, you can overcome any obstacle you face," Pastor Olivia explained. "People hold us to a higher standard, and when we mess up, they crucify us, as if they themselves never made a mistake."

J. Amanda wasn't sure where the conversation was headed, but she had a feeling something bad had surfaced. With so many things on her plate, she hadn't slowed down enough to pay attention to any rumors floating around the church. As the pastor continued to talk, J. Amanda prayed no one in church had seen her do or say something out of character.

"It may not seem fair sometimes, but God has called us to a higher standard. He has trusted us with His Word and equipped us so that we could be a shield for His kingdom. Now, I know that no one is exempt from temptation, but as leaders in ministry, we should know how to fight against it. With that said . . . I had a visit from Patrice Crawford this morning."

J. Amanda's heart felt like it was about to jump out of her chest. Why did Patrice want to meet with Pastor Olivia? She hadn't seen Hunky since the day Patrice showed up at the hotel.

"I don't have to tell you how damaging her words would be to the ministry you're trying to build if she spread them around our church family. I don't even know if the woman told me the truth."

"Pastor, I—"

Pastor Olivia lifted her hand, and J. Amanda stopped talking. "You don't have to explain anything to me right now. You have a sermon to deliver. But before I let you go out there and bless an audience that loves and believes in you, I want you to be absolutely sure that being a leader for God's people is what you want to do."

"I know I messed up," J. Amanda began and dabbed her eyes. The makeup artist had spent an hour creating her look. She didn't want tears to stain what she had crafted. "But I love God, and I love this gift He has entrusted me with."

"Then you've got to stay holy, sweetheart. Because at the end of the day, you not only hurt yourself when you fall, but you also hurt God and you disappoint His children," the pastor informed her. "That's a great deal of pressure for one person to endure, but you have to be special to bear such a precious title. And you are *special,* Reverend King. That's why you're here. There's an awesome ministry inside you, but *you* have to get yourself together and be the woman preacher God designed you to be."

J. Amanda couldn't control her tears. Pastor Olivia could've chosen to tell her about Patrice a day or two after the taping, but God knew she needed to hear those words before she stepped on the stage. J. Amanda was sobbing uncontrollably, and Pastor Olivia laid hands on her shoulders and prayed until J. Amanda felt a breakthrough. When the pastor was done, J. Amanda was laid out on the floor. It was a good thing she hadn't yet slipped into the dress specially made for the occasion.

"Get yourself together," Pastor Olivia said when she was done. "I'll send the makeup artist back in here, and I'll have the choir sing two more songs so you can get ready. If I have to, I'll get up and say a few words. But take this time to get your *whole* self together."

In a sequined dress that clung loosely to her curves, J. Amanda sauntered to the microphone after Pastor Olivia's gracious introduction. Still full of emotion from the talk with her pastor, she placed her Bible on the podium and scanned the faces in the crowd. On the front row, her husband and children stared back at her with smiling faces. Directly behind them were her line sisters, each with eyes on J. Amanda, hoping God had given her a Word that would speak to their specific situation. She was disappointed in her recent actions, but she had promised God that she'd be a better servant from this day forward.

J. Amanda looked down and opened the Bible to First Corinthians. Before welcoming the audience, she closed her eyes and led them in prayer. Moved by the authority in her words, the crowd cried and shouted until J. Amanda said, "Amen."

Now ready for the sermon, J. Amanda quickly welcomed the guests to the station and expressed her appreciation to her pastor for strong leadership and motherly love. She directed everyone to turn to First Corinthians 10:13, and together they read.

"The theme for this year's women's season was inspired by the great women in my life. Pastor Olivia, each of my line sisters, and my outstanding daughter, Tiffany," J. Amanda told the crowd. As she closed her Bible, she said, "Women of God, it's time to get your *whole* self together."

Laughter mixed with praise filled the room as J. Amanda repeated the theme. "Please bear with me," she continued. "God dropped this message in my spirit as I was waiting backstage. What I had planned to say will have to wait. For tonight, I'm allowing God to use me so that I can minister to both you and myself."

Using the verse from First Corinthians as a springboard, J. Amanda spoke about challenges and temptations. At some point she forgot about the cameras and preached as if she were at Faith Tabernacle on a Sunday morning. With the microphone in her hand, she walked around the stage and into the crowd, using random people as props to illustrate a point.

When it was time to wrap up her sermon, she paused by Cynthia, who was sitting in an end seat, and held her hand. Without making direct eye contact, J. Amanda squeezed Cynthia's hand tight. "God will sometimes give you more than you can bear at a time and when you least expect it. He does that so you'll have no choice but to lean on Him," she said, then let Cynthia's hand go. "He'll place a mountain in front of you so you'll learn how to climb. He'll give you an enemy so you'll learn how to defeat him. He'll place an obstacle in your path so you'll learn how to overcome it. God will give you more than you can bear so you'll learn how to handle anything that comes your way."

J. Amanda headed back to the stage and slowly walked up the steps as she continued to speak with passion. "There are achievements for your life that you don't think you're qualified for. Sometimes, God has to push you to reach the potential He sees in you. He has a vision for your life that you can't see. So you've to get your *whole* self together."

Back at the podium, J. Amanda picked up her Bible and concluded her speech. "Sometimes, God has to stretch you further than you ever thought you could be stretched. It's not always the devil that challenges you. I know there are men in the room, but it is women's season, so I stopped by for a brief moment to let the women know that God wants you to get yourself together so that the purpose He has for you can be fulfilled. Life won't always be easy, but in the end, you will be blessed and God will be pleased. So this season, let's get our *whole* selves together!" she stressed, then dropped the microphone on the podium and went to her chair next to Pastor Olivia. As the audience cheered and applauded the delivery of J. Amanda's message, she fell on her knees and prayed.

When the taping was over, J. Amanda hung around and greeted each guest. To show her appreciation for attending the live taping, she had arranged for a caterer to serve appetizers and drinks. As the crowd dwindled, Tiffany stood by her mother's side.

"She's quite the helper," Tionna said as she walked over to her friend, carrying some of the items J. Amanda had left in her dressing room. "Tiffany swept the floor and cleaned off all the tables."

People standing around complimented Tiffany's willingness to help, and the young child hid behind her mother. Unlike J. Amanda, Tiffany was shy around unfamiliar people.

"She's my angel," J. Amanda told the last group of people. As they walked away, J. Amanda gathered her belongings and followed Tionna to a side door. Halfway there, a familiar voice called her name and she turned around. Coming down the hallway in darkened shades was Hunky. He smiled when he had her attention.

"You know him?" Tionna whispered.

J. Amanda nodded nervously. It had been only thirty minutes since she delivered her sermon, and already the biggest obstacle she faced had appeared. She had no idea he was coming to the station. Guests had to reserve tickets well in advance to attend the taping, and most of the tickets had been saved for personal guests and members of the church. Most of the leftover tickets had been taken by members of different churches throughout the city. It was surprising that Hunky had got his hands on one.

I can overcome this obstacle, J. Amanda told herself as she greeted him with a brief hug.

Hunky went to kiss her cheek, and she quickly pushed him away. Tionna stood motionless, staring back at them, and J. Amanda finally introduced him. She knew that was what Tionna was waiting for.

"This is William Crawford," J. Amanda said.

Hunky laughed and extended his right hand. "I'm better known to her as Hunky, but how are you, Ms. . . .

Tionna looked as if she'd seen a ghost, so J. Amanda kept talking to keep the energy in the hallway mellow and light. She knew Tionna was going to lecture her later about this. "This is one of my very best friends, *Dr.* Tionna Jenkins."

Without returning a greeting, Tionna pretended to look at her watch. "I forgot I had a stop to make before nine," she said and backed down the hall. "I'll give you a call tonight."

Tionna was acting weird, but J. Amanda ignored her weak excuse to make a fast exit. She was going to say her last round of good-byes and head out soon too. Tiffany clung to J. Amanda's hand as she pulled her daughter close. "I should probably—"

"Thought I was gonna have to call the firehouse," Hunky joked, cutting J. Amanda off. Since he rarely talked to her on the phone, he wasn't going to let her out of his sight too quickly. "You were on fire tonight, Reverend King. I was proud of you."

J. Amanda tried to relax. It was a good thing David had driven his own car and had already gone home. "I hope you understood the message," she replied. "That's what matters the most."

"I did," he answered and looked down at the bright-eyed little girl by J. Amanda's side. "Who's this beautiful young lady?"

Tiffany looked up at her mother and grinned, exposing the slight gap in her top row of teeth. "I'm Tiffany."

"A fitting name for a princess," he said. "And you're the spitting image of your mother. Did you know that I went to high school with her?"

"Really?" Tiffany laughed, and J. Amanda jerked her close to her side.

"We should probably go," J. Amanda snapped, unaware of her shift in mood. She was afraid Hunky would feed Tiffany more than she should know.

"If I didn't know any better, Jay, I'd think you were trying to blow me off."

Something about Hunky didn't seem right. J. Amanda recalled what Jasmine had told her about an encounter they'd had, and for the first time since she'd known him, she felt uneasy. "Of course not. It's just getting late, and my daughter has camp in the morning."

"Then we'll catch up tomorrow?"

J. Amanda didn't want to lie, so she lowered her voice in hopes that Tiffany couldn't hear her clearly. "I don't think so, and . . . we can't do this anymore. That's the right thing to do."

"For who?"

"For the family we go home to every night. We owe it to them to stop," she replied adamantly.

Hunky's face went cold as he stared at her. "Tiffany really is a gem," he stated. "I guess you do the right thing all the time, huh?" Hunky brushed Tiffany's cheek lightly. J. Amanda wanted to pull her away, but she didn't want to frighten her child. "I used to have a gap in my teeth too," he reminded J. Amanda. "Funny your daughter and I have that in common."

Hunky smirked and waved good-bye to Tiffany before turning to leave. As he strolled down the hall, Tiffany giggled and said, "He's been your friend for a *long* time if you met him in school, Mommy."

"Yes, sweetie. It has been a long time," she answered, realizing that the young man she once knew had disappeared.

On the way home J. Amanda couldn't stop thinking about what Hunky had said. She had totally forgotten about the gap between his teeth. In every picture she had of them, he had never smiled wide enough to show his teeth. He was self-conscious about his appearance and often shied away from meeting new people. Hunky had always said that when he came into a large sum of money, the first thing he would do was buy a set of new teeth.

J. Amanda couldn't believe she had missed that important detail when she ran into him at Whole Foods while shopping with Jasmine, and she couldn't believe she hadn't connected Tiffany's gap to him. Thinking about her child's connection to Hunky, J. Amanda thought about the moment she decided not to go through with the abortion.

"Wait a minute!" J. Amanda cried. "I need another minute . . . please."

Annoyed, the impatient doctor dropped his hands.

"Give us three minutes," the friendly nurse said and asked him to leave. "Are you sure you want to do this?" she asked a trembling J. Amanda once the doctor was gone. "Are you nervous, or are you having doubts?"

J. Amanda listened to the creaky noise coming from the machine by her feet and folded her hands across her belly. "A little of both," she replied. Her grandmother had taught her that abortion was a sin, but she wondered how she'd feel if she knew Hunky was the father. And what would this do to David? Hunky was her true love, but David was the kind of man J. Amanda knew she should marry.

"Follow what your heart is saying," advised the nurse. "I can't tell you what to do, but I will say that there are many joys in motherhood, but motherhood also changes your life forever."

The doctor opened the door and stood in the doorway, straight-faced, waiting for the okay to come inside. "I've got eight more after this one," he grumbled.

The nurse ignored him and repeated her question. "Are you sure you want to do this?"

J. Amanda removed her feet from the stirrups and stood to her feet. "I don't know if I'm doing the right thing, but I'm gonna follow my heart," she stated as she wrapped the cotton hospital robe she was wearing tighter. "And I don't want a cranky doctor to be the one to take my baby's life."

Once J. Amanda was dressed, she met Jasmine in the lobby. "That was real fast," Jasmine said as she closed the magazine she was reading.

"I couldn't do it," J. Amanda mumbled. "I just could not go through with it."

Shocked, Jasmine put the magazine on a table by her chair. "Okay, let's get out of here, then. But . . . have you thought about what you're going to tell David?"

"I have no idea," J. Amanda told her friend as they walked out of the clinic.

"Well," Jasmine responded, "if you want to keep him, you can't tell him before the wedding."

That day seemed so long ago. When she left the clinic, she had planned to tell David after their honeymoon. When that didn't happen, she decided to wait until they moved into their first home. Before she had a chance to say anything, David's mother noticed her weight gain.

"Am I about to become a grandmother?" she had asked as she rubbed J. Amanda's stomach.

In her panic, J. Amanda had blurted, "Yes. I was waiting for the right time to share the news."

Seven months later, Tiffany was born, and Hunky had gone back to Atlanta. J. Amanda thought her secret was safe . . . until today.

~ Chapter 20 ~

Tionna

"This is a pleasant surprise," Casey said, beaming, when Tionna showed up at the precinct. He'd been so busy catching up on cases that he hadn't seen her since he returned from his vacation. Casey reached out to hug her but noticed her strained expression and dropped his hands to his side. "Should we go outside to talk?" he asked, and Tionna immediately headed out the door.

She walked briskly through the parking lot to her car, parked at the end of the first row, as Casey jogged behind her to keep up. When Tionna reached her car, she leaned against the passenger side door and sighed. "Something happened tonight that I'm not sure how to handle," she began and then waited for Casey to get closer before continuing. "A friend may be in trouble."

"And you came to your man to help you solve a problem. I like that," he said lightly. When Tionna didn't shoot back a sarcastic comment, he knew the matter was serious. "Tell me what's bothering you, babe. Are you in danger?"

"No . . . I mean yes . . . well, not really. But there is the potential."

"Did someone threaten you or Brianna?"

Tionna loved that Casey was concerned about her daughter. "No, and I can't give you the person's name, because a patient is involved."

Casey leaned against the car next to Tionna and crossed his arms on his chest. "Let's see. You just left church, so you must've seen the patient there."

Tionna put her hands on her forehead and pushed her hair away from her eyes. "He's seeing a good friend."

"And you're concerned because this patient is in one of your classes. If that's true, then he . . . or she has some kind of serious issue or disease."

"Don't be my detective right now," Tionna urged. "I need you to be my friend."

"I'm always a detective, babe," he said and smiled. Casey's second attempt to make her smile didn't work, but he was determined to help her relax. He put his arm around her and massaged her shoulders. "Did your patient mention anything in your interactions with him to make you think he'd harm himself or your friend?"

The tension in Tionna's shoulders lessened. "He was accused of a crime, but I don't know about any diseases. I want to give my friend a heads-up, but I could lose my license if someone found out I leaked privileged information."

"If this person did time, often the assumption is that he did the crime. That is something your friend should know, but if you can't reveal the details of the information, you need to help her raise a red flag," Casey pointed out. "Wouldn't you want her to do the same for you?"

The answer to his question was undeniably yes. But how was she going to do that without breaking an ethics code?

"Don't forget that the law permits you to tell, if he's a danger to someone else," Casey reminded her. "You also need to be careful when you talk to your friend. People do change. That patient may have changed.

Maybe talk to him first. Perhaps he'll tell your friend about his past himself."

Though he hadn't devised a definite solution to her problem, Tionna was thankful she had Casey to share her concerns with. She kisses his cheek and then walked to the driver's side of her car.

"If you or your friend ever find yourself in a tough or dangerous position, don't hesitate to call me," he said as Tionna got into the car. "I'll stop by later to check on you, okay?"

"I'd like that," she said and smiled. Since Brianna was away at school, she welcomed his company at night.

Tionna lay in bed, wide awake, by Casey's side. It was sweet of him to come over and help clean the house to take her mind off things, but no kind of distraction was going to work. Before going to bed, Tionna had called her best friend but had been unable to talk because J. Amanda was half asleep. Though she wanted to talk, hearing her friend's voice was enough to relieve her stress for the night.

As she focused on the ceiling fan above her, Tionna reflected on the day J. Amanda had walked into her office as a patient. She should've known then that Hunky would show up one day and cause trouble.

"You want me to do what?" Tionna asked J. Amanda, hoping this was a joke.

"Just tell David that I'm one month pregnant," she begged.

"I'm not gonna do that," Tionna stated firmly. "This is my first real job, and doctors shouldn't lie to their patients."

"David isn't having this baby. I am," J. Amanda uttered. "You don't have to say anything. I'll do all the talking. Just don't deny what I say."

"I can't believe you," Tionna responded as she checked J. Amanda's vital signs. "Do you hear yourself? You're acting like your line sister."

"Don't make this about Jazz. This is about me being in a jam."

"A jam you created, soon-to-be Reverend King. How do you sleep with someone three weeks before saying, 'I do'? You're no better than my child's father."

"Will you please focus?" J. Amanda snapped. "This isn't about Brian, either."

Tionna recorded the information she had collected, then asked J. Amanda to lay on her back. "I don't understand how you could sleep with Hunky unprotected."

"For the fifteenth time, the condom broke," J. Amanda told her.

"Whatever," Tionna said and spread gel across J. Amanda's womb. "How do you get pregnant by an old lover, don't go through with the abortion, and then make your husband believe the baby is his? It's just not right. I know they taught you that in seminary."

Visibly frustrated, J. Amanda retorted, "Technically, I didn't lie. I withheld the truth."

Tionna rolled the ball over the gel to try to locate the fetus. "Either way it's wrong, and I don't want any part of it."

"I wouldn't do this if I thought you'd get in trouble. David won't suspect anything," J. Amanda said as she stared at the monitor. "I want to give my marriage a chance. I want to give this baby a chance to grow up in a real home with real parents. I love Hunky, but I know David is the better father for this child."

For the first time since J. Amanda had walked into the office, her crazy plan made sense. Tionna understood how she felt. She wanted the same for Brianna. Tionna found the small mass and sighed. It always amazed her to see the beginning of a life. As she took pictures of the baby from different angles, Tionna decided to give it a chance to grow up with two parents.

"This is the last time I'm gonna follow one of your crazy schemes, Jay. You better pray David doesn't ask me anything specific. I won't volunteer information, but I'm not gonna lie," Tionna replied. "And you better hope the baby doesn't come out looking like Hunky."

Tionna loved J. Amanda like a real sister but wondered when her impulsiveness would end. She was growing tired of rescuing her. Making hasty decisions in your twenties was due to immaturity, but making similar decisions when you were close to forty was just plain foolish. Hunky had been MIA for over a decade. What did J. Amanda really know about this man as an adult?

Hunky called the clinic at the last minute and requested an emergency appointment.

Tionna didn't have any availability, so she carved some time out of her lunch hour to meet with him. She was glad he'd called. After seeing him at the TV station, it would be good to clear up some details. Hopefully, his responses would put Tionna at ease and she wouldn't need to worry about her friend.

Tionna knocked on the examination room door before she entered. "Good morning, Mr. Crawford," she greeted.

"Hello again," Hunky answered from a chair in the corner of the room. "It's amazing, isn't it? We both have J. Amanda as a friend. I'm glad we finally met. I've heard so much about you."

Hunky didn't waste any time getting to the point. Tionna liked that. She wasn't in the mood for small talk. "It's a small world," she replied and sat on a stool across from him. "What brings you in today?"

"I thought we should talk about yesterday. Did you speak to J. Amanda last night about me?"

Tionna was short with her responses. Hunky was not going to get information about J. Amanda from her. "No, we haven't talked yet," she stated.

"I'm sure you'll have a lot to say about me."

Tionna filled out basic information in his chart. "Is there something in particular you want us to discuss?"

"Are you trying to blow me off too?"

Tionna noticed Hunky's demeanor had changed, and looked up. "No, Mr. Crawford. I have a lot of patients to see today. I want to make sure we discuss what's on your mind before I have to leave."

"I don't believe you," he replied blandly, and before Tionna had a chance to respond, Hunky leaped from the chair, lifted her from the stool, and covered her mouth as he pushed her against the wall. "If you want to live, don't think about screaming, don't bang on the wall, and don't give off any sign that you're in trouble," he demanded. "I know you can't tell J. Amanda any-thing about me. There's laws that say you can't, right? And I know an overachiever like you won't risk your career by violating any laws."

Tionna tried not to flinch or display any sign of fear, but she was afraid. On any other day her intern would've barged into the room to ask a question, but not today. Today Tionna was left alone with a madman.

"Maybe I should tell your boss about Tiffany." Tion-na's left brow rose, and Hunky laughed. "Yeah, I know you delivered the baby. J. Amanda told me that. I also know that Tiffany is mine."

It was hard to breathe with Hunky's hand over her mouth. Every time she inhaled, faint traces of gasoline on his hand nauseated her. When that became too much to take, she tried to open her mouth, but the taste of his hand made her feel worse.

Hunky pressed his body deeper into hers and touched her inner thigh with his free hand. As he slowly moved up and down her thigh, he got so close to her ear that she could smell what he'd eaten for lunch. "Stay out of my way, Dr. Jenkins. Jay and I have unfinished business," he said as his hand moved closer to her private area. "Don't cross me. You have no idea what I'm capable of. If I get a whiff that you opened your mouth, I'll take a trip to Temple and visit that pretty little daughter of yours."

Hunky removed his hands and smirked. "It's a shame I didn't meet you first," he said before turning to leave.

Tionna stayed against the wall for five minutes and then quickly locked the door. She needed a minute to digest what had happened. Hunky knew too much, and now she was in an even bigger bind. There was no way Tionna was going to put her daughter at risk. But something had to be done. She wasn't going to live the rest of her life in fear.

~ Chapter 21 ~

Zora

"I can't wait to get home to my husband," Zora announced as she parked her car in Kenya's condominium complex. In honor of Cynthia's last radiation treatment, the women had gone to the Cheesecake Factory to celebrate. Cynthia needed to follow up with the doctor in a couple of weeks, but for now she was free to get back to her normal daily routine.

"I'm gonna miss you two," Kenya said and grabbed a doggie bag of food as she got out of the car. "No one keeps me in check the way you do."

"I'm only a phone call away," Cynthia chimed in. "Whenever you get that urge to do something crazy, stop, get your phone, and call one of us."

"Should we come in and say hello to Mack?" Zora asked.

Kenya leaned into Cynthia's opened window. "Mack is not your friend anymore. But if you want to speak to him, just hang around out here for a bit. He thinks he's gonna spend the night, 'cause it's so late, but I've got news for his old behind."

As Kenya made fun of her son's father, Zora smelled faint traces of smoke. "Is there a warehouse or something around here?" she asked Kenya.

"In Chestnut Hill? I don't think so?"

"You guys don't smell smoke?"

Kenya stood up and looked toward her condo as she sniffed the air. "Maybe someone burned a bag of popcorn or fried chicken."

"No, silly. I'm pretty sure that's—"

Cynthia cut Zora off. "I think your building is on fire. Look!" she exclaimed and pointed to Kenya's bedroom window.

Kenya dropped the bag in her hand and ran toward her condo. "Someone call the fire department!" she screamed.

While Cynthia stayed behind to call nine-one-one, Zora jumped out of the car and ran after Kenya. If that were her child in the house, she would risk her life to save him too. On her way to the front door, Zora saw someone's shadow race from behind the condo and disappear into the forest of trees. Zora didn't have time to alert anyone of his presence. She had to keep an eye on Kenya.

"My son's in there!" Kenya screamed as she banged on the door and rummaged through her purse for her keys. "Somebody help me please! Call the fire department!"

Slowly, people started running from their homes. When the main door of the building was opened, Kenya charged in against the flow of people running outside. "Oh, God, please no!" she cried.

Zora relieved Kenya of her purse and frantically tried to find the house keys herself. "We've got to hurry before the fire starts to spread," she shouted, praying that God would send His angels.

In a panic, Kenya banged on her front door, yelling Mack's name over and over until he charged out of the condo with their son in his arms. Kenya snatched Tyree from Mack's arms just as the flames became brighter, and they all raced out the main door into the parking lot.

Kenya sat on the edge of the sidewalk, rocking Tyree back and forth while thanking God for his safety. As they both cried, Mack stood over them in astonishment. "Did you do this?" she snapped, directing the question to Mack. "Answer me! Did you set my house on fire?"

"I can't believe you'd ask me a question like that," Mack barked.

Cynthia pulled Mack away so that he wouldn't become enraged by Kenya's questions. This was a highly sensitive matter, so there was no telling what Kenya might do to him.

Zora sat down next to her friend. "We don't know what happened, so let's not jump to conclusions. I don't think Mack would do anything to put Tyree at risk," she said and told Kenya about the man she'd seen running into the trees.

Kenya's mascara started to run down her cheeks. "Thank you, Zora. I hate to think what could've happened if you didn't smell the smoke. Tell the cops what you saw. If someone tried to hurt my son, I want to know who it is. They'll be sorry they messed with me and Tyree."

~ Chapter 22 ~

Jasmine

Though the fire at Kenya's condo was unfortunate, it gave Jasmine the opportunity to clean out her closet. Kenya had lost an entire summer wardrobe, so Jasmine planned to give her a few things until she was able to replenish what was destroyed. One of the firemen had said a half-lit cigarette that fell on the carpet in her bedroom had started the fire, but that was strange. Kenya didn't smoke. Neither did Mack, who had been there all night. An investigation was still pending, but in the meantime, Kenya and Tyree were staying with Tionna until she could figure out her next steps.

After learning about Kenya, Brianna left school to spend a few days at her mother's, in case she needed help. Brianna was visiting with her half sisters today, which was good for Jasmine. While she cleaned, Brianna could keep the girls entertained.

Jasmine had no idea where Brian was. He'd taken her car to run errands. If he didn't come back soon, he was going to miss spending time with Brianna before she left.

As Jasmine threw clothes into a large garbage bag, she sang along to the music blasting from Sasha's room. Usher was an entertainer whom the younger generation adored, but he'd gained a more mature fan base with some hits adults could also enjoy. The upbeat song "Yeah!" was one of them.

Out of nowhere Jasmine felt something hit her arm, and when she turned to see what it was, Brian slapped her with a cell phone. "You dirty little liar!" he barked.

Jasmine grabbed her face and felt blood. The phone had cut her cheek. "What's wrong with you?" she yelled as she tried to exit the walk-in closet.

Brian blocked her path and shoved her deeper inside the closet. As she stumbled over the clothes on the floor, she noticed a pack of birth control pills. Though she'd hidden her pills in the back of her glove compartment, Brian must've found them while he was out. *I knew I shouldn't have let him drive my car!* Jasmine thought.

"Let's have a baby," he mimicked in a female voice and knocked Jasmine to the floor. "I want to have your son." Brian kicked Jasmine in the side, and she curled into a ball. "Why'd you lie to me, Jazz?"

Jasmine tried to squirm toward the door, but Brian continued to kick her back in place. She was trapped and feared her husband was going to kill her.

"I was looking for a pen, but guess what I found instead?" he yelled and picked up the pack of pills. "You tried to hide them, but you're not so smart, are you?" Brian threw the pills in her face, and his foot quickly followed. Seeing his foot come down, Jasmine twisted her body and turned her head just in time.

"Then," Brian continued in between kicks and hard slaps to her head, "I come home and our neighbor wants me to relay a message to my wife. He says to make sure Orion gives Kierra a permission slip to attend some musical in New York. Orion, Jazz? You can't be serious," he shouted. "That's why you want to dance again, isn't it? You want to be near your lover. Well, let me show you what happens to liars."

Enraged, Brian dropped to his knees and continually beat Jasmine as he called her derogatory names. Jasmine should've fought back or hollered, but the girls were in the other room and she didn't want them to see their father in this state. So she took the beating until her body became numb and the taste of blood trickled into her mouth. As if he hadn't damaged her enough, Brian wrapped his hands around Jasmine's throat and banged her head against the floor. Jasmine thought for sure her life was ending. Tears escaped from her eyes, fueling Brian's rage. "You ought to cry for disrespecting me!" he exclaimed.

Jasmine prayed the insanity would end. *If there is a God,* she said to herself, *only He can save me now.*

In that instant Brianna barged into the bedroom and screamed at the top of her lungs. "Daddy, let her go!"

Alarmed, Brian loosened his grip on Jasmine's throat, and her head fell hard to the floor. Without saying a word, Brian flew out of the room and then out of the house. Brianna rushed to Jasmine's side and yelled for Sasha to call nine-one-one. While she held Jasmine's hand, Brianna grabbed the cell phone in her pocket and called her mother.

"Mom, Daddy hurt Jasmine. It's real bad," she cried into the phone.

That was the last thing Jasmine heard before everything went dark.

~ Chapter 23 ~

J. Amanda

"She's going to be so happy to finally meet you," J. Amanda told the lady on the phone. She'd just driven home from Washington, D.C., when Roxanne McDaniels called. Rather than return the call when she was settled inside the house, J. Amanda kept the car running in her driveway and answered.

Thanks to Kenya's detective skills and social work resources, J. Amanda was able to locate Roxanne, Jasmine's birth mother. Roxanne cried for twenty minutes when J. Amanda explained her reason for contacting her last week. Though Roxanne lived in Florida, after thirty minutes on the phone, she anxiously agreed to come back to Philadelphia in a few months to surprise Jasmine for her birthday.

When the call was over, J. Amanda dragged her weary body into the house. She couldn't wait to get in the bed. Since her television debut, she'd been traveling to different churches to teach a class or preach. Instead of catching a train to D.C., she had decided to drive and leave at 5:00 A.M. to get ahead of the heavy traffic. She'd been moving nonstop since then.

"I'm home," she announced, expecting her children to come charging at her. But no one did. J. Amanda locked the back door and dropped her briefcase by the nearby water cooler. The house was unusually quiet.

"David!" she called as she walked through the kitchen. Maybe David took the kids out and left a note, she thought. "Anybody here?" she said, unable to find a message from her husband or the kids. Maybe they ran to the store," she whispered.

Part of her was relieved. With the kids out of the house, she could get a quick nap in before they returned home. J. Amanda strolled out of the kitchen and paused at the stairs to remove her shoes. As she started up the steps, she glanced into the family room and noticed David sitting in his chair in the dark.

"David?" she called. "Didn't you hear me come in?" When he didn't respond, J. Amanda nervously backed down the steps and went into the family room. "David, are you okay?" she asked as she approached him. David's eyes were open, but they didn't blink. Something was definitely wrong.

J. Amanda turned on the lamp on the end table and then faced her husband again. Sitting tall in the clothes he had worn to work, he clung to a newspaper clipping in his hand

"Why are you in the dark, David?" she questioned.

David finally blinked but did not look his wife in the eyes. "I've been sitting here since four o'clock."

"You're scaring me, David. Where are the kids? Did something happen?" J. Amanda asked, trying not to panic.

"Tiffany and David are with my mother," he stated.

"Okaaay . . . so why are you acting so weird? Did something happen to you?"

David lifted the clipping in his hand and gave it to his wife. From the wear and tear of the edges and its faded coloring, J. Amanda knew the clipping had been cut from a newspaper some time ago. She sat down under the lamp to get a better view and almost dropped it on the floor.

"Where did you get this?" she wanted to know.

"William Crawford stopped by today."

J. Amanda didn't know what to say. The clipping explained why Hunky was at the house, though she questioned how he got ahold of it.

The picture was taken the day of J. Amanda's visit to Planned Parenthood for the abortion. When she had left the building, there was a protest going on. Lots of flashing cameras and angry people screaming harsh words had bombarded her when she walked out the door. J. Amanda hadn't paid attention to the flashes going off as she walked through the disgruntled mob. But the cameras had caught J. Amanda holding up her arm to block the blinding lights. Though not all of her face was visible, you could tell it was her. Jasmine, who walked beside her, was easily recognizable. With attitude written on her face, Jasmine practically stared into the camera lens.

As J. Amanda read the article, which highlighted the rise in the number of abortions taking place in the city, David continued to speak. "He came here to tell me that Tiffany was his daughter. I thought he was mistaken, so he put that clipping in my hand. Still, I told him that my wife was a decent woman. She wouldn't lead me to believe something that wasn't true. But then I looked at the date on the article," David said, and his voice cracked. "The article was written one week before we got married. So even if Tiffany is really mine, you were pregnant before our wedding day and the baby you were carrying wasn't mine."

J. Amanda could've come up with another excuse to dance around what the photograph conveyed, but her conscience wanted to come clean. "David . . . let me explain."

"What is there to explain? That man says Tiffany is his daughter. Is that true?" David asked and waited for a response.

J. Amanda opened her mouth, but nothing came out.

"You don't have to answer, Jay. I can go get tested and find out myself," David said in a raised voice. "How could you do this to our family?"

J. Amanda had never seen David this angry. "I tried to tell you, but—"

"There is no but," he shouted and stood up. "You should've told me."

J. Amanda's hands trembled at the thought of what else Hunky might have shared with her husband. Seeing him this way, she wasn't going to add fuel to the fire by asking.

"And to think . . . you had me racking my brain for months, trying to figure out why you were so upset with me, and you've been keeping this from me. Were you ever planning to tell me?"

Still unable to speak, J. Amanda closed her eyes and cried silently.

"I want you to leave," David told her.

J. Amanda looked at her husband in disbelief. "I can't leave," she sobbed. "I'm not gonna leave my kids."

"Then I'll leave, and we'll work out visitation."

"You're angry right now," J. Amanda cried and went to her husband. She tried to touch his arm, but he pushed her away. "I'm not gonna let you leave, either. I messed up, but we can get through this."

"I thought I married a godly woman," David said with disappointment and turned to leave.

"David, wait a minute," J. Amanda moaned as she reached for him again. This time David yanked his arm away from her with a little more force, and she dropped to the floor. As she listened to him climb the stairs, she knew his heart had broken, and there was little she could do to change that now.

With her marriage at risk, J. Amanda remained on the floor until the sun had been replaced by the moon. She didn't know how to make this better, but J. Amanda knew she had to speak to Hunky and resolve whatever was on his mind.

J. Amanda got off the floor and walked into the kitchen. She had a bad headache but needed answers. As she reached for her cell phone and removed it from the briefcase by the cooler, she couldn't believe how her life had changed in a matter of months.

The first ring hadn't completed a full cycle when Hunky answered the phone. "I've been expecting your call," he said.

"Just tell me why, Hunky. Why would you do something like this?"

"Why would you lie to me?" Hunky returned. "How could you deny me the chance to be a father? How do you know I wouldn't have been good enough?"

"My decision wasn't about your ability to be a father. You seem to forget that I was engaged at the time," she reminded him.

"You can't have everything your way, Jay," retorted Hunky. "You can't manipulate every bad decision to your advantage. Tiffany is *my* daughter. I wasn't sure when I saw the article years ago, but when I looked into her eyes at the station, I knew. And your response confirms that I'm right."

J. Amanda sat down and sighed. "You could've come to me, Hunky."

"Really?" he answered. "I tried to, but you were too busy for me after we made love. Once again, J. Amanda got what she needed and then went on to the next chapter in her life."

"You know that I'm busy, Hunky. But . . . my distance was because of the guilt. Nothing more."

"I know that you left me to go to college. You stayed away from me because of your sorority, and now you have the church and a family to keep us apart."

"What's happened to you, Hunky? I've never seen you be this cruel."

"Don't you get it? This is who I became when you left me."

"So . . . where are we now? What is it that you want from me?" J. Amanda asked. It was clear that the friend she once knew was long gone.

"I won't say anything to your husband about our night together," Hunky replied. "But I want Tiffany to know I'm her father."

J. Amanda had a tough decision to make. Should she push David's buttons more or potentially scar a young girl for life? "You're being irrational," she snapped.

"And you're being selfish," he retorted. "Imagine how I felt sitting at Thirtieth Street, waiting for my train to Atlanta. Seeing you in that paper brought tears to my eyes as I thought about the baby I thought you had aborted. I shed *real* tears for you at that station." Hunky sounded as if he was about to shed more tears as he remembered that day. "I was shocked to learn that you were pregnant so soon after you got married," he continued somberly. "That's when I started keeping tabs on you. You posted so many pictures of Tiffany on your personal Web page. Every time I saw a new picture of her, my heart ached. You robbed me, Jay, so no . . . I don't think I'm being irrational at all. Because of you, I missed out on the early years of my only child's life."

It didn't matter that Hunky was right. She had robbed him of his fatherhood, but there was no way she was going to let him be a father to Tiffany now. "I'm not going to let you disrupt her life right now. She's only eight," J. Amanda replied firmly. "Maybe . . . we can come up with another solution that will work for everyone involved."

"I guess I can—"

"Hold on one second. I've got an incoming call," J. Amanda interrupted and switched to her other line.

"I need you to come to the hospital," Tionna told her. "Jasmine was badly beaten."

Forgetting that Hunky was on the other line, J. Amanda tossed her phone inside her purse, put on her shoes, and rushed to the hospital.

~ Chapter 24 ~

Tionna

Tionna was the first person Jasmine saw when she opened her eyes. "Isn't it ironic that *my* daughter would be the one to save you?"

Jasmine tried to laugh but stopped when she felt pain. "I'm glad she was there," she replied groggily.

"The doctor says you're gonna be fine," Tionna informed her. "You have a few bad bruises, and you'll have a mean headache for a few days, but he thinks you can leave in two to three days."

Jasmine lifted her arm, and Tionna held her hand. "Sorry about Brianna's prom."

"I've already forgotten about it," Tionna assured her. Seeing Jasmine lying in a hospital bed with swollen lips and eyes, and bruises in random places, she understood why Jasmine was often on edge. She could only image how long the abuse had taken place.

All these years she had imagined what life would be like if she were married to Brian. Today those thoughts were officially squashed. Brian led a life that was not acceptable for any family, and especially not for her precious daughter. The brief episode of violence that Brianna had witnessed had tormented her. Tionna shuddered at the pain Brian's other daughters had suffered as a result of watching abuse regularly. She'd heard patients share their stories all the time in group sessions. Kids who came from homes where domestic violence was prevalent either became spousal abusers or date abusers or withdrew completely from life.

How or why Brian had changed, Tionna had no clue. His father wasn't an abuser, and his mother didn't tolerate abuse. But as Tionna replayed conversations she had had with Mrs. Dorothy, she wondered if she had played a part in Brian's behavior. Many times she would say, "Jasmine turned my baby into a different man." At the time, Tionna had agreed, but now she knew Brian had a hand in his own fate. Nothing a woman did should be an excuse for a man to hit a woman.

"Brian was arrested," Jasmine mumbled as a tear rolled from her eye.

Tionna studied the floor. How was she supposed to respond? Brian had done a terrible thing, but she couldn't forget that he was the father of her only child. How would this affect Brianna?

"His mother is furious with me," Jasmine continued.

Tionna sighed. As much as she cared for Brian's family, there was no way she could let anyone justify his horrendous behavior. "I love Mrs. Dorothy," she said, "but . . . send her a picture of your face and let her know that you're furious too."

Jasmine turned her head as far as it could go without causing her too much pain. "Brian's never gotten over you," she muttered. "That's why—"

Tionna couldn't let her finish. "There's no excuse for what he's done, and . . . there was no excuse for my poor behavior, either. I was mean to you, and I'm sorry for all the years I kept Brianna away."

"Do you think we'll ever be friends again?"

Tionna rubbed the top of her hand gently. "You're my sister, Jazz. We'll always be more than friends.

We're family. Now, stop talking so you can rest. We have plenty of time later to catch up."

Tionna pulled a chair closer to the bed and read a book as Jasmine zoned in and out of consciousness. Either God had softened her heart or she was reacting to Brianna's change of heart. Maybe it was a little of both. Either way, she welcomed Jasmine back into her life.

J. Amanda flew into the room five minutes before visiting hours were set to end. Instead of disturbing Jasmine, Tionna let her sleep and told her line sister the story she had been told by Brianna.

Jasmine stirred when she heard J. Amanda's voice. "We were doing so good," she mumbled. "I don't understand why—"

"Hush, Jazz," J. Amanda told her. "We've been through this talk before. This is not *your* fault. God is *not* punishing you. God loves you, sweetie."

"Brian found my pills, and then Hunky told him about Orion owning the studio."

"Hunky?" Tionna asked, in shock. She'd forgotten he was Jasmine's neighbor.

"Let's not worry about Hunky," J. Amanda stressed. "Let's focus on getting you better. I'll take care of him from now on."

Tionna remembered his words about unfinished business. That business seemed to be hurting the lives of the people she loved. Tionna became worried, and a thought crossed her mind. "I don't want you to go back to your house for a while, Jazz. You and the girls can stay with me. Kenya's there too, but there's plenty of room for more. It'll be like old times."

"My girls may be cute, but they are a handful," Jasmine tried to joke.

Tionna thought about sweet little Gabrielle. Yes, she was sure. With everyone under her roof, she'd be able to keep an eye on them in case that evil side of Hunky reared itself again. "I can make the adjustment. You and your girls are worth it."

In the lobby, J. Amanda told Tionna what happened before Tionna had called her. Tionna's heart dropped. Was that the unfinished business Hunky was referring to? Maybe now he could go away and leave all of them alone.

"Make sure you handle him gently," Tionna urged. "I don't want him to turn on you the way Brian did on Jasmine. I don't like coming to hospitals to visit people I love."

"I can't let him tell Tiffany the truth," J. Amanda replied. "It may be selfish, but . . . David has been there for her since she was born. I can't turn her world around because of my stupidity."

"I understand, but Hunky is . . ." Tionna had to catch herself before she said too much. "Just be careful with him. Think this through so that no one else gets hurt."

J. Amanda took in her advice and sighed. "In other news," she said, "I talked to Jasmine's birth mother today. She's gonna come here in a few weeks for Jasmine's birthday."

"Now, that is good news. Where is she, and what's her story?"

"Well, she got pregnant when she was fifteen, and her parents made her give Jazz up for adoption. She went to college for dance, just like Jazz, and she still teaches dance to active seniors," J. Amanda said. "She's been married for twenty-two years and has one daughter and one son. I think she has two grandsons as well."

"And what about the father? I wonder if she still knows him."

J. Amanda shook her head. "I think he was older than Roxanne. She said he was a drummer for a local band and traveled a lot. They lost touch when the family moved out of Philly."

Tionna could only imagine what Roxanne had gone through. Many of Tionna's relatives had encouraged her to give Brianna up for adoption. Looking at the woman Brianna had grown into, Tionna thanked God every day for giving her the strength to tell her family no. She also had to admit that it felt good to prove them wrong. God had given her a wonderful support system, and thanks to that, she was able to obtain her goals while raising a child. "I'm so glad you and Kenya found her. Jasmine really needs some good things to happen right now."

J. Amanda agreed and said, "So do I."

"You'll get your happy back, Jay. You just need to stay focused on God," Tionna said encouragingly. "He's gonna get you through this. He's gonna get all of us through this period in our lives."

In honor of Jasmine's birthday, Tionna had planned a special dinner party. Jasmine had been released from the hospital a week ago, and Tionna felt an intimate celebration would help lift her spirits. With the exception of her wounded heart and a thin gash on her cheek, the injuries Jasmine received the night she was beaten had healed. As Tionna washed the china plates, she looked out into her backyard, where everyone was gathered. The permanent smile on Jasmine's face let Tionna know that her goal had been accomplished.

"You have a minute?" Kenya asked as she entered the kitchen.

"Sure. What's up?" Tionna asked, laughing at Casey, who was splashing water on Sasha and Brianna in the pool. No matter how many times she told them to wear caps on their heads, they refused. It wasn't the cool thing to do.

"You promise not to get mad when I tell you?" Kenya asked as she sat at the counter.

"I don't know. The secrets we keep always end up hurting someone," Tionna half joked. "What did you do?"

"Mack gave me a gun," Kenya stated bluntly.

Tionna put the china plate in her hand down. On any other day, she would've lectured Kenya about the dangers of keeping a gun around, especially in a house full of kids. But she thought about the day Hunky accosted her at work. Knowing there was a weapon within her grasp somehow eased some of her worry.

Kenya was shocked at Tionna's calmness. "So . . . I'm not gonna get yelled at?"

"Until we take self-defense classes, I'm afraid your weapon of choice will have to do. Where are you gonna keep it?"

"On me at all times," Kenya replied. "I'm gonna start carrying my tote bag as a purse. The inside pouch is big enough to hide it in there."

"You're scared, aren't you?" Tionna asked and finished the last dish.

"Casey said someone definitely opened a window in the condo and somehow started the fire. It had to be the guy Zora saw running away that night. I don't know who would want to hurt me, but I have to protect myself," Kenya said sincerely.

"Do you even know how to use the thing?" questioned Tionna. She feared the weapon would end up harming Kenya more than any would-be assailant.

"Of course not," Kenya said and laughed. "Mack gave me a bootleg lesson, but don't worry. I signed up for lessons for the week before Tyree and I move into the new place."

Tionna was relieved to hear that her friend had sought professional lessons. Next, she hoped Kenya would consider counseling to tame that fireball personality of hers. One could only imagine the kind of trouble Kenya could get herself into now that she was armed. Tionna only prayed that the gun was registered with the state.

Thinking about registration, Tionna froze. Since the gun came from Mack, it was highly likely that the gun was "hot." This made her more nervous than having the gun in her house.

"So . . ." she continued, "where did Mack get the weapon from?"

Kenya shook her head. "I knew the lecture was coming," she replied. "I'm not gonna lie to you. Mack got it from one of the young guys in his neighborhood."

"And that doesn't bother you?"

"Not at the moment," Kenya quickly answered. "But as soon as I am licensed, I promise I'm going to buy my own. Right now I need to protect myself and my son."

Tionna gazed out the window. While she didn't agree, she definitely understood. "Well . . . let's just pray there won't be any reason to use it."

"I already had a little talk with Jesus," Kenya chimed in playfully. "He knows me, so I think He'll keep trouble away from me. And Mack prayed too. He said the city wasn't safe with me carrying a loaded pistol."

Tionna laughed aloud. "You and Mack need to get married, because you're both crazy!"

"On that note . . ." Kenya grabbed an orange from the fruit bowl on the counter and then went back outside.

Tionna sighed when she left. What was she going to do when Kenya moved into her new place next month? She was getting used to having her and Tyree around.

J. Amanda walked up to the window and mouthed, "It's time."

Excited, Tionna rushed to the front door to welcome Jasmine's special birthday surprise. As she led Roxanne and her husband into a small room next to the foyer, she heard Jasmine singing the birthday song to herself. Tionna giggled softly. She didn't plan on presenting the birthday cake until Jasmine had met her birth mother.

J. Amanda walked ahead of everyone and stood next to Tionna. When the crowd made it into the foyer, they were surprised there wasn't a cake sitting on the table.

"There will be cake," Tionna told the mumbling crowd, "but first we have a surprise for Jasmine."

"Jazz, your past is behind you. From this day forward, there's no looking back. No feeling sorry for what was or could've been," J. Amanda said. "So to start off this wonderful life that's ahead of you, we'd like to introduce you to your birth mother."

Escorted by her husband, Roxanne gracefully walked into the foyer. Already in tears, she paused when she saw her daughter. Jasmine's legs grew numb, causing her to lose her balance. As the adults behind her kept her steady, she covered her mouth with her hand to muffle the sounds she was making.

Walking toward Roxanne, Jasmine saw herself in twenty years. "Is it really you?" she cried and touched her mother's face.

"My darling daughter," Roxanne said and pulled Jasmine into her arms, where they stayed stuck together like glue for the next five minutes.

"Why is Mommy crying, Auntie?" Amber asked Tionna.

"She's happy, sweetie," Tionna answered. "She's found a part to a puzzle that's been missing for years."

~ Chapter 25 ~

J. Amanda

"Are you sure about this?" J. Amanda asked Jasmine as she helped her put a set of dishes inside a box.

Jasmine taped the box in front of her closed. "No, but Brian hasn't parted his lips to apologize yet. If he's not going to change, I have to start thinking about what's best for me and the girls," Jasmine answered. "Besides, I don't think we can get past this. His mother's been calling me every day, trying to make me feel guilty about his short-lived jail time."

"She ought to be happy you dropped the charges," J. Amanda observed, highly annoyed by Mrs. Dorothy's actions. She couldn't believe how this incident had changed Brian's mother. Mrs. Dorothy had her ways, but J. Amanda had never seen her act so rudely toward another person, especially her grandchildren's mother.

"If it wasn't for my girls, I would've let him rot in that cell," Jasmine replied and exhaled. "But I'm okay with everything now. I just want to move on with my life."

Happy to see Jasmine taking control of her life, J. Amanda was saddened to hear that she'd filed for a separation. It reminded her of the conversation she had with David a few nights ago. He wanted a divorce, but J. Amanda had refused to accept it, though she wondered how long she could reside in a house divided. They were living like strangers in their home.

David had moved all his things into the guest room and initiated conversation only when it concerned the kids. It didn't bother David that the kids were behaving differently as a result of their new living arrangements. He argued that it would make the transition easier once he was gone for good.

Despite David's desire to be apart from his wife, J. Amanda continued to suggest other alternatives, even though he denied them all. To him, spending time alone was a waste of time, counseling was pointless, and a separation delayed the inevitable. The rejection was painful, but not as painful as what she'd done to him. That was why she continued to try.

J. Amanda heard Hunky's voice through the opened kitchen window and rolled her eyes. The chills she used to feel were replaced by feelings of disgust. Not hearing from him in almost a month had given her time to reflect on his recent behavior. Hunky was right about J. Amanda manipulating things to her own advantage. She had never seen it that way before, but when she dissected her past, J. Amanda realized his accusations were true. Still, what he did to her family wasn't justified.

For several weeks after hanging up on him the day Jasmine was hospitalized, she had attempted to contact him to discuss a reasonable solution to his demands, but Hunky refused to answer the phone each time she called. After a while, he grew tired of her persistence and had sent a text. You had me on hold for fifteen minutes. I hung up, and you never called back. This is the last time you'll disrespect me.

J. Amanda walked on eggshells for weeks in anticipation of what he might do next.

"I know you'll be happy to get away from him," J. Amanda said as she watched Hunky toss small trash bags into a large bin in his backyard.

"That's an understatement," Jasmine agreed. "I know you loved him, but that man gives me the creeps."

J. Amanda closed the blinds and pulled herself away from the window. "I'm done over here," she said. "Anything else you want to take?"

"No, this is it. My new apartment can't hold half of the things the girls and I own," said Jasmine. "I'll have to come back before winter and put some stuff in storage."

"Okay," J. Amanda replied and walked to the kitchen door. "Want me to close this, or do you have more to do in the yard?"

"I'm done, but leave the door open," Jasmine requested. "There's a nice evening breeze coming through the screen."

"Okay. I'm gonna run to the store while you finish up," J. Amanda told her. "I forgot to pick up some eggs and cheese for breakfast tomorrow."

The line sisters had planned a girls' weekend at Tionna's house to celebrate the sorority anniversary they had missed in early September due to the problems each of the them had faced over the past few months. Once Jasmine was finished packing up enough clothes and toys to last until the end of the year, they were headed to Tionna's house for fun.

J. Amanda grabbed her car keys from the table, then joined her other line sisters in the living room. "Anyone want to ride with me to Giant?"

Zora and Kenya decided to take the ride and followed J. Amanda to the front door. As she drew closer, J. Amanda froze when she saw Hunky staring back at her from behind the screen door.

"The gang's all here," he said coyly.

"What do you want?" J. Amanda responded, slightly annoyed.

He smirked, then said, "You know the answer to that. I can be out of your hair for good if you'd just cooperate." Hunky caught a glimpse of Zora eyeing him suspiciously as she stood to the left of J. Amanda, and he smiled. "Remember me from the hospital?" he asked to jog her memory and then pointed at J. Amanda. "This is the woman who dumped me. She still won't give me a chance."

"He approached you in the hospital?" J. Amanda inquired, and Zora nodded apprehensively.

"I don't want any trouble," Hunky stressed. "All I want is my daughter."

Kenya pushed her line sisters aside and tried to reason with the man at the door. "I'm a manager for a social service organization. If you give me a call on Monday, we can talk about your options."

Hunky shook his head. "I need to work this out now."

"But you can't. I need the mother's information and a computer—" Kenya tried to explain, but she was cut off.

"I see Jay keeps secrets from her sorority sisters too," Hunky noted.

Don't do this, Hunky," J. Amanda pleaded, but Kenya was already agitated. She wanted an answer.

Kenya turned around to look at the other women in the room. "Does anyone know what he's talking about?"

With Kenya's back turned, Hunky opened the door and invited himself inside. "You shouldn't have made a fool of me," he said to J. Amanda. "I thought you loved me."

Hearing the commotion, Jasmine entered the room and, at the sight of her unwelcome neighbor, shouted, "Why is he is my house? He needs to leave."

Cynthia got up from the couch and walked up to J. Amanda. "If you know something, Jay, now would be a good time to talk. Tell him what he wants to know so he can leave."

"Let's go outside," J. Amanda said and pulled his arm, but Hunky didn't budge. His feet were firmly rooted in front of the door.

"I tried to reach out to you a few weeks ago, but you hung up on me. I tried to make you love me again, but you chose to love David over me again. Do you know what that does to a man? You can have him now. I'm done trying. Just give me Tiffany."

"Tiffany?" Kenya was confused. "For the third time, what is he talking about?" she asked, then covered her mouth with her left hand. J. Amanda confided in Kenya about her indiscretion. "This can't be . . ." she muttered.

J. Amanda stared at her former high school love in disgust as she told her line sisters, who were unaware of this facet of her past, about the day she went to Planned Parenthood and how she lied about Tiffany's paternity to save her new marriage.

"Oh, Jay," Cynthia said and frowned.

Kenya walked over to the couch and sat down. "This isn't good."

"There's got to be another way to handle this. Why don't you step outside and talk about it?" Zora calmly insisted.

"I like you," Hunky interjected. "You've got a kind heart. That's why I didn't bother you the way I have the others. I don't hold you responsible for what J. Amanda's done."

Jasmine snapped, "None of us are responsible, and I really wish you would go home to your wife. Maybe I need to call her."

"Listen to you. You're so tough now," Hunky said as he stared at the permanent scar on Jasmine's cheek. "Jay and I were once good friends. We shared a lot.

Honesty was the glue that held us together back then,"
he explained. "She consulted with me about the abortion, but ultimately, it was her line sisters she listened
to. She told me you all adored David. Kenya was the
one who told her about abortion. I chose to be sup-
portive because I thought she'd come back to me. But
Kenya told my love to leave the past behind. You didn't
even know me."

"I'm not gonna lie to you. I was looking out for my
friend," Kenya said in her defense. "She had too many
positive things going on for her at the time. The timing
for you and her was not right."

"I should've been a part of that!" Hunky shouted,
alarming the women. He moved toward Kenya, and
she jumped up.

"Back up, Hunky," she commanded. "I'm a loose
cannon these days."

"I like feisty woman," he replied and stepped back a
little bit. "I didn't know your son would be home that
night."

Kenya lunged forward, and Tionna and Jasmine
grabbed her and held her back. "He's not worth it,"
Tionna urged at the same time Jasmine begged Hunky
to leave and then threatened that she'd call the police.

"I didn't do anything wrong," he said as he slid back
toward J. Amanda. "If you want to punish me, you
should do the same to Jay. She's done a lot of things
too. Isn't that right?"

He placed his arm around her and kissed her cheek.
J. Amanda cringed and pushed him away. Feeling
rejected, Hunky dropped his arms and looked at Jasmine. "I'm gonna be in your lives until my daughter is
safe with me or I get total revenge," Hunky said and
smirked. "Revenge for you was easy, Jazz. I thought it
was Christmas when the house next to you went up for

sale, and I learned that Brian beat you. I just needed the right time to pull his strings. I hope your girls won't have any unfortunate accidents when they're here with Brian."

Hunky took a few steps to his left and faced Tionna. "My dear sweet, Dr. Jenkins. You're so smart and so strong. You shouldn't have hid the truth from me. Especially when J. Amanda isn't so loyal herself." Hunky pointed to Tionna and Jasmine at the same time. "Did you ladies know that she was the author of the letter that ended your friendship?"

J. Amanda turned red. "Hunky, that's enough. You're bringing up stuff that doesn't matter anymore."

Hunky disagreed. "Look at their faces," he demanded, but J. Amanda couldn't bring herself to. Though the letter had exposed deceit, it had also jump-started a stream of turmoil that had lasted through the years. When J. Amanda didn't comply, he continued. "This is the woman you've known all this time. The one you call the preacher."

"The longer you keep Tiffany from me, the more I'll do to hurt you. Isn't that right, Tionna?" he said. "But I got to give you credit. I thought by now they would know about the rape I committed or the intimate encounter we shared in your office. I have an eye on my next victim now," he told her. "Either you help me get my daughter or I'll start hanging around your daughter at Temple a little more. Now, I'm tired of talking. C'mon, Jay," he said and turned toward the door, tugging J. Amanda with him. "Let's go home and get Tiffany."

While his back was turned, Tionna reached for Kenya's bag, which was lying on the couch, and pulled out the gun she kept inside it. "Get off her!" she screamed, in tears.

"Please put that thing away!" Cynthia yelled in shock. "Let's let the police handle this."

Hunky stared at the gun, which was shaking wildly in Tionna's hands. "No need to call them. She's not going to shoot me. She doesn't have the heart."

Jasmine started to breathe heavily. J. Amanda was about to go tend to her, but without warning, Jasmine whispered, "Forgive me, Father," then took the gun from Tionna's hands. "She may not have a heart to hurt someone, but I do." And just like that, she pulled the trigger.

Hunky fell back and landed on J. Amanda's feet. Everyone in the room stood still for several seconds and then moved forward at warp speed. Cynthia fell to her knees and prayed, while Zora rushed to Hunky's side.

"He's still breathing!" Zora cried.

With the gun still pointed at Hunky, Jasmine stood still as tears rolled down her cheeks. Behind her, Tionna and Kenya walked back and forth, trying to take in what had happened. J. Amanda couldn't move with Hunky on her feet. Afraid to look down, she closed her eyes and began to pray. *This has gone too far,* she thought, *and it's all my fault.*

Suddenly, the back door slammed, and on impulse, Jasmine jerked to her left and fired again. The bullet sailed through the open space of the living room and dining room and landed in the left side of the person in the kitchen.

"Oh, God, not again!" Cynthia screamed as she ran into the kitchen. "Who is *that* woman? Someone please call the ambulance!"

Jasmine carefully laid the gun on the couch and fell to the floor when she realized that she'd just shot Hunky's wife.

"He's bleeding too fast. What should I do, Tionna?" Zora yelled, afraid to lay her hands on him. "Tionna! What should I do?"

Tionna stood over Hunky, motionless, careful not to step in the pool of blood near him.

When he was able to open his eyes, he smirked and said, "Are you going to let me die?"

Tionna shook her head but didn't move to try to help him.

As Hunky struggled to breathe, he called on J. Amanda. "Don't let me die, baby. I promise I'll be a better man. Please save me."

J. Amanda looked at Tionna, who was still shaking her head, and covered her face with her hands. As she listened to Cynthia pray in the kitchen, she wished the bullet had struck her too.

With the little strength Hunky had, he grabbed her right ankle. "If you ever really loved me, you'd s-s-save me," he stuttered.

J. Amanda looked down for the first time as Hunky slowly loosened his grip. His eyes rolled as he fought to live. But when blood started coming from his mouth, J. Amanda knew his life was coming to an end. She slid her feet out from under him and kneeled by his head. "Oh, Hunky," she cried, and he looked up at her as he struggled to take his next breath. In his eyes, J. Amanda saw the soft soul she knew when they were young. She prayed over him, asking God to take care of his troubled soul. Within seconds of ending her prayer, she saw that Hunky was gone.

With the exception of Cynthia, the women stood around Hunky, in tears. "We've got to call the police," Zora said. "It's the right thing to do."

"And what are we gonna tell them?" Kenya asked.

"Self-defense," Tionna said numbly. "This was all self-defense."

"But the gun . . . it's not registered to any of us, and our prints are all over it," Kenya replied nervously. "What are we gonna do?"

"You've got to be kidding me," barked Cynthia as she walked into the room with bloodstained hands. "You actually had an unmarked gun in your purse? Kenya . . . you're a mother! How could you—"

"Don't judge me, Cynthia!" Kenya snapped. "You have no idea how it feels to be a single parent and feel helpless."

Zora jumped up from the floor and gave her line sisters a reality check. "This is not the time to lecture one another. There is a dead man on the floor and possibly another dead person in the kitchen. Unless we come up with the story we want to tell the police, we're *all* going to jail."

Kenya rolled her eyes at Cynthia and asked, "Do you think anyone heard the gunshots?"

"Who knows!" Cynthia replied and then headed back to the kitchen.

Jasmine backed away from the lifeless body and picked up the gun. She lifted her shirt and cleaned the weapon as best she could. "I pulled the trigger, so I'll tell the police he was after me."

"Someone needs to call nine-one-one," Cynthia demanded.

Jasmine walked back to Hunky's body and knelt by it. She put the weapon in his hand. His body was still warm. Jasmine shuddered at the thought of touching a fresh corpse, but she rubbed his hand on the gun. "His prints are on the gun, and so are mine. I'll tell the police that we got into a wrestling match and the gun went off. So please . . . go ahead and call the cops now."

"I'm not gonna let you take the fall for this," J. Amanda told her and took the gun from Hunky's loose grip. "I want all of you to leave. I'll tell the police I did it."

"I'm not leaving you, Jay. This is my house and I pulled—" Jasmine started to cry harder. "I did this. Oh, God," she moaned. "What's gonna happen to my girls?"

J. Amanda gathered her line sisters close and begged them to let her handle this. Self-defense was the story she was going to tell the police, but she did not want the women there when they arrived. In less than two minutes, J. Amanda came up with a story. "Now get out of here, and don't call Casey until you get in the car," she told Tionna.

As the women exited the house, J. Amanda walked into the kitchen. Patrice was still breathing. She said a quick prayer for her and then paced the floor in a daze. Sobbing sounds in the living room caught her attention, and she walked back to the scene of the crime. Jasmine was sitting a foot away from Hunky with her arms wrapped around her legs.

"I'm not leaving you," she cried, "so don't make me."

J. Amanda eyed the gun, which she was still holding in her hand. Slowly, she headed back to the kitchen. "We're gonna be all right," she moaned, though she wasn't confident they would be. The more she thought about what happened, the more frightened she became. "Hunky is dead," she silently repeated several times, as her body slowly fell to the floor. "I can't believe he's gone."

J. Amanda crawled across the room and leaned against the refrigerator. In her eyes, her life was over. There was nothing she could do to fix the mess she created. Holding tight to the gold cross dangling from her necklace, she closed her eyes and silently begged for forgiveness. "I'm so sorry, God" she moaned.

J. Amanda pointed the gun to her head and listened to the sirens in the distance grow louder. In a matter of minutes, the police would storm into Jasmine's home and demand answers. Though she was prepared to recite the story she and her line sisters had rehearsed, J. Amanda didn't want her sorors to shelter the burden of her foolish mistakes.

As her hand trembled on the trigger, J. Amanda squeezed her gold cross tighter and looked at Patrice, who was struggling to breathe beside her. It was now or never. She started counting backward from ten, and when she reached seven, a soft and friendly voice whispered in her ear. *Your life isn't over yet. You shall live and not die!*

Slowly, she lowered the gun to the floor and sobbed as policemen charged inside the house.

Leading the pack, Casey raced straight to Jasmine, and she screamed, "He tried to kill us, Casey!"

As policemen and medics ran to the bodies on the floor, Casey quickly gained control. He ordered someone to console Jasmine and stared into the kitchen. He pointed at J. Amanda, and immediately a female cop rushed to her side. Everything around J. Amanda started to blur. She watched Hunky, who lay lifeless on a gurney. It was hard to believe that the man she had loved in her youth was gone. As they rolled him out of the house, J. Amanda prayed that Tiffany would never find out the truth. How could J. Amanda face her daughter, knowing that she was partially responsible for his demise? Tiffany didn't need to know that her real father was a troubled man, and that her mother had hurt him by hiding the truth of her pregnancy.

The policewoman asked J. Amanda a series of questions, and she did her best to answer them just as she had rehearsed before the police arrived. "He was my first love," she said blandly. "He blamed me for the way his life ended up. He became angry with me because I wouldn't take him back, and he was mad at Jazz because she wouldn't try to change my mind. I don't know what happened today, but . . . he came here unannounced and let himself in. He must've seen my car out front. Things just got out of control, and then he pulled out a gun." J. Amanda tried to get through the story without crying, but it was hard to talk about Hunky as some kind of deranged monster. That wasn't the man she knew and loved.

While J. Amanda waited for the interrogation to end, she observed Jasmine in the other room, hysterically telling the officer about the struggle that took place and how the gun went off by accident. "Then we heard a noise in the kitchen, and we were so scared that the gun went off again. We didn't know that Patrice had come into the house," Jasmine cried. "She was my friend. She probably heard all the arguing and came to check on me. She did that a lot when my husband and I would fight."

Behind Jasmine, Casey was studying markings on the floor. J. Amanda prayed there were no clues that would lead him to the truth. Medics rolled Patrice out of the kitchen, and J. Amanda cringed at the sound of the wheels scraping against the floor. J. Amanda didn't know how long Patrice had been listening outside the house or what she heard after she'd been shot. J. Amanda and her sorors would have to wait patiently for Patrice to regain consciousness to know those answers. But as she watched Patrice being taken from the house, J. Amanda prayed Patrice's story would coincide with what she and Jasmine had told the police.

Casey strolled into the kitchen and knelt by J. Amanda's side. "I know you've been through a terrible ordeal," he said sincerely, "but . . . I'm gonna have to take you and Jasmine down to the precinct."

J. Amanda numbly stared at the floor. "I understand."

As Casey helped J. Amanda to her feet, he hesitantly asked, "So . . . just you and Jasmine were in the house?"

"Yes," she lied and followed Casey outside to his police car.

~ Chapter 26 ~

Zora

Months Later . . .

After Renee opened what everyone assumed was
the last gift of the evening, Zora crawled close to the
Christmas tree and removed a square-shaped box.

"*More* presents?" Cynthia asked as she balanced
Lawrence Jr. on her lap.

Zora smiled and crawled back to where her husband
was sitting on the floor. "Just one more for my number
one guy. Just a little something to let you know how
much your support this year has meant to me."

Reggie leaned forward and kissed his wife. "We're a
team, babe. Always and forever," he said and removed
the box from Zora's hand.

"Don't they remind you of us at that age?" Jerome
commented, and Renee gave him the eye.

"You're getting senile, old man," Renee stated in jest.
"We were on our way to divorce in our thirties."

"But we're still together," Jerome sang. "Now, hurry up
and open that gift before I talk myself into more trouble."

As Reggie laughed at his parents, he carefully ripped
the bright red wrapping to expose the Macy's box underneath. "What could this be?" Reggie said playfully
and shook the box by his ear.

Cynthia's husband got off the couch and pretended
to listen to the sounds coming from inside Reggie's gift.

"It's something very light," he said and returned to his wife and child on the couch.

"Just hurry up, babe," Zora demanded.

Reggie lifted the lid on the box just a little, and everyone yelled at him. Seeing that his crowd was restless, he removed the lid and pulled out a stuffed basketball the size of an orange. Before he realized what the gift symbolized, Renee and Jerome had jumped out of their seats and performed an old-school dance.

"Merry Christmas, Daddy," Zora said and placed his free hand on her belly. "I'm nine weeks."

Reggie was speechless. He tossed the stuffed toy back inside the box and lifted his beautiful wife to her feet. "Thank you, baby," he said and kissed her until Cynthia had to break them apart.

This came as a surprise to everyone in the room. Zora was certain she wasn't going to have children at all. But the smell of death had overwhelmed her, and she had decided not to deny her husband the right to be a father. When she made it back to New York that week, she'd thrown away her birth control pills without telling anyone. As she'd stared down into the wastebasket, she'd released all her fears and let God take control.

Renee didn't waste time calling the rest of the family. Both she and Jerome excused themselves and went into a different room to make calls.

While Reggie bonded with Lawrence Jr. and his father, Zora and Cynthia retreated to the kitchen and started putting away the leftovers from the holiday meal.

While Zora stuffed buttered rolls inside a large Ziploc bag, she noticed that Cynthia was standing over the sink in a daze. Whenever Cynthia seemed distant, Zora worried that her cancer had returned. "You all right over there, Cyn?"

"I can feel something brewing in the pit of my stomach," she answered and poured the leftover eggnog in a container. "I couldn't be happier about you becoming a mom, but Hunky's been on my mind a lot lately."

Zora put the rolls on the counter and then walked to the sink. "He's dead, Cyn. Hunky can't harm us anymore. His wife may be paralyzed, but she's alive. Let's forget about this year and get ready for the next one. You're cancer free, my book will be in bookstores in February, and I'm gonna be a mama. Can you believe that?"

"You're right," Cynthia replied. "I won't mention his name again."

Though Zora had told Cynthia not to worry, she had the same feeling too. But she refused to let Hunky haunt her from the grave. The year ahead was full of possibilities and new beginnings, and she was going to embrace it filled with joy. God had been too good to her to do otherwise.

~ Chapter 27 ~

Jasmine

Hiding behind a side door that led to Faith Tabernacle's sanctuary, Jasmine stared at J. Amanda, who was waving her hands as a soloist sang "Alabaster Box" from her soul. J. Amanda had been away at a speaking engagement when Jasmine said the prayer of salvation a few weeks ago. She was also unaware that Jasmine had joined the liturgical dance ministry. So J. Amanda had no idea that Jasmine had requested the song selection for her debut performance as a member of the liturgical dance ministry. She was going to be so surprised when she saw Jasmine dancing for the Lord with her mother, Roxanne.

Every time Jasmine thought about God's mercy and grace, her soul leaped. She still didn't understand why God had chosen to spare her life after she had rejected Him for so many years, but she was eternally grateful. Now that she knew God as her savior, she vowed to live the rest of her life praising His name.

The soloist hit a high note and held it steady until it faded. That was Jasmine's cue to come inside. Jasmine turned to her mother, who was standing next to her, and grabbed her hand. "Ready?" Roxanne nodded, and when Jasmine opened the side door, they gracefully danced their way to the center of the sanctuary together.

Jasmine couldn't see J. Amanda or her family and friends, but she heard J. Amanda shout behind her. Jasmine remained in sync with the music, and as the soloist brought the song to a dramatic close, she gave a performance alongside her mother that she prayed God would approve of.

When the song ended, J. Amanda ran from the pulpit and threw her arms around Jasmine. In words Jasmine didn't understand, J. Amanda spoke to her spirit. Jasmine was oblivious to the standing ovation taking place. She couldn't hear the praises of the congregation or the moans coming from her mother. She didn't know all her line sisters had formed a circle around her, with tears of joy, to pray. All she knew was that God was present, and so she focused all her attention on Him through her personal dance of praise.

After the service, Jasmine waited for her daughters in the lobby with Roxanne. They had spent the weekend with Brian, and he had promised to drop them off at church. On Friday Jasmine's lawyer had served him separation papers, so she prepared for the worst. She hadn't seen Brian since the day he picked her up from the police station and drove her back to his mother's house. At that time, Brian had insisted he was a changed man, but when Jasmine refused to move back in, he threw an African statue across the room. Jasmine didn't wait around to see more of his rage. She immediately ran out of the house and walked to the gas station two blocks away and called herself a cab.

Jasmine saw Amber running toward her and smiled. Her girls had been gone only a few days, but after the scare with Hunky, it was hard not to have them in her presence. The girls were just as eager to see her, and that made Jasmine feel good.

When Brian and Mrs. Dorothy reached her, Jasmine didn't bother to introduce him to Roxanne. He didn't need to know, and she didn't want a reason to talk to him longer than what was necessary.

"That dance was absolutely beautiful. I couldn't stop crying. I don't think I've seen a duo perform like that before," Mrs. Dorothy said and looked at Roxanne. "You made all women over fifty proud this morning."

Roxanne hugged Jasmine and pulled Sasha close to her side. "We're working on a trio for fifth Sunday. Sasha here is pretty good too."

Jasmine took a set of keys from her purse and handed them to Roxanne. "Okay, girls. Go ahead to the car. Aunt Tionna wants us to help with dinner, so we better go."

"You and Tionna are getting along good, I hear," Brian said when the girls left.

"Yeah, we learned the hard way that life is too short to hold on to grudges," Jasmine answered.

"I agree," Mrs. Dorothy said solemnly. "I've been waiting for the right time to apologize to you, Jazz, for anything I may have done or said—"

"It's all right," Jasmine interrupted at the sight of her mother-in-law's tears. "I've blocked out everything that happened in the past. We'll be celebrating a new year in a few days, and I'm excited about starting everything anew. That's why I'm not gonna fight you, Brian, about visitation. You're their father, and you have a right to see them as much as you want. All I ask is that you let me know in advance."

Orion walked out of the sanctuary and waved as he passed them on his way out of the church. Brian's mood shifted, but he remained calm. "I guess you two are dating," he said, and Jasmine giggled.

"Orion is my friend. He's everyone's friend."

"About that . . . I'm almost finished with my classes," Brian replied. "I hope that you'll reconsider the separation when I'm done. I'd like us to start over again as friends."

Mrs. Dorothy pretended not to listen, but Jasmine knew she was taking in every word. "I'm glad you followed through. I know how hard it can be to face your issues," responded Jasmine. "But . . . we'll see where things are when you're done. I'm happy right now, and I'm gonna enjoy that for as long as God allows me to. So let's hold off on us for a while. I'm enjoying being free."

Brian looked as if he'd lost his best friend, but that was no longer Jasmine's concern. God had given her a new view on life, and nothing from her past was going to steal her joy.

~ Chapter 28 ~

Tionna

Something was on Casey's mind. He had been quiet all through dinner, and for the past hour he had listened to Tionna and Brianna reminisce about favorite Christmases past without saying one word.

"I was invited to an Eta Omicron Pi New Year's party," Brianna told her mother.

Tionna tried to hide her excitement, but she was proud of her daughter. Brianna's first semester at Temple had been successful. Though she'd received her first B in an English composition class, she had earned an A in her other courses. Brianna had made a few new friends and was considering trying out for the cheerleading squad. She was adjusting well, but Tionna didn't want her to take on too many extracurricular activities too soon.

"I know your aunts will be happy to hear that," she replied.

Brianna's cell phone rang, and she practically sprinted across the family room to answer it. *Some things don't change,* Tionna thought. Though Brianna had matured some, she still exhibited signs of an anxious teenager. From the look on her daughter's face, she could tell Quentin was on the line. Tionna had hoped they would have separated by this time, but Brianna seemed more in love now than she was in high school.

Brianna ended her call and then put on the new wool coat Casey had given her as a Christmas present. "I'll be back in a few hours," she said and grabbed her car keys from the table. "I'm going over to Quentin's house."

"Aww," Tionna pouted. "I thought we were gonna hang tonight."

"You can have me all day tomorrow," Brianna responded. "Quentin's going to Rhode Island for a few days with his family."

"Gee, thanks for making your old mother feel special," Tionna teased, then looked at Casey. "See how she disses me, babe?"

Casey pretended he didn't hear Tionna speaking to him, and Tionna became concerned. As soon as Brianna left, she would find out what was on his mind.

Tionna turned back to Brianna. "Don't stay out too late. I don't want you on the road with all the holiday drivers."

"Yes, Mother. I'll be in before midnight," Brianna said to amuse her mother, then headed out the door.

Now that they were alone, Tionna moved from the love seat to the sectional, where Casey was sitting, half watching a basketball game on television. "Hey, fella," Tionna said as she sat next to him. "Kenya's in her new home, and Jasmine and the girls are in Florida, visiting Roxanne. We finally have the house to ourselves. What do you want to do? Play Scrabble or maybe one of those kid computer games? That might be fun."

Casey reached into his pocket, pulled out the studded bracelet he had given Tionna a few months ago, and dangled it in her face.

"Is that why you're moping around?" Tionna said and took the bracelet from his hand. "I'm glad you found it. I was worried it fell off my arm at the clinic. I was going to tell you—"

"I found it at Jasmine's house the night Hunky was shot," interrupted Casey.

The smile on Tionna's face subsided when she thought of that night.

Casey moved to the edge of the couch and stared Tionna in the eyes. "Were you there when Hunky was shot?"

Tionna nervously fiddled with her bracelet as she tried to remember the lie she'd told him. "I've been at Jazz's house a number of times. Maybe—"

"I knew you'd say that," Casey remarked, cutting her off mid-sentence. "You must've forgotten that I'm a detective, and a good one at that. I knew something was strange when you called me that day," he continued. "You told me you were home, but I heard a lot of traffic in the background. You were calling me from your car, weren't you?"

Tears rolled down Tionna's cheeks. She didn't want to tell Casey any more lies, but she couldn't speak the truth.

Casey got up and looked at the Christmas tree he had helped Tionna decorate with Jasmine's kids. "You don't have to answer that. It's best I don't know." Casey walked out of the room and stopped before entering the kitchen. "Was it self-defense?" Through the glass in the china cabinet, Casey saw Tionna nod her head. "Then let's leave it at that."

Inside the kitchen, Casey poured himself a glass of lemonade, then walked to the patio doors. He stared at the snowman he and Jasmine's girls had put together on Christmas Eve, and sighed. Tionna came up behind him. She wanted to touch him, but fear of what he might have discovered about that night plagued her. The case had been closed, but . . . was there new evidence that pointed in her direction?

"It really was self-defense," she stated.

Still gazing into the backyard, Casey spoke with little inflection in his tone. "I believe you. I just wish you had trusted me enough to tell me the truth. I told myself to let it go, but . . ." Casey turned to face Tionna. "I couldn't move forward in this relationship or the New Year without getting it off my mind. I removed evidence from the scene of a crime, Tionna. . . . I've never done anything like that before."

Tionna backed into the kitchen table and sat in the chair closest to her. Although Hunky was out of her life, he was still taunting her from his grave. What if Casey was found out? He could lose the job he loved, and Tionna could lose his love forever. "I'm so sorry," she cried.

Casey put his glass on the table and got down on his knees. As he wiped her tears, he looked Tionna in the eyes. "I'm not going anywhere, Tionna. No matter what happens. But we've got to trust each other enough to share everything. You and I can't have any secrets between us. That's the only way you and I are going to make it together. Understood?"

Tionna nodded. She didn't want to lose Casey now that God had opened her heart, but she didn't want him to risk his career for her, either. As Casey gently rubbed her hands, Tionna's spirit stirred. God had blessed her with a great man, one full of integrity and honor. She wasn't going to let anything damage what they were trying to build together.

In that moment Tionna made a huge decision. If Casey's career ever came into question because of what happened to Hunky and his wife, she would go against her promise to her line sisters and tell the truth. That was the right thing to do. And she believed it was what God would want her to do to save the relationship.

~ Chapter 29 ~

J. Amanda

In less than five hours, J. Amanda would stand before thousands of people at Faith Tabernacle, ready to deliver a message for the New Year. Though she had preached a number of times over the years, this was the first time she'd usher in the New Year as the main speaker. To her, this was a sign of new beginnings. More than anything, she desperately needed a new start.

Since Hunky died, J. Amanda had taken some time off from serving at the church. She needed to regroup and consecrate herself so that she'd be ready to embrace life and minister to women again. Two months seemed like a long time to be away, but when she stepped into the sanctuary, it felt as if she'd been gone only a few days.

J. Amanda inhaled and took in the smells of fresh flowers and scented shampoo on the carpet. She'd come to church early so she could seclude herself from family and friends and reacquaint herself with the pulpit. The message she had for the congregation was important, and she didn't want to risk bumping into a distraction. During the course of the year, life had taught her many lessons. The most valuable was the lesson on faith. She had preached it every Sunday and had shared it in sessions, but when her spirit became restless, she had forgotten that lesson and had given in to her weakness.

What a year this has been! She walked onto the pulpit and covered it in prayer. She'd been through some tough times, yet through it all God had continued to bless her. Starting in January, she would co-host a segment on a nationally recognized radio show and preach once a month on Pastor Olivia's television broadcast. *I don't deserve this,* she said to herself as she walked across the pulpit, *but I thank you. I don't know why you love me so, but I thank you.*

J. Amanda gazed toward the area where David and the kids used to sit every Sunday. *One day things will return to normal,* she thought. No matter how long she had to wait, she was determined to patch the broken places in her marriage. She and David were still living in the house as roommates, but there was some progress. David had agreed to counseling, and eating dinner as a family unit had been restored.

As she left the pulpit, J. Amanda saw a young girl wheel a woman down the center aisle. Members didn't usually get to church this early on New Year's Eve, so J. Amanda guessed they were part of the staff or one of the ministries participating in the service. But as the wheelchair drew near, J. Amanda recognized Patrice and her daughter, Kierra.

J. Amanda hadn't seen Patrice since medics rolled her away on the gurney. Through the grapevine, she had discovered that Patrice was paralyzed from the waist down and was unable to speak with ease. J. Amanda had donated a large sum of money anonymously to help pay for funeral costs for Hunky and for Patrice's medical bills. But money would never be enough to erase the memory of what happened that fateful day.

J. Amanda walked toward them, wondering if they had come early to pray. It seemed only right that she say hello before leaving them alone. Standing close to Patrice, J. Amanda read the sadness in her eyes. The look was different than the one she had had the day she appeared at the Doubletree. This sadness was piercing, and it rattled her soul.

"My mother wanted to see you today," Kierra began. "She's still paralyzed, but she can talk much better now."

J. Amanda praised God for Patrice's breakthrough. As she prepared to say a few words to Patrice, her daughter continued talking. "There are a few questions that we'd like you to answer."

Something told J. Amanda that this wasn't a conversation she should have inside the sanctuary. She suggested they go to her office for more privacy, but Kierra declined.

"I won't be long," she said. "Does Tiffany know who her father is?"

Perplexed, J. Amanda looked down at Patrice. What had Hunky shared with her?

Kierra didn't wait for an answer. She obviously had more to say, so J. Amanda prepared herself for more.

"How could an unarmed man be a danger to you? I know you were his lover. I know you didn't pull the trigger, and if you don't come forward with the truth, I'll share your poor behavior with the world. You'll suffer for what you've done to my family."

"I—I don't understand. Why are you doing this?" J. Amanda stammered.

"My dad was good to me and my mother until you came along. You took our happiness away, and now we're going to take away yours. My mom will never walk again or complete a sentence fluently. I'll have to take care of her every day, and I'm only fourteen. I think you owe it to us to come clean. I'm not gonna rest until you do."

If J. Amanda didn't know any better, she could've sworn Patrice had a smirk on her face. "Are you looking for money? Is that what this is about?" She was grasping for an answer other than the one she had received.

"Money can't change this, Reverend King," Kierra replied. "I suggest you think about what I said. And . . . unless you're going to come clean tonight, I wouldn't set foot in the pulpit if I were you."

J. Amanda stood in the aisle until Kierra and her mother were gone. What was she going to do?

A few hours before the New Year's service was set to begin, J. Amanda sat behind her desk, finishing a resignation letter. She had to hurry so that Pastor Olivia could prepare a sermon for tonight in her place. She hated putting her pastor and the church in a bind, but Kierra had her between a rock and a hard place. Though she could address the threat, J. Amanda didn't want to ruin her line sisters' lives, and she especially didn't want to hurt Tiffany.

As she wrote, snippets of the sermon she had delivered for women's season came to mind. God had equipped her with the tools she needed to combat any challenge. *Though I walk in the valley of the shadow of death, I will fear no evil.*

J. Amanda ripped up the letter she had started, and threw the pieces in the trash can beside her desk. She was ready for battle. As she sat in the chair, rubbing the Bible next to her hand, J. Amanda prayed for her line sisters. She would do her best to shield them from her confessions, but it was time for the truth to come out, and J. Amanda wanted to be the one to share it with her church community. She wasn't going to let Kierra or her mother blackmail her and keep her from living her best life.

J. Amanda didn't know what Kierra and Patrice had planned, but she was going to show up for the New Year's service and preach until her soul was free.

Readers' Guide Questions

1. J. Amanda believed that Hunky was her true love, but David was the kind of man she knew she should marry. How do you think this affected her marriage?

2. Should an unhappily married couple put off divorce because of their children? What are the pros and cons of staying in this type of marriage?

3. We often hear about men suffering a midlife crisis. Do women go through this as well?

4. Is it ever all right to deny your husband in bed?

5. Zora wanted to pursue her career before considering having children. Can a marriage survive if one spouse doesn't want to have children?

6. Is separation or divorce the best option when infidelity in a marriage has been exposed? How did you feel about the way Zora handled Reggie's interaction with Valencia?

7. Zora waited for her husband to become established before pursuing her goals. Cynthia chose to be a stay-at-home mother. Should a married woman always make a sacrifice when it comes to her career?

8. Have you ever been caught in the middle of a situation that involved a good friend and you had to keep something a secret? How did you handle it? How was the situation resolved?

9. What are some early signs of abusive relationships?

10. Do you think Mrs. Dorothy knew her son was emotionally and physically abusive toward his wife? What should she have done, if anything, about Brian's abusive behavior?

11. What role should family and friends play in domestic violence situations? What are the reasons why some people remain silent?

12. Why do you think Jasmine stayed in her marriage? Is there anything she should've done differently? How were her children affected by the abuse?

13. Did Jasmine do the right thing by dropping the abuse charges against Brian?

14. Kenya was very protective of her son. Discuss her relationship with Mack. Were her rules realistic? As a single mother, should Kenya have had the right to set all the rules and boundaries?

15. How would you define an emotional affair? Are emotional affairs more damaging than intimate/physical affairs?

16. Holding on to the past sometimes hinders you from moving forward. How was Tionna's life affected by her past? What areas of your past are you still hold-

ing on to? Why is it difficult to let things in the past
go?

17. How would you describe the women's relationships
with one another? Do you have a circle of friends?
What impact do those friends have on your life?

18. How do you handle a friend who struggles with ac-
cepting Christ? Does this affect your friendship in
any way? Did Jasmine's struggles with Christ affect
her relationship with her line sisters?

19. Which character did you identify with the most,
and why? Did you learn any lessons from the characters?

20. If you could have a conversation with one of the
main characters, which one would it be, and why?
What would you say to her?

About Author

When Nicole S. Rouse's parents decided to name their firstborn after their favorite literary icon, Nikki Giovanni, they didn't expect their daughter to share the famous poet's birth date. They also had no idea their child would one day become a published author.

Happily Ever Now is Nicole's debut novel and has ranked consistently on the Top 25 Christian Independent Publishers Bestsellers list. *Happily Ever Now* also received the 2008 EDC Creations Best Book Award. Her sophomore novel, *Someone to Love Me*, was picked up by the Black Expressions Book Club. *Be Careful What You Pray For* was released in October 2010. *Still Standing* was released in November 2011.

During her spare time, she serves as an undergraduate advisor at Temple University, for Zeta Phi Beta Sorority, Inc., and in that capacity she encourages young adult women to dream beyond their expectations. She also teaches writing workshops to aspiring writers. Nicole resides near Philadelphia, Pennsylvania, and is currently working on her sixth novel.